Without Warning

Without Warning

ELLEN'S STORY

1914–1918

DENNIS HAMLEY

CANDLEWICK PRESS
CAMBRIDGE, MASSACHUSETTS

This is a work of fiction. Names, characters, places, and incidents are either
products of the author's imagination or, if real, are used fictitiously.

Copyright © 2006 by Dennis Hamley

All rights reserved. No part of this book may be reproduced, transmitted, or
stored in an information retrieval system in any form or by any means, graphic,
electronic, or mechanical, including photocopying, taping, and recording,
without prior written permission from the publisher.

First U.S. edition 2007

Library of Congress Cataloging-in-Publication Data is available.

Library of Congress Catalog Card Number pending

ISBN 978-0-7636-3338-7

2   4   6   8   10   9   7   5   3   1

Printed in the United States of America

This book was typeset in M Baskerville.

Candlewick Press
2067 Massachusetts Avenue
Cambridge, Massachusetts 02140

visit us at www.candlewick.com

FIC
HAMLEY

For Pam Royds,
to whom I owe so much

Contents

PART 1

·1914·

RECRUITING

CHAPTER ONE

It's dark now. The church clock has long struck midnight. Betty and Madge, my younger sisters, went to sleep the moment I blew their candle out, but I can't sleep and I'm wondering if I ever will again.

I'll never forget today. Everybody's been so happy, cheering and waving flags. But I don't think they're happy, not deep down, and I'm not happy at all. Our Jack has been a good brother to me, and we've always been very close. But soon he'll be going away, and we might never see him again.

There's a war starting. I don't know much about wars except soldiers and sailors get killed and Jack might get killed with them. But grown-up people say different—that wars are nothing really; they're a chance for young men to go off to foreign parts and be brave and come home heroes and, besides, the Hun needs a taste of his own medicine, going through Belgium and killing all the babies and the nuns.

Jack works for Crispin and Thacker, the local builders. He's an apprentice bricklayer, but he can turn his hand to anything. For instance, he loves taking my bike to bits and putting it back together again. He'd love to have a motorcycle—a Rudge or a Royal Enfield—but he can't afford one. He loves his football too and plays center forward for Lambsfield. Pa wanted him to leave building and work on the railway, the same as he does, but he wouldn't. He wants to join up, and he's been waiting for the recruiting officer from the Sussex regiment to come to our village of Lambsfield. Well, the recruiting officer did come today. As soon as he heard about it, our Jack said, "You see if I'm not a soldier of the king by this evening."

Ma cried and said, "Please don't, Jack," and Jack answered, "Don't worry, Ma. Everybody wants to go and, besides, we've fought in every war there ever was and we've won the lot, and we'll win this one too. I'll cut the kaiser's mustache off myself."

I didn't like Jack talking like that, and neither did Ma, because she cried into her apron, though nobody noticed but me. Pa said, "You go, boy, and good luck to you. If I was twenty years younger, I'd go with you." Jack's nineteen now and old enough to be taken by the army. I'm sixteen next January. Betty and Madge, the twins, are eleven.

Today was Saturday. In the morning a stage made of trestle tables was set up in the market square, and on it was another table spread with a Union Jack. Word traveled through the village that something unusual was going to happen. Suddenly, early in the afternoon, the high, clear tone of a bugle echoed through the village, like a summons. Jack and Pa were sitting in the living room quietly digesting Ma's roast mutton, potatoes, and cabbage. At the sound they both stood up. "It's the call," said Jack. "The army's here. I've been waiting for this. I'm going."

"I'm coming with you," said Pa, and they dashed out of the house together. I ran out after them.

The call had brought most of the men in the village to the market square and quite a few women as well. I arrived just as the bugler's last echoes were dying away. Now he stood at attention with the bugle at his side. A soldier with a drum stood beside him. Next to them, standing ramrod straight, was a big sergeant with a red face and a bushy mustache. His boots twinkled in the sunshine.

An army officer sat behind the table. With him sat Lord Launton, Mr. Brayfield the vicar, and old Colonel Cripps, with his medals on his chest and his right sleeve pinned up because he'd lost an arm. People said a Zulu warrior chopped it off in a terrible battle in Africa years ago. He hadn't been seen in the village much since his wife died last year, and I could tell that people were pleased he was here today.

There was a roll on the drum. The noise made me feel strange inside, as if it called me somewhere I didn't want to go. Before you could blink, the market square was full. When the soldier had finished the drumroll, he lifted the drumsticks smartly up level with his chin and stood at attention. The officer stood up.

"Men of Lambsfield," he said. He didn't mention women, though there were just as many there. "My name is Anstruther, Major Anstruther. You know that our beloved country is in dire peril. The British Army is our sure shield and has never shirked its duty, but our danger is so great that we need every able-bodied man in the land to flock to the colors. You, and you alone, good men of Sussex, can rid us of the scourge that threatens us and every right-thinking person in the world."

People were very quiet when he said this, until someone at the back shouted, "God save the king," and then everybody roared, "God save the king, God save the king."

Major Anstruther lifted his hand for quiet. "I see you are full of the patriotic fervor that the army needs. I am proud to be an officer in the Royal Sussex Light Infantry, and Sergeant Witherspoon and Private Slack here are proud to be soldiers."

The sergeant said, "Very true, sir."

Major Anstruther went on. "And so should all you good men here today. Once you join our ranks, I promise you pride in yourselves and the knowledge that you are doing your duty for your country."

Then Mr. Brayfield got up, and people started fidgeting because they heard him every Sunday. He talked about God's purpose and how we must rid the world of the devil and all his works and the need for sacrifice, and people stopped listening because he was going on too long. At last he finished. "Those who do not return will truly be martyrs and will be revered as the church reveres all its martyred sons and daughters." This didn't go down well. Nobody had said anything about being martyrs.

Lord Launton talked about duty and valor, and how he wished he were a young man again because he'd be at the head of the line. Nobody took much notice; he wasn't much liked for the way his wife treated the servants, and he was too weak to stand up to her, so they said.

When he sat down, there was silence for a moment. Then somebody shouted out, "Three cheers for the British

Army. Hip, hip, hooray!" Then three cheers for King George, three cheers for Lord Kitchener, three cheers for the Sussex Light Infantry, three more for the Royal Navy, and three for France. Someone started singing, "We're the men of Sussex, Sussex by the sea," and everyone joined in. Then somebody shouted, "Kill the Huns," someone else took up the cry, and suddenly everybody was chanting, "Kill the Huns! Kill the Huns!" It sounded horrible, as if they would kill them with their bare hands if they were there to kill. One moment everything was good-humored; now it seemed ugly.

I knew who had shouted "Kill the Huns" first: a big man with a hard face standing quite near to me. Fred Straker his name was, known in the village as someone best not to get on the wrong side of. His son, two years younger than me, stood with him. Everyone called him "Bully," which was about right for him. I didn't like Bully, and I was scared of his father—and I wasn't the only one.

The chanting didn't stop until Major Anstruther stood up again and raised his hand. One by one people left off shouting until he could make himself heard. "My friends," he said. "We have someone else here to address you, some-one for whom I have the greatest admiration. If I am ever half the soldier he has been, I shall be well pleased. Please continue, Colonel Cripps."

Colonel Cripps stood up. His medals clinked and sparkled. His voice was quiet, and the crowd hushed be-cause people respected him. "My friends here are right," he said. "We are indeed fighting a dangerous enemy, and if we do not destroy him, he will destroy us. But be careful. We will do our duty, but our foes believe they do theirs, and love for their country burns as strong in them as it does in us. A soldier who starts the battle blind with fury is a bad soldier." I was near enough to see sad eyes in his grizzled, sunburned old face. "That is why the cries of 'Kill the Huns' that I have just heard in this square are wrong. Yes, my friends, wrong. This is no spirit in which to go to war. If we are blinded with hate, twisted by revenge, drowned in the cries of the rabble, then we are no true soldiers. We will descend to the level of those we detest. War is always detestable, but there is never a war in which there are not good men on both sides."

There was muttering in the crowd, as if nobody quite understood. Then someone shouted, "Shame," and someone else joined in with "There are no good Huns, Colonel."

"That is where you are wrong, my friend," said Colonel Cripps. "There are many good Germans, as there are many good Englishmen, Scotsmen, and Frenchmen. And as many bad ones too."

"Well said, sir," a voice near me murmured when the colonel had finished. I turned and saw Mr. and Mrs. Randall. Mr. Randall worked for the colonel. When they were both in the army, Mr. Randall was his servant, and when the colonel retired and came to live in Fieldfare House, Mr. Randall came too and brought his wife as the colonel's cook. "But I don't think the people here understand what he meant," he continued.

I thought he must be right. Everybody looked nonplussed; killing Huns seemed the whole point of going to war. It was surprising that an old soldier who must have seen so much fighting was trying to tell them different. The muttering changed to a sort of mutinous rumble.

Colonel Cripps's speech was not what most people wanted to hear.

Mr. Randall was speaking again. "He's the best and truest man I know, and I've stood by his side in battle more times than I care to think of. If he doesn't know what he's talking about, then nobody does."

"Shame on you, Colonel," somebody shouted. For a moment I feared more might join in. But then another piercing bugle call soared over the noise, not a call to arms but haunting, sad. I'd heard it before—the Last Post, played at the end of the day as the sun goes down or when there is death. Its mournful, healing notes dropped down from the air until there was a guilty silence, as if those who wanted to shout knew they'd gone too far.

All this time, the men on the platform had watched, unmoving. I couldn't tell what they were thinking. But when every eye was turned to him again, Major Anstruther said, "Thank you. May I say that I agree wholeheartedly with what Colonel Cripps has said. It expresses perfectly the sort of spirit we need in this regiment. We are soldiers, not butchers. Please remember that. Now, any man here who wishes to volunteer, will he please step forward and give his name to Sergeant Witherspoon."

Nearly every young man in the market square stepped forward to give his name to the sergeant. Jack was one of the first. The mood changed again; now people cheered and sang "God Save the King." The sergeant spoke to Major Anstruther, who called for silence and said, "You will be proud to hear that twenty-seven of our fine young friends have volunteered for king and country. The gratitude of the nation is due to them all."

Well, that started it. Somebody shouted out, "Three cheers for the British Army. Hip, Hip…" and hoorays split the air until people began to leave the square, happy and excited. Many of the men made for the Plough, Lambsfield's only pub; I saw Jack among them.

Colonel Cripps had stepped down from the stage and was coming toward us. "Time to go home, John, I think," he said to Mr. Randall. "It seems I caused something of a surprise just then." He saw me and said, "Ah, you're Charlie Wilkins's girl, I believe. Look after that brother of yours. He's exactly what our country needs."

"Are you all right, sir?" said Mr. Randall.

"All right? Why shouldn't I be all right?"

"That shout of 'Shame.' It was aimed at you."

"John, if that was the worst thing ever aimed at me, I'd still have both my arms, as you well know. But I mustn't be flippant. It was not good. It struck a note I never thought to hear in this village."

I plucked up my courage to say something. "Sir, was it the bugle that calmed them down?"

He looked closely at me and said, "Yes, my dear. I believe it was. 'Music hath charms to soothe the savage breast,' as they say."

Mr. Randall had brought the pony and trap. He helped the colonel up, then Mrs. Randall, then jumped up himself, and they trotted off.

As I watched them go, I heard a boy's voice behind me. "He's a daft old twerp, that Colonel Cripps. My dad says he doesn't know what he's talking about." I turned round. Bully Straker and his friends were walking past. Bully was a real little bruiser. His inseparable hangers-on were Percy Pinkney, who was pale with a puffy face, and Oswald Langley, who was tall and always looked as if there were a nasty smell right under his nose—his family thought they were a cut above everybody else.

I knew Bully wasn't speaking to me, but I felt I had to answer. "No, he isn't," I said. "He's right."

Bully stopped and the others did too. He looked as if I didn't know what I was talking about and said, "My pa says if we took notice of people like him, the Hun would go through us like a dose of salts."

"It's the Hun's fault we're at war," said Oswald.

"That colonel must be in league with them to say we ought to like them," said Percy.

"That's not what he said at all," I replied.

"Yes, it was," said Bully. "Anyway, what's it got to do with you? You're only a girl. Are you two coming?"

And off they went, with me feeling, once again, that I didn't like any of them very much.

Pa was back home before me. "Were you in the square, Ellen?" he asked.

"Yes," I replied. "Pa, shouting 'Shame on you' to Colonel Cripps was awful."

"Yes," said Pa. "Bad business. It spoiled the day. Things are bad enough anyway without that. It's that troublemaker Straker's doing. Still, nobody can say Lambsfield isn't doing its bit for England. It made me proud to see all our young lads going up to volunteer."

Jack came in late, long after the supper things were cleared away. He'd had a few drinks at the Plough. I could smell the beer on his breath. "I've joined up!" he shouted, as if daring us to say he hadn't. "I've signed on. I'll be going." He stood there. Big and burly, with his sandy, almost ginger hair, he looked just like Pa must have looked when he was young.

Ma screamed. "No!" she cried. "No, you're not. You don't have to. Nobody's making you. I won't let you!"

"You can't stop me," said Jack.

Ma turned on Pa, who was sitting in his chair in his shirtsleeves. "Charlie, don't sit there grinning. Stop him. Tell him he's not going."

"That I won't," said Pa.

"Madge and Betty, get upstairs," said Ma. "This isn't for your ears. Go with them, Ellen, and make sure they keep quiet."

"Can't I stay?" I asked. "They'll be all right on their own."

"What's a shrimp like you know?" said Jack. "You're too young for this. It's man's work."

That wasn't fair. I may be little, with dark brown hair and brown eyes like Ma's, but people say I'm pretty, and besides, I'm sixteen in January.

Betty and Madge scuttled up the stairs like frightened rabbits, but I stopped halfway up to see what went on. Jack smiled, which made Ma even angrier. I couldn't believe what she did next. She slapped him across the face, a real stinger. "It's nothing to laugh at," she said. Jack stepped back, holding his hand to his cheek, and looked too shocked to speak.

Pa jumped out of his chair. "What do you think you're doing, woman?" he shouted. "He's my son as well as yours. I say he's going to France, and good luck to him. He couldn't look anyone in the face if he stayed. Neither could I on his account. Is that what you want?"

"I want my son home and safe, and let the others get on with their war," said Ma.

"You know nothing," said Pa. "This is man's work, man's business, and you're to let the men get on with it."

I could see a red mark on Jack's face where Ma had hit him. "I'm sorry, Ma," he said quietly. "But I must go. Can't you understand that?"

"No, I can't," said Ma.

"That's your fault, then," said Pa, putting his jacket on and shoving his cap on his head. "I'm off to the Plough. You coming, lad?"

Jack hesitated, having only just left it. Then he said, "All right, Pa."

"Pint of wallop puts all to rights," said Pa.

"That's your answer for everything," said Ma, but they'd already gone. I heard her crying, so I came downstairs to comfort her. She dried her eyes on her apron and said, "Well, at least you girls will never leave."

"Our place is here, Ma," I answered. Ma gave me a kiss and said, "Oh, Ellen, what would I do without you?"

I lit a candle in a holder—we don't have gaslight in the bedrooms—and tiptoed upstairs. I tucked the young ones into bed, told them to say their prayers, with an extra one for Jack going off to the war, blew the candle out, and went to bed myself.

Ma crept upstairs quietly at about ten o'clock. Half an hour later I heard Pa and Jack come in, laughing, singing, and knocking into things. I could tell they'd had too much to drink. They made a terrible noise, and one of them fell all the way back downstairs, but it only made them laugh all the more. I heard Pa say, "Are you awake?" when he got into the bedroom, but Ma didn't answer and I guessed she was pretending to be asleep.

So that's why I'm lying awake tonight unhappy. Our Jack's going away, and Ma's upset about it, and Pa's angry with her, and Jack and Pa are drunk, and Straker tried to stir the crowd up to make mischief. And it's all because of this war.

It took Ma a week to get over that night. The day after Jack left, she gave up crying and was more like her usual self. "Now Jack's gone off to be a soldier, we're losing a paycheck in the house," she said.

"But we're one less now," I replied.

"It doesn't matter," she said. "We were short even with his money. You'll have to go out to work."

"But Ma, only last week you said I'd never leave, and I agreed."

"That was then. I'm thinking straight now. I don't want you to leave the village. Get a nice little job in Lambsfield—go out in the morning, and come home in the evening."

"Ma, don't be silly. What is there for a girl round here?"

"What every other girl does. Go into service. Be someone's maid."

"Whose?"

"I don't know. The vicar's? Dr. Pettigrew's?"

"They've already got maids. There's nobody else in Lambsfield."

"What about Colonel Cripps?" said Ma.

"He's got Mr. and Mrs. Randall," I replied.

"They're old. He needs a nice young girl to open the door and welcome visitors. Besides, I'm sure Mrs. Randall could do with some help."

"All right, Ma, I'll try, though I don't think there's much chance. I'll write him a letter. Mr. Spendlove said I was good at letter writing." Mr. Spendlove was headmaster at the village school.

"Don't bother with letters. Just go and ask him straight out."

"Ma, I wouldn't dare."

"If you don't ask, you won't get," she replied. "Now, help me with the washing while you're still here."

CHAPTER TWO

I'm standing on Beacon Hill. It's a bright day now, but clouds are massing over the Downs, and it looks like it may rain soon. From the top of the hill, I can look down on Lambsfield as if it were on a map. There's St. Botolph's Church at one end of High Street. The market square where the recruiting happened is halfway along. At the other end is the Plough. The village green is a little farther on, with its emerald-green grass, the lighter patch of the cricket square in the middle, and the big elm trees surrounding it. I can see Sheep Street, where we live. The gleam of water beyond the church is Oldwood Mere. If I turn the other way, I can see the bare, green South Downs and just make out where the sea meets the sky beyond them. The sun is shining, and a light breeze rustles the grass. I can't believe that anything's wrong in the world, that Jack won't soon be sailing over that horizon and thousands of young men with him. Why can't things stay the way they were?

When Pa came in from work last night, he had a lot to say. "They were talking in the Plough," he began.

"They're always talking there," said Ma. "Most of it's nonsense."

"Wilfred Langley's just come back from London," said Pa.

"Oswald's father?" I asked.

"That's him. Thinks because he's a commercial traveler he's God's gift to the world. Anyway, he's full of what he found in London. He says people there are really worked up. There's an MP—what's his name, Horatio Bottomley, that's it—going round making speeches about the 'Germ-Huns,' as he calls them. There are German waiters in hotels being hauled out and beaten up because everyone thinks they're spies or soldiers sent here secretly years ago. The other day a German band playing in a park had all its instruments smashed up."

"I don't believe it," said Ma. "It's the drink talking."

"I'm only saying what Langley said. I didn't say I believed it."

"I should hope you don't, Charlie," said Ma.

"Then Straker joined in," said Pa.

"Then definitely don't listen," said Ma.

"He's got this bee in his bonnet about the colonel. He reckons the Germans are paying him to make us weak and spineless so we won't be any trouble to them."

"I've never heard such rubbish in my life," said Ma.

"Me neither," said Pa. "But there was a funny mood in the Plough when I left, as if someone could get hurt, and it all springs from Cripps's speech."

"Surely Mr. Straker wouldn't do anything against the colonel, would he?" I asked.

"I'd put nothing past that man," Pa replied. "If Fred

Straker wants to light a fire, I reckon Wilfred Langley's given him the matches."

"So what does he think the colonel is?" said Ma.

"A spy or a traitor, something like that."

"Well, what can Straker do?" replied Ma.

"You don't know him. If he says 'jump,' half the village jumps."

"But what Colonel Cripps said was right," I said.

"Maybe," said Pa. "Whatever he said and whatever he is, there's no call for Straker to keep this thing going. He could rouse people up so much there might be mischief done—and Cripps might not escape scot-free. We're all patriotic round here, or I hope we are, but I can't understand why those who make the most song and dance about it are the ones who drink most and are readiest with their fists. And who'd probably run a mile if they ever saw a German soldier."

I think about all this as I walk down from Beacon Hill to Fieldfare House, where the colonel lives.

When I reached Fieldfare House, lovely and trim, with its garden of flowers in neat borders, nobody was there. I thought I'd better knock at the front door, but my nerve failed me. He won't want a maid, I thought. He'll laugh at me.

Then a man's voice said, very gently, "Well now, young lady. What can we do for you?" I looked round, and there was Colonel Cripps, looking different from the man who spoke on recruiting day. He wore plus fours, and there were no medals pinned to his chest. He was leaning on his walking stick. A beautiful golden retriever sat at his feet and looked at me with big soft brown eyes.

Plucking up my courage, I said, "Please, sir, I was wondering if you needed a maid."

"A maid?" he said. "Do you know, the thought has never crossed my mind. Come and sit down, and we'll talk about it. Mrs. Randall will make some lemonade. Barney, walk." The beautiful dog stood up at once.

We sat on deck chairs on the lawn at the back of the house with glasses of homemade lemonade. Except at vicarage fetes, I'd never seen anything like it—the short grass, rosebushes, and flower borders. And it was all his. He didn't have to pay rent to a landlord like we did.

"How's your fine brother? Jack's his name, I believe."

"Yes, sir. He's just gone off to train to be a soldier." I hesitated, then asked a question. As soon as it was out of my mouth, it seemed very stupid. "Please, sir, do you think he'll be killed?"

"Please don't call me sir," he said. "I had enough of that in the army to last a lifetime. Well now, as to Jack, yes, of course he may be killed. Every soldier may be. I've seen thousands die, including some of my best friends."

"But it won't be so bad in this war, will it? We'll soon have won it. Everyone says it will be over at Christmas."

"Ellen," he said. "That is your name, isn't it? I'm afraid that this time, everyone is probably wrong. This war will last a long time, and we may not win. The pity is, it's against people very much like us, who should be our friends."

"But you said . . ." I started, then stopped.

"Go on," he said.

"You said we had a dangerous enemy who we must destroy or he would destroy us."

SIMMS LIBRARY
ALBUQUERQUE ACADEMY

"I know," he replied. "Sadly, war changes people for the worse. We had a good example of that when the recruiters came."

He stopped. I waited for him to continue.

"Wars," he said at last, "are caused through the vanity of people who don't have to fight in them." With his good arm, he patted the empty sleeve of his jacket. "Years ago, even as that furious man in Africa, defending the land he and his ancestors had lived on for thousands of years, struck at my arm, I remember thinking, *What am I doing on this alien soil? Who sent me?* Well, a bit more of the world was colored red for the British Empire as a result. But I wonder for how long."

"The vicar and Mr. Spendlove say the empire will last forever, because it's a gift to us from God," I said.

"What do you think German vicars and German schoolmasters are telling German children now?" he replied.

"The same, I suppose. But they're wrong, aren't they, Colonel Cripps?"

He sighed. "Yes, they're wrong. So are the vicar and Mr. Spendlove."

"But how can everybody be wrong? Someone has to be right."

"My dear young lady," said the colonel. "I never thought I would live to see the world overtaken by such madness. Millions of young men all over Europe looking for a little adventure to brighten their dull lives. Their families sad to see them go but proud as well. They are answering their nations' call. That's not wrong. It's wonderful. But what will these young men find on their adventures? We've unleashed a monster that we can't stop.

People wanted this war for years, and now they've got their excuse for it. But they don't know what they've started." He was silent again for a moment. Then he said, "They'll soon find out, I fear."

"My brother thinks he'll be in France in the New Year," I said. "Won't it be over by then?"

"I'm afraid not," he said quietly.

Pa always said the colonel was "one of the toffs who'd never speak to the likes of us." But Pa was wrong. The colonel had spoken to me as if I were a friend.

The clouds I saw as I stood on Beacon Hill had arrived. Big drops of rain began to fall, making me shiver. "Well, you can't go home in this downpour," he said. "Let's go indoors and continue our chat." He got to his feet. Barney rose as well, and I followed them into the house.

The colonel's sitting room was full of dark, heavy furniture, and there were spears on the walls, souvenirs of old African campaigns. On one wall was a huge framed engraving: soldiers on horseback looking defeated, their heads hanging low, their horses exhausted. It was called *The Retreat from Inkermann.* The opposite wall was taken up entirely by a huge wooden bookcase, its shelves crammed with books. Three framed photographs stood on the table. I recognized one, his wife. The next was of a man in an army officer's uniform, the third a woman.

He saw me looking at them. "The man is my son, Edmund," he said. "He's a soldier too. Following in his father's footsteps. The other photo is Daphne, my niece. Remarkable woman, Daphne. Perhaps you'll meet her one day."

Suddenly I remembered Straker's threat. Dare I tell the colonel? I was almost too scared. But he had to know. I took a deep breath and told him what Pa said. He listened gravely, then said, "Ellen, I'm afraid it doesn't take much to make a crowd angry, even if, left on their own, no one in it would say boo to a goose. I've heard about our friend Horatio Bottomley and what he says. Not such a savory character, I think. I should be sorry if the hysteria in London were to come here."

"Pa says Fred Straker is the one causing the trouble."

"I've had dealings with Mr. Straker before," said the colonel. "He and his friends can do a lot of damage, and not only with their fists. They could split Lambsfield down the middle if they try to stir up hatred. Perhaps I should have one of these newfangled telephone things installed."

"Why?" I asked.

"In case they come here looking for me. I might need help."

"They wouldn't, would they?"

"The good soldier aims for the best and is prepared for the worst. These are strange days." He chuckled. "Anyway, if anything's to happen, it's too late to have a telephone installed."

I finished my lemonade, feeling rather silly. He was laughing at me after all. I should never have come here.

He must have read my thoughts. "Ellen, I take what you say extremely seriously. I don't think any trouble from Mr. Straker will get as far as this house, and I have no intention of saying anything to the police, because that could have exactly the wrong effect. But you did right to warn me, and I'm grateful to you, believe me." He paused and smiled. "I seem to remember you came here to ask if I needed a maid."

"Yes, sir—Colonel Cripps."

"I'm sorry to disappoint you, Ellen. The Randalls look after me very well. Besides, the army sees fit to expect its old
officers to live on half-pay. I couldn't possibly afford you."

"I wouldn't want much."

"But you'd deserve more. The laborer is worthy of his
hire; that's what the good book says, and I agree with it.
Besides, we'd be trying to find things for you to do that
Mrs. Randall would admit she couldn't do better herself,
and that, I can assure you, would not be easy. You
couldn't spend all day answering the front door."

He must have seen my crestfallen face, because he
added, "I'll keep my eyes and ears open on your behalf
and let you know if anything turns up. Now, run along."
And even though I'll be sixteen next year and he hadn't
given me a job, I didn't mind him talking to me as if
I were a little girl. As I came to the top of Beacon Hill, I
thought what a wonderful man he was and how much
I would have loved working at Fieldfare House. And how I
hoped that Mr. Straker wouldn't ever come down here to
do mischief.

Chapter Three

A letter from Jack came the next morning. He told us about the barracks, his uniform, marching, drill, the sergeant major. He's never been so tired in his life. He's made friends from all over Sussex, but they've got a Scottish sergeant major, and they can hardly understand a word he says. He hopes he might get a few days' leave before they go to their first training camp, where they'll really learn to be soldiers. If all goes well and they pass muster, they may be out in France early next year. When I read that, I went cold. We keep hearing about great victories, and most people believe the war will be over by Christmas. But Jack must think it will last longer.

So does Colonel Cripps, and when I think about what he said, I fear for Jack and the other twenty-six boys who joined up when the recruiting officer came.

This morning I told Pa I might be going into service. He was furious. "Service?" he shouted. "No daughter of mine goes into service. I won't have her at the beck and call of a lot of toffs."

"What are you talking about?" said Ma. "You work for toffs, the directors of the London, Brighton and South Coast Railway. People like us, we all work for toffs. They're the only ones with the money to pay us. We'd starve without them."

"When I'm in my signal box, I'm my own master and make my own decisions and nobody interferes. If our Ellen's someone's scullery maid, she won't have a minute to call her own. Keep out of the way of toffs—that's the best rule. They always let you down."

"I might not find work anywhere," I said. "I asked Colonel Cripps if he wanted a maid, but he told me he didn't."

"With any luck nobody else will either," said Pa.

"We need the money," said Ma.

"Not that badly," Pa grunted. He put his jacket on. "I'm on shift this morning," he said, and stalked out of the house.

When Pa came home from work this evening, he slumped down at the table. Ma gave him a mug of strong sweet tea and a plate of stew and dumplings, which he ate silently. I could see he had something on his mind. He finished the stew, swallowed the last of his tea, and said he didn't want any more. Then he sat in his chair by the fire and lit his pipe.

"Billy Fawkes was talking this morning," he said. Billy Fawkes was a porter at the station. "It seems a lot more was said after I left the Plough the other night. The colonel will need his wits about him. There's some in the village determined to do something, though I don't know what. But whatever it is, it spells trouble for him."

"That's what I told him," I said.

Pa almost jumped up out of his chair. "You did what?" he shouted.

"When I went to his house to ask if he wanted a maid, he was very nice to me. I like him, and I thought he ought to know about Mr. Straker. So I told him what you said."

"You'd no business to," he said angrily. "This is nothing to do with you, or any woman if it comes to that, so keep your nose out of it. Now I wish I'd kept my mouth shut."

"Your father's right, Ellen," said Ma. "It's nothing to do with us. Let the men deal with it, like they deal with everything else."

I felt so angry that I nearly shouted back, "Don't we have a say in anything?" But there was no point in setting Pa off again, because there had been trouble enough in this house over the last few days. So I did what Pa wished he'd done and kept my mouth shut. But after he'd gone to the Plough, I felt mutinous, because it had taken a lot to do what I did, and what he had said was so unfair.

CHAPTER FOUR

I'm in bed now, edgy and restless. The church clock strikes eleven. It's hot; there's no wind—it's the sort of night when tempers can snap. Something's going to happen. I can't stay here in bed. I've got to get out and be moving.

I look out of the window. Moonlight makes everything clear as day. I see Mr. Daines's grocery, Jones's Family Butchers, and the cottages beyond them. The Strakers' cottage has a light in the window. At the end of the street is the Plough. Its doorway is open and lit up.

Suddenly there's shouting. Men are coming out of the Plough, and Fred Straker's voice is loudest of all. "It's time to teach the traitor a lesson he won't forget. Who's with me?"

There's a confused noise. Some are saying, "Count me in" and "We're with you, Fred," and I see one or two creep back inside the Plough. Someone breaks away from the crowd and walks quickly this way. It's Pa.

Fred Straker calls after him, "Let the coward go home." There's mocking and jeering at the ones who leave. It's a nasty noise. Windows all down the street are opened, and heads look out. There are a few cries of "Shut up! We're trying to sleep," but they may as well shout at the moon.

Fred Straker yells, "Wait a minute. I'm getting my son up. He should come with us because he's a young lad with a long way to go, and it's only right that he should see what happens to traitors."

Straker's on his way. They'll march to Fieldfare House, and the colonel won't know what's happening. What they'll do I've no idea, but he has to be warned they're coming, and I'm the one to do it. I pull some clothes on over my nightgown. *Now,* I ask myself, *how am I to get out, with Pa already opening the front door?*

A window overlooks the back garden, and the water barrel is directly underneath. If I'm careful, I can let myself down and get a foot on top of it. I push the sash up, gingerly climb out, put one hand on the windowsill, turn so I face the wall, and feel down with my foot. I pull the window sash down a little, so it looks as if I'd opened it to get some air in. My foot's now on top of the barrel. Thankfully, the lid's on, so I lower myself down, put both feet on it, and jump off. I dart up the garden and hide behind the runner beans. The beans are high and thick and make good cover. I reach the fence at the side of the garden and climb over it into the lane that runs round the side of the cottage.

There's still shouting in the street. Straker's lot hasn't gone yet. Perhaps lazy Bully wants to stay in bed, though he'll get a beating from his father if he does. I've got a few minutes' start.

I run and run until I can hardly breathe. Then a wonderful second wind floods through me, and I carry on until I reach Fieldfare House and I've beaten the mob.

*   *   *

The front lawn is silver in the moonlight, like Oldwood Mere when it freezes over in winter. The flowers stand at attention like gray soldiers. A faint glow shows through a downstairs window. Perhaps the colonel isn't in bed yet. I knock on the door. No answer. I knock again, louder.

Someone's coming to the door. It's Mrs. Randall. There's a light in the kitchen: the smell tells me that she's making a pie for tomorrow's dinner.

"You again," she says. "This is a funny time to call."

"I've got to see Colonel Cripps," I gasp.

"Cheek," she answers. "You're seeing no one. You go back home, and don't you dare come round here again or I'll get Mr. Randall on to you, and then you're in trouble."

But Colonel Cripps is coming down the stairs. He's in his nightshirt and carries a lighted candle. He looks old and defenseless. "What's the matter, Mrs. Randall?" he says.

"It's that girl again. I'm just telling her…"

"It's all right, Mrs. Randall. Ellen is welcome here at any time, and I think this may not be a social call. You may go now, and please don't wake that hardworking husband of yours."

Mrs. Randall sniffs and goes back down the hallway. "Now then," says the colonel. "What's this all about?"

I blurt it all out in one breath. When I finish, he says, "How long do we have?"

"Well, I ran all the way here," I answer. "I don't suppose they can run. Half of them sound drunk. They must be at least five minutes away." But I'm too optimistic.

There's shouting, and lights twinkle on the hill like little glowworms. "They're on their way," I say.

"Go home, Ellen," says the colonel. "Don't let them see you. Just get away for your own safety."

But they are very close now, and I wouldn't get past them even if I tried, which I've no intention of doing. I hide behind a bush in the garden and watch the crowd of men, still shouting, most now carrying stout sticks and big stones. They stop right outside the garden. Then I look back at the house.

Outside the front door, framed in the light from the hall, are two figures, tall and proud in the dark. One is Mr. Randall, so his wife woke him after all. Younger than Colonel Cripps, but not by much, he wears an old-fashioned army uniform, a red jacket with buttons that gleam in the moonlight and dark trousers. I feel he ought to be carrying a rifle, but he's armed with only a spade. Just for a second, I don't recognize the other. No longer old and defenseless, Colonel Cripps stands straight, wearing a magnificent dress uniform, red tunic, gold braid and medals, a shako on his head, and a gleaming sword at his waist. I imagine him years ago in battle at the head of his men, and suddenly I know why the Zulu warrior struck at him. He was to be feared, and to take off his arm was the best compliment an enemy could pay. Barney sits quietly at his feet. A third joins them. Mrs. Randall. She carries a rolling pin, and for a moment I want to laugh, and then I'm ashamed for even thinking of it.

Three of them, and there must be twenty facing them. When I was at school, Mr. Spendlove once read us a poem about how three warriors stood at the gates of Rome and fought off whole hordes of enemy soldiers. I remember the name of one of them—Horatio. The same name as that MP everyone's talking about. Now Colonel Cripps is like the Roman Horatio, with his comrades on either side.

I can hear what the crowd is shouting: a chant, repeated over and over again. "Traitor Cripps! Traitor Cripps!"

Fred Straker leads them. Bully is by his side, grinning like he's in his element at last. Straker kicks the gate open, and they stream across the lawn. When they are almost at arm's length from the three who await them, he shouts, "Stop!" At once they are still, and the shouting dies.

Colonel Cripps speaks. What he says amazes me. "I admire you for that, Straker. You have a real hold over your party. You are obviously a leader of men. I would to God you were at the front in battle rather than making mischief here."

Fred Straker answers. He doesn't shout. His voice is soft and all the more dangerous for it. "Nothing o' that, Colonel. I see we've got three traitors here to tell us what nice people our enemies are and how we mustn't be beastly to them."

"What are your intentions, Mr. Straker?" says Colonel Cripps.

Straker is silent and so is everybody else, as if nobody's thought about what their intentions are. I wonder if Straker has any idea himself. "Something, Colonel," he says. "Something you won't like."

"Such as what?" says Colonel Cripps. "Are you a lynch mob?"

"Now there's an idea," says Straker.

Suddenly there's a scrape of metal against metal. Colonel

Cripps has drawn his sword. It gleams bright in the moon-
light. "So that's how you want it, is it?" says Fred Straker.
"Everyone mark this. The colonel drew his weapon first.
That means we can do what we like."

"Being prepared and ready in the face of superior forces
does not constitute an act of aggression, Straker," says
Colonel Cripps. "Something you should remember." It's all
too quiet, too polite. I don't like it.

"We'll see about that," Mr. Straker replies. His voice
isn't just quiet now; it's menacing as well. Barney rises to
his feet and growls softly.

Everything's still, like the churchyard when you're
among the gravestones. Colonel Cripps and Straker look at
each other as if willing the other to snap first. Then Straker
says, "Lynch mob. Yes, I like that. Come over here,
Colonel, and then you'll find out if we are."

"I defy you, Straker. So do my friends here. We support
each other, just as we supported our soldiers long ago."

"Much good it did them," says Fred Straker. Now he's
sneering. "How many came home? If you looked after
them so well, how come you did while they didn't?"

"You're contemptible," says Colonel Cripps.

"And you're supposed to be the officer, yet you want us
to be soft on the Huns. There's no place for the likes of
you here. Enough said."

Colonel Cripps raises his sword. "Don't think of using
that," says Straker. "You won't do much with only one
arm."

"And I say I defy you."

"Then on your own head be it," Fred Straker replies,
and makes a circular motion with his outstretched right

arm. "He thinks we ought to be gentle with the Huns who invaded Belgium, and he doesn't care who they killed or how many houses they destroyed," he yells. "Well, let's see how he likes being invaded." The men with sticks and stones understand and run round the side of the house.

I suddenly remember something else that Mr. Spendlove read to us. It was from a play by Shakespeare called *Julius Caesar*. After Caesar had been killed, his friend Mark Antony made a speech to all the people of Rome and started them rioting because they were so angry. As he watched them rampaging, Mark Antony said, "Mischief, thou art afoot. Take what course thou wilt." Mr. Straker's doing the same as Mark Antony did. I rush out from my hiding place and scream, "Colonel, stop them."

A man pushes me. It's Albert Stover, Lord Launton's under-gamekeeper. "Out of the way, missy," he grunts. I try to keep on my feet but can't. I fall and roll out of the way so as not to be trampled underfoot.

Straker doesn't move. He's watching the men set about the job he's given them. Then, something odd happens, and I can't quite explain it, but I see him change his mind. There's something about his eyes, his expression. It's as if they shift and make him look almost a different person. He cups his hands round his mouth and bellows, "Stop!" Amazingly, the shouting and sound of breaking glass cease at once. "Leave it, lads, till I tell you different."

The men come back, grumbling. "I were enjoyin' that, Fred," one shouts.

I scramble to my feet. Colonel Cripps has stepped forward. "If you must, then take me," he says. Straker takes a stride forward himself, his eyes gleaming with triumph.

"Yes," he says. "This is a better way, isn't it, Colonel." He says the word "Colonel" with a sneer. "I knew you'd see sense, traitor Cripps."

There's an uncanny silence. I shiver, thinking I might see something terrible. Then Straker says, "You were wrong. We're no lynch mob. I'm not swinging for the likes of you. No, what I want, and what I'm going to get, is for you to repeat now, nice and clear, exactly what you said on recruiting day and then tell us, so we all hear, that it was nonsense and you can't fight a war if you don't believe the Hun is pure evil, a scum on the face of the earth, the devil's own spawn, and must be wiped out forever. Then tomorrow you'll come with us to the square and say it again to the whole of Lambsfield. Have you got that, Colonel?"

"I will never do such a thing," says Colonel Cripps. "Never. I would rather you were a lynch mob than make me speak such filth."

Straker doesn't answer. Then Mr. Randall—spade in hand, his old uniform making him look like a picture in our history books at school—advances right up to Mr. Straker and says, "Look here, Fred, you and me, we've had a few pints together in the Plough, and I've never thought ill of you, not like some in Lambsfield. But me and the colonel and Mrs. Randall, well, this is our place, you see, it's our castle, and we don't take kindly to folk coming here like you have and threatening us."

"And what are you going to do about it?" says Straker. "This isn't a threat; it's telling you what's to happen whether you like it or not."

Mr. Randall lifts his spade. Straker laughs. "You touch

me with that, and I'll make sure you're inside for the rest of your life. You're past it, John Randall. Your day's done."

"Oh, is it?" says Mr. Randall. "We'll see."

So there they stand, the three of them and Barney, and I wonder if the warriors at the bridge in ancient Rome had a dog with them too. On a sudden impulse, I run up to join them.

"Well, look who it is," says someone. I know the voice. Wilfred Langley. "Won't your pa be pleased, Ellen?"

Suddenly, someone throws a stone. Straker wheels round. "Who did that?" he snaps angrily. Well, he doesn't know, but I do. It's Bully. The stone hits Colonel Cripps on the forehead and he falls, blood masking his face. Mr. and Mrs. Randall stoop down to him, and Barney looks too. Then Barney, with a growl and a bark that I never thought to hear from so gentle a creature, turns and springs at the nearest man, wraps his teeth round his arm, and holds on. The man screams, "Get off, you bloody mongrel," and tries to kick him. "Let me do it," yells the man next to him, and swings his stick. It hits Barney sickeningly on the head— the lovely dog falls and is still.

Now Bully is nowhere to be seen.

The sight of Barney dead, and quite likely the colonel as well, quiets everybody. Fred Straker faces his friends and says, "I want to know and I want to know now. Who threw that stone?" There's no answer. I want to shout "Bully did" but stop in time. If the others saw, they don't dare tell his father. "Come on," says Straker. "Who threw it? If I swing for the colonel, I'll take someone with me, sure as God made me."

Colonel Cripps is unconscious. Mrs. Randall brings hot water and iodine and sponges away the blood on his forehead. Fred Straker joins us, strangely quiet and cowed. "Let me see him," he says.

"Haven't you done enough?" says Mrs. Randall.

The colonel stirs. Slowly, with difficulty, he sits up and looks at Mr. Straker. "Are you satisfied now?" he says. Then he sees Barney. Tears fall from his eyes as he awkwardly leans over and clasps the dog in his arms.

I want to cry too. But I look up away from the house toward Beacon Hill and Lambsfield. Two tiny lights are coming down the hill, nearer and nearer, until I see Pa on my bike, and Officer Foster on his. Officer Foster dismounts, lights up his bull's-eye lantern, and pushes his way through the silent crowd. Pa follows him.

"What's all this, then?" says Officer Foster. No one answers. "I think I can see for myself. Fred Straker, I reckon you could get five years for this."

"I'll not argue with you now, George," says Straker. "We'll all go home quietly, and you and I can sort this out between us at the police station tomorrow." He turns to the others. "All right, lads. We'll go back now."

Mr. Randall and his wife help Colonel Cripps indoors. He still carries Barney, and I know he won't easily part with the dog. Pa stands next to me, still holding the bike. "I'll talk to you later," he says.

"I want to see the colonel," I say.

"All right, Ellen," he answers. "But be quick. I'll wait out here."

Colonel Cripps lies on the couch in the sitting room. He

is pale as death, but conscious and alert. Barney's body is on the couch at his feet.

"I'm sorry," I say.

"You shouldn't be, Ellen," he says. "You came to warn me. If you hadn't, Straker might not have held back his hordes and this house might have been destroyed with us inside. At times like these, we must all find out how we stand, what the real truth is."

"But I don't know what the real truth is," I blurt out.

"No more do I, Ellen, no more do I."

"Poor Barney. Colonel, I'm so sorry." It sounds silly and weak.

"All wars have casualties," says Colonel Cripps. "The pity is, they are too often the innocent ones." His face is somber, stern. "I saw your father outside. He will be waiting for you. Ellen, don't worry about me. Go to your father. And thank you."

I expect Pa to be furious, but he speaks mildly. "George Foster's right," he says. "Fred Straker could go to prison and others with him. Still, I suppose he came good in the end. He's his own worst enemy, is Fred."

He turns the bike round and begins to wheel it away. "We'll go," he says. "We're not needed now."

As we leave the house and set off along the road, I hear sniveling. Pa points the cycle lamp toward the sound. Bully Straker is crouching behind a bush. He tries to hide when he sees us.

"Leave him be," says Pa. "He's learned a good lesson tonight."

"Why are you here?" I ask as we walk quietly together.

"You can't fool me, girl. As soon as I saw you weren't in the house, I knew where you'd be. I knew where Straker's gang was going. I found George Foster and brought him here. Just in time, I reckon."

"Pa," I say, "I'm sorry. I thought you'd be angry with me."

"What about?" he says.

"You said I should keep my nose out of it."

He laughs. "It looks like it's a good thing you didn't," he says.

We walk on for a while. Then he says, "Yes, it is a good thing. There could have been murder done here tonight. But this will get around now, and when people hear, they'll know where they stand and they'll know what it could lead to. Things should be better in Lambsfield now." He's quiet again, then says, "On the other hand, if Fred Straker goes to prison, it might split us down the middle even worse. All things considered, though, and on balance, I think you did all right."

The lights of Colonel Cripps's house are far behind us now. Pa speaks again. "You know what saddens me most?" he says.

"No, Pa. What?"

"You had to take sides with a toff to do it."

"But, Pa," I cry. "Colonel Cripps isn't a—"

"Yes, he is, whether you like it or not."

"But he's nice; he's good; he's not like Lord Launton. Perhaps not all toffs are alike."

"Perhaps not," says Pa, as if he's never considered such an idea before.

As we turn onto High Street, Pa says, "If this war goes on a long time, we'd all better hope you're right."

Yes, perhaps we had. I know I've done something good tonight, and I vow again that I'm going to do something more in the years that this war lasts, and be worth my weight. Though I said to Ma "My place is at home," now I'm not so sure. I've learned from the past few days, and next time I'll make sure things happen the way I want them to.

PART 2

·1915·

HARTCROSS PARK

Chapter Five

Some mornings I walk to the railway station with Pa's dinner—a bowl full of mutton stew or Ma's steak and kidney pie keeping nicely warm in a hay box. He's always forgetting it, and he can't go through the day starving. This fine May morning I go through the ticketing hall, and Billy Fawkes shouts, "Morning, Ellen. He didn't forget it this morning as well, did he?"

"He did," I reply, and Billy says, "Daft old coot. He'd forget his head if it wasn't screwed on." I go out onto the platform past the notice saying PASSENGERS MUST NOT PASS THIS POINT, crunch along the cinder path to the signal box, climb the steep wooden staircase, open the door, feel the heat from the fire, which keeps burning even on the hottest day—and there's Pa, standing in front of the double row of signal levers. The telegraph, with its dial showing "Train entering section" and "Train leaving section," tinkles now and then to say that a train is on the way. The needle moves from red to green, and Pa answers it. I like to think of him as one of a line of sentries, talking to each other to keep the trains and passengers safe. If one signalman is missing, the engine drivers could steam on, not knowing the danger, until they feel the grinding shock and the fire creeping through the wooden carriages as the gas lamps explode.

When I open the door, Pa's looking toward the station at the passengers waiting for the early-morning train. Then he turns to the home signal nearby, the distant signal beyond, and farther still to where the tracks meet in the distance. This is his little kingdom, where he makes everything happen. He looks round and sees me, smiles, and says, "Ah, Ellen, I knew it would be you. Have you brought my dinner?"

"You are a one, Pa," I answer, and he says, "I wouldn't have gone hungry. The early-morning goods is due. If driver Bob's chickens have laid this morning, we'll have a right feast. Perhaps they'll give you some too."

I say I'll wait, because the engine men often bring something worth waiting for. Soon there's a *ting* on the telegraph, and Pa answers it. Then he wraps a handkerchief round the top of a lever and pulls it back. Far away, the distant signal goes down. He pulls another and the home signal goes down as well, and I can hear the signal arm's heavy *clunk* as it falls. He pulls another lever back to set the points into the siding, because this is the morning goods train and there's loading and unloading to be done.

It steams off the main line into the siding and stops at the loading bay. Perhaps a couple of cattle trucks or baskets full of squawking chickens will be unloaded. On some mornings there are wicker baskets, which the porters open. A fluttering gray cloud rises into the air—homing pigeons set free to fly far away to their homes in Yorkshire and

Lancashire. The engine is uncoupled, steams slowly forward along the siding, and stops outside the signal box.

We go down the steps to where it simmers and hisses away to itself, and its heat hits me like a wall. The driver and fireman are here with cheerful, soot-streaked faces, and when Pa says, "Morning, Bob; morning, Alf," the driver answers, "Well now, Charlie, how about a fry-up? And Ellen too, if she'd like some. The chickens did well this morning." Alf the fireman adds, "Me uncle killed a pig last week. He's given me some rashers."

They don't need a frying pan. Alf puts his shovel into the firebox till it glows hot and comes out shiny and then spreads a pat of lard on the blade. As it melts, he puts the rashers on. Bob cracks the eggs open, and they sputter and crackle in the open air. I go back up the steps and bring out four tin plates, knives, forks, thick slices of bread, and hot, dark tea in tin mugs. We sit on the grass beside the rails and eat happily. Pa, Bob, and Alf talk about how the war's going, and I listen, thinking how wonderful it would be if there were no war and this moment could last forever. But it won't, and when I walk home, I know I'll feel sad.

This morning, when the eggs and bacon are eaten, the engine coupled up again, and the goods train gone, Pa says, "Don't worry, I'll still have room for my dinner. Your mother's pie'll go down well." He changes the subject. "Are you sure you want to do this?" He means me going into service.

"We need the money," I reply. Pa doesn't like the idea much and neither do I. I still feel sad about Colonel Cripps not taking me on.

That awful night at the colonel's house was six months

ago now. Fred Straker didn't end up in prison because the
colonel refused to press charges. If he had, Straker would
have been in court the next day. The village has quieted
down a lot. If anybody still thinks Colonel Cripps is soft
toward the enemy, they don't show it.

"It's a shame there was no job at the colonel's," says Pa.
"I'd have been happier if you were there. Now look what's
in store for you. I never thought a child of mine would
have to work for those people."

"Perhaps they aren't as bad as you think," I reply.

"Don't make me laugh," says Pa. "Everyone knows what
they're like, and a good many carry the scars. Nobody has
cause to thank them. Especially not *her*."

He's talking about Lord and Lady Launton from the big
house, Hartcross Park. Now, I'm sixteen, I've had to apply
for a position as a housemaid there, because I don't know
how to go about doing anything else, even though people
say Lord Launton's a nasty little man and if he wasn't a
lord, people would laugh at him.

"But, Pa," I say, "lots of girls like me end up working
there. He's the only one round here with a full staff of servants. Look at Dottie Langley. She went in as a housemaid
and she's the lady's maid now, second only to the housekeeper, and she's not thirty yet."

Pa looks at me sadly. "Oh, Ellie. Do you call that an
ambition? Those Langleys would walk ten miles for a sniff
of Lord Launton's dirty laundry, especially Wilfred. I'd
rather stand straight and be beholden to no man. Our
Jack's in the army doing his bit like all young men should,
yet all that's left for a young girl is to make things comfort-

able for toffs, just to get us a few extra pennies. It's all wrong, Ellen, it's all wrong."

"What else can I do, Pa?" I ask, and he says, "Ellen, I wish I knew."

I must write to the housekeeper and ask for an interview. I don't want to, but there's no alternative.

CHAPTER SIX

It's July and I've just come home from my interview at Hartcross Park. I got up early this morning, put on my best dress and new boots, and set off on my bicycle to see the housekeeper, with references from the vicar and Colonel Cripps. I thought Lady Launton might interview me, but Pa said she'd be too grand for the likes of us. It's four miles to Hartcross Park, and by the time I was pedaling up the long tree-lined drive, I was tired and hot. I'd started off so neat, and by then I must've looked a sight.

Mrs. Pardew, the housekeeper, is a stern lady with iron-gray hair. I sat in her parlor on a hard chair at a table with a green cloth on it. Mrs. Pardew sat down opposite me, put on a pair of glasses, and read my references. Now and again she looked up as if to match the person she saw with the one she was reading about. She read them twice, put them back in their envelopes, and said, "Those gentlemen seem to think quite highly of you." I could tell that, to her, men's opinions weren't worth the paper they were written on. The next question made me angry. "Are you pregnant?"

"Of course not; I'm only sixteen," I replied indignantly, adding "Ma'am," out of politeness.

"You do not call me ma'am. I am Mrs. Pardew to you." She looked at me with narrowed eyes. "I trust you have no callers, no gentlemen friends."

"No, Mrs. Pardew."

"Sixteen, you say. Age hardly seems to matter nowadays, even for respectable girls. Lady Launton insists upon the highest standards for her servants, and I agree with her completely. I need to be assured that your behavior will be beyond reproach."

"I shall do my best, Mrs. Pardew."

"You must do more than your best. Any slipup means instant dismissal." She waited for this to sink in, then said, "I trust you can read?"

Didn't she know I was at the village school till I was twelve and had been at the top of my class for reading and arithmetic? "Of course I can," I said.

"Don't be hoity with me," said Mrs. Pardew. "A simple 'yes' will suffice." She gave me an envelope. "Here is a list of rules for servants. Regard it as your bible. It shows both your duties and your privileges."

"Thank you, Mrs. Pardew," I replied, and opened it.

"Not here," said Mrs. Pardew. "You read it in your own time. Miss Langley, my under-housekeeper, will show you your room and tell you your duties."

"Mrs. Pardew," I said. "I don't want to be a live-in servant."

"Beggars can't be choosers," she replied. "If you work here, you'll do as you're told. Lady Launton wants her staff here and will not entertain servants living out. If these arrangements are not suitable, I suggest you leave at once. Plenty of girls your age would give their right arms for such an opportunity. Free board and lodging, seven shillings and sixpence a week for yourself, and Sunday afternoons off except for special occasions—I should say that's a chance not to be missed for a girl of your station in life."

I did some calculations. If I lived and ate free at Hartcross Park, then the whole of the seven shillings and sixpence could go to Ma. Betty and Madge could give Ma a hand in the house. I didn't like it one bit and nor would she. Pa would be furious. But what else could I do? At least I'd be home most Sunday afternoons. "The arrangements suit me very well, Mrs. Pardew," I replied.

"I should hope so." She tugged on a bellpull on the wall behind her. There was a knock on the door. Mrs. Pardew said, "Enter," and a tall, thin, youngish woman in a black dress and white apron stepped inside.

"Miss Langley," said Mrs. Pardew. "This is Wilkins. Show her the room she will sleep in if you please, and outline her duties."

Dottie Langley. Pa doesn't like the Langleys, and they don't like him. When we were outside, she smiled meanly and said, "I expect you Wilkinses think working here is a real comedown. Well, you'll soon find out which side your bread's buttered. I'm not Dottie here—I'm Miss Langley to you. I am numbered among the higher servants; housemaids are among the lower." She led me up a steep, narrow staircase to a landing with doors opening off either side. Dottie unlocked one. "This is your room," she said. "Read your duties when you're inside. Then lock the door, come downstairs, and wait outside Mrs. Pardew's parlor."

The attic room was tiny, with a sloping ceiling on which I could bump my head if I sat up suddenly in bed. The bare floor had a worn rug in the middle. There was a washstand with two large jugs and a washbowl, all old and cracked. There was no closet or mirror. The little fireplace looked as if a fire hadn't been lit for years.

I sat on the narrow iron bedstead to read the rules of the house. A lot of rules but precious few privileges. I was to keep out of the way of the family at all times. Up at six o'clock to do the chores before they got up. I must never talk loudly, sing, or whistle in case Lord and Lady Launton and their guests hear me. If I meet them accidentally, I must stand back out of their way. I must never hand them anything directly but instead place it near them. Only the butler, housekeeper, and lady's maid were allowed to speak to the family. I could have one bath a week, in a tin bath I must lug upstairs myself. When there are weekend house guests, I will lose my Sunday afternoon off. Last year I'd stood outside Colonel Cripps's house and vowed that in the future things would happen the way I wanted them to. Now look where I was.

I counted the steps going down. Seventy-four. Mrs. Pardew's parlor was locked. When she returned, she said, "Be here in two days' time. Meanwhile, Lady Launton has a gift for new servants." She handed me a roll of thick black cloth and a paper pattern. "I trust you can sew," she said.

"Yes, Mrs. Pardew," I replied. "I made the dress I'm wearing."

"Indeed." She sniffed, as if she didn't think much of it. "Lady Launton's generosity means you are spared the expense of buying your uniforms. You are required to make two dresses to the pattern provided. The cost of aprons and caps will be stopped out of your wages."

Was I supposed to be grateful? The cloth was rough and would be hot and uncomfortable. But I dutifully said, "Thank you, Mrs. Pardew." She answered, "Don't thank me. You should thank Lady Launton."

Even if I got the chance, I wouldn't. Riding home, I felt really unhappy. What sort of life had I let myself in for?

Jack's out in France now. He came home on leave over Christmas. He looked really well and very smart in his uniform. If he was frightened about going off to war, he never showed it. His regiment left in January, and since then his letters have had the bits that might tell us where he is crossed out. When I got home, Ma showed me his latest letter, which he'd written a week before. "I've been promoted to lance corporal," he'd written. "We're going up to the front tomorrow. Wish me luck and say a prayer."

There and then we did both. Then I thought of something terrible and said, "Oh, Ma, he might have been killed already."

Ma looked at me and I could see she'd been crying a lot more than I had today. "I know that, Ellen," she said. "I know that."

Tomorrow I must start making my uniforms.

CHAPTER SEVEN

I've been here a month now, and I'm getting the hang of it. Up at six, tidy my bed, make myself presentable, and go down to the servants' hall, where Mrs. Pardew and Mr. Gudgeon, the butler, inspect us before we start work. Mr. Gudgeon's quite old. He looks kind—kinder than Mrs. Pardew, anyway—but something about him says he won't let us get away with much.

Before I left home, I tried my uniform on. "You look nice," said Ma. But Madge said, "No, you don't; you look silly," and I thought she was right. I packed the old tin trunk, Jem Medley the carrier took me to Hartcross on his cart, and I dragged the trunk up the stairs to my room. With no closet, my things would have to stay in it. Still, Ma had found me a little mirror, even though it was cracked.

There are four other housemaids. Beatie is the oldest, about twenty-one; then there's Enid, Meg, and Cissie. Beatie has red hair and can get really cross. She doesn't like Mrs. Pardew, and she hates Dottie. That's in her favor, anyway. Enid, Meg, and Cissie are all about the same age—eighteen, I should think. Enid looks a bit prim and

proper, always tidy even after making the fires. Meg's tall
and thin, with fair hair. She says what she thinks and
doesn't try to dress it up. Cissie's small, with dark hair.
When she laughs, there are dimples in her cheeks. I think I
like her best. So that's who I've got to work with, and I
reckon I could do a lot worse.

After the inspection, there are hours of sweeping, dust-
ing, polishing, and laying fires. Then we serve breakfast in
the dining room. Beatie says that before the war, the footmen, Reginald and James, served, but now Reginald's in
the army and James is in the navy, so there's no one to do
it but us. Lord and Lady Launton often have guests. Already a duke and duchess have come and somebody from
the government as well. On those mornings the sideboards
are loaded with bowls of porridge, dishes of bacon, eggs,
kippers, kedgeree, racks of toast, and pots of honey and
marmalade. The guests pile their own plates high, though
we have to stand by the sideboard in case they want us to
do it for them. They never do, but they usually want us to
pour their coffee. They talk away in braying voices and
laugh at each other's jokes as well as their own. I know Pa
would hate the things they say about the lower orders. Still,
they can't eat all that good food, so we usually get what's
left. I think cook makes too much on purpose.

I mustn't sound bitter. I daren't upset anyone or I'll be
dismissed without a reference. When they've gone to do
whatever it is rich people do, we clear up, bring the bowls
and plates to Effie the scullery maid to wash up, then go upstairs to make the beds. Silk sheets and feather mattresses.

We serve lunch and clear up after it, then have a couple

of hours off, though we can't go in the gardens in case they see us; then it's preparing for dinner. At six o'clock we meet in the servants' hall for our meal and then serve dinner in the big dining room. At nine thirty we meet again, Mr. Gudgeon says prayers, and we're in bed for ten o'clock sharp.

There are very few men among the servants. Mr. Gudgeon, old Mr. Crabtree the head gardener, Sam the groom, and Ben the bootboy are the only ones left. Sam's sixteen and Ben's not fifteen yet. The others have joined the army. Albert Stover the under-gamekeeper, one of Straker's henchmen, has gone, which I'm not sorry about. Mr. Cox the head gamekeeper has to do the work on his own.

"Lady Launton didn't like them volunteering," Beatie told me this morning. "She even told her husband to make the army send them back. He tried to as well, but I reckon they laughed at him." I remembered Lord Launton speechifying at the recruiting meeting, all those fine words, yet when it applied to him, he'd tried to wriggle out of it.

"But he did keep Arthur back," said Beatie.

"What are you talking about?" said Meg. "Arthur didn't volunteer." Arthur Dunhill was Lord Launton's chauffeur.

"Of course he didn't. He's got a sense of duty to his employers," said Beatie. "He's too loyal—that's Arthur all over."

"Arthur, loyal?" said Cissie. "Pull the other one. Lord Launton couldn't bear losing the only person who can drive that noisy thing in the garage—that's all it was."

"The army took the horses," said Meg. "Pity they didn't take Arthur."

"Arthur's much too important," said Beatie, simpering.

"You only say that because you fluttered your eyelids and he came running," said Meg.

Arthur Dunhill is two or three years older than Beatie. He's got shiny dark hair, and he laughs a lot, especially with her. I can see how the land lies between them. Woe betide Beatie if Mrs. Pardew finds out.

Nobody said much as we ate that night in the servants' dining hall, not with Mrs. Pardew there, until Arthur told a joke. "There was this man, and he said to his next-door neighbor, 'I haven't seen your wife lately,' and his neighbor says, 'No, she's been ill.'" Mr. Gudgeon gave him a warning look, but he didn't stop. "'Is that 'er coughin'?' says the first man. 'No,' says the other. 'It's a chicken coop I'm making!'" He nudged Sam with his elbow. "Get it? Chicken coop. He said 'coffin,' not 'coughin'.' He thought the chicken coop was a coffin." Only Beatie laughed. Her face lit up, as if to say, "Isn't he wonderful?"

Mr. Gudgeon said, "You need not explain the joke, Mr. Dunhill. We see the point, such as it is, for ourselves. After such unseemliness, I shall seriously consider a rule of silence at mealtimes."

Sam whispered, "One in the eye for Dunghill," and Ben spluttered behind his napkin.

Anyone could see that Mrs. Pardew and Mr. Gudgeon had their eyes on Beatie and Arthur. I wondered whether I should warn her. Dottie was smirking to herself. She's got eyes to see as well, and she'll make trouble if she can.

After prayers, Enid, Meg, Cissie, and I climbed the seventy-four steps to our rooms, and at the top Cissie said, "Where's Beatie?"

"You know as well as I do," said Enid. "In Arthur's room over the garage. I saw her slip out after prayers. If they find out, she won't work in service again."

"That's her fault," said Meg. "I've no sympathy for her."

"If Beatie's dismissed, that's all the more work for us, and I work hard enough already. They won't find a new maid that easily," said Cissie.

"Why not?" I asked. "They found me."

"You live right on the doorstep," said Cissie. "There are new munitions factories in the towns that want girls to make shells for the big guns. Better money and your life's your own. That's where girls go now, and for two pins I'd join them."

"I wouldn't," said Enid. "Horrible, rough places."

"I could see Beatie going there," said Meg.

"She might be filling shells sooner than you think," said Cissie. "There'll be real trouble if she's caught creeping in after ten o'clock."

"There's nothing we can do," said Enid. "I'm going to bed." The thin sound came of the clock over the stables striking ten. "Wait," said Cissie. "She's here." Beatie was creeping up the stairs, her face red and flustered.

"You should be careful," Meg told her. "You could lose your place."

"I don't care. If I go, Arthur goes. He told me so."

"If you believe that, you'll believe anything," said Meg.

"You don't know him. Or any man, if it comes to that." Beatie was angry, and I was afraid someone might hear, Dottie for instance.

"He's like all men—he looks after himself first," said Meg.

"You're too young to know about men," Beatie replied.

"I've got a father and three brothers," said Meg. "Don't tell me I don't know about them."

I heard a door closing downstairs. "Shhhh," I said. "Someone was listening."

"Don't be silly, Ellen," said Beatie.

"We'd better get to bed," said Enid.

So here I am in the dark wondering who was listening and how much they heard and what it would mean. The more I thought about it, the more I was sure that the eavesdropper was Dottie Langley.

CHAPTER EIGHT

Sunday afternoon at home. It was strange being a visitor to the house I've lived in all my life. Ma made Irish stew, one of my favorites. Betty and Madge treated me as if I were back from foreign parts. Pa asked what I thought of it, and I told him, warts and all. "Don't let them wear you down," he said. I answered, "I won't, Pa," and he said, "I know you won't."

Ma showed me Jack's latest letter. He's just had a week in the trenches, but it was quiet except for a few whizbangs coming over. He's hardly seen a Hun, though they're only two hundred yards away, in their own trenches. "It's live and let live at the moment," he wrote. "If it stays like this, there's no need to worry."

"There you are," said Ma. "It's not half as bad as we think."

"It'll get worse," said Pa as he took the stopper out of a bottle of brown ale and poured it into a glass. He sat in front of the fire, puffing on his pipe, and didn't speak again until it was getting dark and time for me to go. "Good-bye, Pa," I said.

"You watch yourself," he replied.

So I pedaled back to Hartcross Park, full of Irish stew and wishing I could have stayed at home.

Next day, Mrs. Pardew spoke to us after her morning inspection. "Pay attention," she said. "Stop sniggering, Ben." Ben quickly pulled his face straight. "As you know, there's a war on."

"Who does she think she's talking to?" whispered Beatie. Mrs. Pardew looked at her sternly, then went on. "Lady Launton has decided that it is time for us all to do our bit for our brave soldiers, and I know you will not shirk in your efforts."

This sounded better. Perhaps now we'd do something worthwhile.

"You all know where Pembury Camp is," said Mrs. Pardew.

Of course we did. A big army camp about five miles away. Soldiers went there for training before they were sent to France.

"Lady Launton has arranged with the brigadier that we offer hospitality to our brave men before they embark."

Soldiers coming to Hartcross Park? I looked at Cissie. Her eyes were shining.

"Next weekend the house will welcome thirty officers from Pembury Camp who are going to France on the next draft. On Saturday there will be a ball, so the ballroom must be decorated to the highest standard. Suitable young ladies are invited as dancing partners. The officers will stay overnight on Saturday and leave on Sunday, ready to embark for France the following Wednesday. This means there will be no time off for anybody."

There was a deep silence. Cissie's face fell. Then Beatie said, "Excuse me, Mrs. Pardew. Is it only officers? What about ordinary soldiers?"

I heard Arthur mutter, "Well said, Beatie."

"Don't be impertinent, girl," said Mrs. Pardew. "Other ranks are not Lady Launton's concern."

How proud Pa would be if I'd had the nerve to say what Beatie did. With every floor I polished, every chair and table I dusted, I felt how unfair it was. At breakfast I wanted to empty the coffee pot over Lady Launton's head so she might realize we had feelings too. As I changed her bedsheets, I recalled how Jack once made me an apple-pie bed. I got the shock of my life when I tried to get into it. Why not make one for Lady Launton? I would have, too, except that I'd be sent home straightaway.

In the afternoon we met in Beatie's room. "I can't believe this," she said. "I've been fuming all morning."

"Surely you didn't think the likes of us would be invited?" said Enid.

"Everyone's as good as everyone else in a war," said Beatie.

"I don't think it works like that," said Enid.

"Well, it ought to," said Beatie, and I said, "That's right; it should." *Wouldn't Pa be proud of me now,* I thought.

"We can't do anything to change things," said Enid.

She's right, of course. That's the way of the world we live in.

* * *

It's Friday night and the ball's tomorrow. We've been getting Hartcross Park ready all week, on top of our usual chores. We made the guest bedrooms ready for the higher-up officers, then opened up rooms usually closed off and prepared them for the young ones. The rooms were dusty and the beds needed mattresses, sheets, and pillows. The doors between the drawing room and the ballroom were thrown open to make a really big space, and we polished the dancing floor till we could see our faces in it. We could only walk on it if we tied bits of old blanket round our shoes.

On Monday Mr. Gudgeon told us that Lady Launton wanted a tent for a buffet set up on the lawn. Sam laughed about it that evening. "She's got a hope," he said. "There's no one left here to put it up."

"Lady Launton is not 'she,'" Mr. Gudgeon said severely. "Watch your tongue, my lad."

"That won't stop her," said Arthur gloomily. "Get ready to pull on a rope, young Sam."

"In the present circumstances, Lady Launton will hire outside contractors," said Mr. Gudgeon.

The contractors arrived on Wednesday, six of them. They set about their work in the morning. We weren't allowed to talk to them, even though Meg said one was her uncle Cyril. By Thursday lunchtime the tent was up, and the men were gone. In the afternoon, Arthur, Ben, and Sam were set to work putting up trestle tables. On Friday we laid white cloths on the tables. Dottie supervised us and she was horrible, complaining if there was so much as a wrinkle. On the day of the ball, we brought in flowers from the garden. They were picked by Mr. Crabtree and his boy, and Mrs. Pardew arranged them in vases. Dottie was finicky to the half inch about where the vases were placed. I liked the tent. Sunlight filtered through the canvas roof and gave a lovely cool light, and there was a smell of grass underneath the tarpaulin floor. I thought how wonderful it would be to be a guest at the ball and meet a handsome young officer and dance with him all night, just like in a book. Then I said to myself, *Those rich young ladies can have all the gentlemen friends they want, but if we do we're dismissed on the spot. It's not fair, but there's no helping it.*

Sam, Ben, and the gardener's boy hung lamps along the terrace between the house and the tent. All day long, lovely smells came out of the kitchen, of baking cakes, roasting beef, lamb, and pork, and—not so nice—of partridges and pheasants shot by Mr. Cox and hung until they were well ripe. In spite of myself, I couldn't help being a little bit excited.

In the servants' hall at midday, Mr. Gudgeon said, "Well done, everybody. You may feel pleased with yourselves. I'm sure you have the gratitude of Lord and Lady Launton."

"They won't show it," muttered Beatie. Dottie gave her a dirty look.

"Mr. Gudgeon," said Arthur. "Don't you think that it's a bit much that we've worked ourselves half to death this week and won't get a bonus in our wages or a bit of extra time off?"

"Mr. Dunhill," said Mr. Gudgeon severely. "I will not tolerate such Bolshevik remarks. You know the terms on which you are employed."

"Yes, I'm employed to drive the car," said Arthur. "Nobody said anything about this."

"And other duties as may be required," said Mr. Gudgeon. "I should not have to remind you. There's a war on. We must all pull together."

"War, war, war. Just an excuse to put upon us even more," said Arthur. "What's so good about this malarkey? Some big people have given their houses to the army as hospitals and convalescent homes. If the old bat here did the same, I might be a bit more impressed."

"I'm warning you, Mr. Dunhill," said Mr. Gudgeon. "Disrespect to Lady Launton can lead you into serious trouble."

"See if I care," Arthur muttered. If Mr. Gudgeon heard, he didn't let on.

Chapter Nine

Sunday night. The ball is over, we've cleared up the mess, and I'm worn out.

We'd worked all afternoon, putting the finishing touches to the ballroom and laying out the buffet in the tent— bowls of chicken legs, chops, cold pheasant, salads, fruit, cheeses, joints of ham and beef for carving; jellies, custards, blancmanges—such a spread. Bottles of champagne in buckets full of ice, fine wines from Lord Launton's cellar, whiskey, brandy, gin—Sam's eyes popped out at the sight.

The officers began to arrive at three o'clock, some on horses and a few in cars, looking very dashing in helmets and goggles.

In the ballroom, the orchestra was tuning up. Soon the young ladies began to arrive, some with lady's maids, some with older chaperones, in cars, phaetons, ponies, and traps. Their dresses were beautiful, the height of fashion. It was another world, and I couldn't take it all in. But there was no time to stare. As dusk fell, Ben and Sam, in the footmen's uniforms Reginald and James used to wear, opened car doors, helped young ladies out, and took their parasols and coats to the cloakrooms. The lamps on the terrace were lit. It was all so beautiful that I wanted to cry.

But not because of the lovely sight. I thought of Ma struggling at home on Pa's wages and my seven shillings and sixpence a week, a scrag end of beef from the butcher, vegetables from the back garden, eggs from the chickens when they decided to lay; Pa in the signal box, bacon and eggs on the fireman's shovel; Jack away at the war. That was my world, and I could hold my head up high in it. We did better than some, anyway. But here—yes, I was really watching another world, a world closed to me. *Ellen Wilkins, are you envious? Wouldn't you love to be a guest with a chauffeur to drive you, and Sam to open the car door for you? No, I wouldn't,* I told myself.

I stood at the table holding a carving knife for slicing ham, and Mr. Gudgeon stood next to me behind a joint of beef. Music and laughter drifted over from the ballroom. Soon officers in dress uniforms came into the tent with their partners. "Be ready, Miss Wilkins," said Mr. Gudgeon. "Neat slices and not a word except 'Yes, sir' and 'Yes, ma'am.'"

I concentrated hard, feeling the sharp knife cut through the ham, taking pride in making the slices thin and putting them on plates without crumbling them. The chatter and laughter, the tang of the cool night air softened by the heat of bodies, the wreathing blue smoke and the rich smell from cigars almost put me in a trance as I carved, lifted, and placed, carved, lifted, and placed, over and over again. But my thoughts whirled away beyond the reach of anybody there, and that gave me great comfort.

A familiar voice brought me back. "Good evening, Ellen.

I heard you were here." It was Colonel Cripps, looking very impressive in his uniform with all his medals. "No, I haven't gone back to the army. I'm far too old," he said. "I'm here because of this reprobate."

The man beside him looked far from a reprobate. It was his photo in the colonel's sitting room. He was tall, I should think about forty, and also wore a dress uniform.

"Let me introduce my son," said Colonel Cripps.

"Edmund Cripps, major in the British Army, at your service," said the man. "My father has told me how brave you were on the night those ruffians came to call. I congratulate you."

"Thank you, sir," I replied. Mr. Gudgeon glanced at me.

"Edmund and his regiment leave England for France on Wednesday. Wish him luck, Ellen."

"I do, sir, oh I do," I said, and Edmund smiled at me.

"Good luck to you too, Miss Wilkins," he said.

"We had hoped Daphne, my niece, might be with us," said Colonel Cripps. "Alas, it was not to be." He changed the subject. "How is your brother faring?"

"Quite well, I believe, sir." Somehow I couldn't talk to him in the free way I did at home. "He was safe the last time we heard."

"Long may it continue," said the colonel, and they moved away.

"Miss Wilkins," murmured Mr. Gudgeon so nobody else could hear. "I told you not to talk to the guests."

"But they talked to me."

"The colonel had no business to. It destroys the system." He turned back to his joint of beef.

He really means it, I thought. If he didn't, he couldn't do his job. But I didn't believe it. I couldn't see myself still here in ten years' time, a lady's maid, wondering whether I'd take over from Dottie if she became housekeeper after Mrs. Pardew retired. I watched Beatie moving between the guests with a tray of drinks. Would she still be here? Never.

What's to become of us all? I said to myself. I went on carving ham like a little machine, knowing inside that something was about to change.

CHAPTER TEN

A week has passed since the ball. Everyone's edgy and bad-tempered. Dottie has been really nasty—on at Cissie and me about nothing, really sarcastic to Beatie and Meg, and finding fault with Enid, who deserves it least. Arthur is sullen, and I've caught him and Beatie exchanging glances as if they know something we don't. Only Ben and Sam seem happy, because Mr. Gudgeon told them they could go on wearing the footmen's uniforms, even though they look like scarecrows in them. Mr. Gudgeon and Mrs. Pardew go around with grim faces, and I don't think it will be long before there'll be harsh words spoken. It's as though someone is blowing up a balloon and one more puff will burst it.

Yesterday being Sunday, I went home for the first time in three weeks—the longest I've ever been away. Pa was still angry about it. Ma said, "Don't be so silly, Charlie. It's part of her job that she can't always get away when she wants. We knew that before she went."

"That doesn't make it right," said Pa.

I asked if Jack had written. "Not since you were here last," said Pa.

That's a long time for Jack. Ma and Pa were suddenly quiet.

"What's the matter?" I said.

"There's two families in Lambsfield had bad news," said Pa. "Ronny, the eldest Carter boy, has been killed, and so has Billy Fawkes's youngest."

I felt guilty. I should have been worrying about what would happen to Jack and about all those young officers at the ball going away and perhaps never coming back, not my own silly little concerns. It didn't matter a scrap that we had extra work while the guests at the ball had a wonderful time. They could be killed just as easily as Ronny Carter and Harry Fawkes.

"Jack'll be all right, Ma," I said. "He always is."

I stayed at home for longer than usual, rode back furiously in the dark, and was in bed only just before ten o'clock. Luckily Dottie didn't find out that I was so late getting in, but it meant that getting up this morning was very hard. My maid's uniform felt scratchy and uncomfortable. Going down the seventy-four steps wore me out worse than climbing them.

"Enid's overslept," whispered Cissie. "Now she's in for it."

"Wilkins, fetch her down here," Dottie ordered.

I dragged myself up the stairs again, knocked on her door, and called, "Enid, come on." No answer. The door was locked. "Enid," I shouted. Still silence. She wasn't there. I ran downstairs so fast I nearly fell headfirst. "I don't think she can be back from her afternoon off yet," I panted. She'll really be in trouble now.

"I'll speak to her when she returns," said Mrs. Pardew. Dottie ordered us to share Enid's duties between us and not to skimp on them.

It's been a long morning, but we're back in the servants' hall to eat. Mrs. Pardew, not angry now and holding a piece of paper, comes in with Dottie.

"I have received a telegram," says Mrs. Pardew. "It's from Enid's vicar." That's the first time I've heard her call a housemaid by her first name. "Her brother has been killed. I have wired the vicar back with our sympathy. In the circumstances, she is allowed an extra day at home."

Beatie nudges me and whispers, "Big of her." There's a quiet sniff on the other side of me. Cissie's weeping and trying not to show it.

"Don't snivel," says Dottie. "It's not your brother."

No one's hungry. When we're on our own again, Beatie says, "Mrs. Pardew might let her off for a day, but I bet Lady Launton wouldn't."

"Ooh, you are hard," says Cissie. "Why don't you think about Enid for a change?"

"Why should I?" Beatie answers. "Enid's not the only one who's going to lose a brother in the war."

"You're worse than Arthur, the things you say," says Meg.

"Arthur's the only one round here who talks sense," Beatie replies.

"You'd better be careful," says Cissie. "Dottie might catch you at it."

"Why should we care about Dottie?"

"She'll get you both dismissed."

"Let her. I'd go and work in a factory." She laughs. "In fact, I will work in a factory, unless…"

"Unless what?" says Meg.

Beatie smiles and then says, "Unless Lady L gives a ball for ordinary soldiers, with us as their partners."

We're thunderstruck, at a loss for words. Then Cissie says, "You're daft. She'd never do that."

"Won't she, though," says Beatie. "She will when she hears we're all going to work in a factory."

"But we're not," says Cissie.

"She won't know that," Beatie answers. "But it's what she'll hear."

"There's no way the likes of us can make her," says Meg. "Mrs. Pardew and Mr. Gudgeon wouldn't let us near her."

"She'll change her mind when we go on strike," says Beatie. Now I feel frightened but excited as well. Wouldn't Pa love to hear this.

Monday is over. Lord and Lady Launton didn't want the car that afternoon, so Beatie crept out to Arthur's garage. The rest of us spent our time off talking over her plan. Cissie thinks it's silly. Meg and I aren't so sure, though the thought of it makes my heart beat faster.

Beatie still wasn't there as we were setting the dinner table. Ben said, "I saw 'em both. They were being all lovey-dovey."

"Shut up," said Sam. "Don't let her hear." He inclined his head toward Dottie, who was arranging the candles at the far end of the table. Then Beatie ran in, looking flustered. Dottie didn't look at her but said, "I shall report your late arrival to Mrs. Pardew. Be thankful I won't tell her the reason. Watch your step in the future." She was enjoying herself.

Beatie didn't flinch. I thought she might say, "Tell her, if you like." Instead she said demurely, "Of course, Miss Langley. I always do." I heard the sarcasm, and I wondered if Dottie did as well.

The week has gone by, and it's Saturday night. I'll be glad to get away tomorrow. It's been quiet here, but there's a lot swirling away under the surface. Now that Beatie knows Dottie is watching her, she sticks with us all the time. If she's seeing Arthur, then we don't know about it, though Dottie's got a gleam in her eye like a dog digging up a bone.

I keep thinking about what Beatie said about a strike. It's a lovely idea, because none of us are happy. All those young ladies at the ball—they could have gentlemen followers. If Beatie and Arthur had been born into their class in life, they wouldn't be forced to skulk around like criminals. It's only fair that the house should be opened for us to invite ordinary soldiers and give them a good send-off. But is it worth striking over? Men go to prison for striking, and, besides, this isn't a lockout and it's not about our wages and conditions. What if we're all dismissed? It's all right for Beatie to say she'd work in a factory. How could I ever get to a factory? Another thing: if Beatie's with us every afternoon, where's Arthur? I know the Launtons haven't ordered the car this week. I suppose he has to oil it, or whatever he does, but that can't take all his time. I hope he hasn't got another lady friend. It would be terrible if he's leading Beatie down the garden path. I've heard the car start up a few times, and once I saw it going down the drive. I suppose he might be testing it, but what if he's going to see someone in the village?

Enid's back. She's very distant, and when we tell her how sorry we are, she just says "Thank you" so quietly that we can hardly hear her.

I'm on my bike, just coming into Lambsfield. It was raining when I started, but the sun comes out as I pass the Green, the Plough, and Billy Fawkes's house. The curtains are drawn because there's a death in the family.

The cottage seems deserted. "Ma? Pa?" I call. I hear a little cry. "In here, Ellen." It comes from the front room. Ma's sitting in her chair. She's been crying, and Pa stands over her. There's a newspaper on the table.

"It's Jack, isn't it?" I say.

"We don't know," says Pa. "It would be better if we did."

I look at the paper. There's a great battle at Loos in Belgium, and it says the British are beating the Germans. "But we're winning," I say.

"If it's as easy as they tell us, how come the war isn't over?" says Pa. "The telegrams still keep coming. Another young Lambsfield lad has gone."

"But it's not Jack," I say.

"Not yet," says Pa, and Ma starts crying again.

"Have you had anything to eat?" I ask.

"I couldn't," says Ma.

"You must," I say. "I'll make a pot of tea and see what I can find."

But there's nothing: no vegetables, no meat, and the shops are shut. All that's there is a stale loaf and a bowl of beef drippings. Well, drippings put a lining on your stomach, so I slice the bread and spread some on. I'm hungry myself.

I make the tea and bring it in with a plate of bread and drippings. Ma drinks her tea but doesn't eat anything. Pa eats his. So do I, and I'm glad of it. Ma says, "It's the waiting, Ellen. That's what I can't stand."

Madge and Betty have been playing in the fields. When they come in, I ask them if they've been good and helped Ma all they can. "Yes, Ellen," they answer, and Ma smiles at last and says, "They've been real little treasures."

The long September nights are beginning to come in. The sun sinks and the light goes. "Ma," I say. "You've got to get food in or you'll all starve. I'd have brought something over from the kitchens if I'd known."

"I know, love," she replies. "I don't seem to have the heart for anything lately. But I'll try, Ellen. I'll really try."

"We miss you here, Ellen," says Pa.

I know they do, and I miss them. My heart is heavy as I light the bicycle lamps and start the lonely ride back.

Chapter Eleven

There's been a crisis. Dottie isn't daft. She's gotten hold of Ben and wormed it out of him that he'd seen Beatie and Arthur being "all lovey-dovey." "Oh lor'," said Beatie when she heard. "That's done it."

"But you haven't been near the garage for a week," I said. "You've been with us every afternoon."

"No," said Beatie in a meaningful sort of way. "I haven't been to the garage in the afternoon."

At once I knew what she meant. "Oh, Beatie," I said. "You've not been stealing out at night?"

"She mustn't find out," she replied. "Or I'll be fired."

"But then you can work in a factory," I said.

"If I leave to work in a factory, I'll go when I choose to, not be pushed out by the likes of Dottie Langley."

"You'll have to stop seeing Arthur," I said.

"That I won't," she said defiantly. "In for a penny, in for a pound. I'll see him more than ever."

"It's nothing to do with us," said Enid when I told the others. Another time I'd have said, "No. It's everything to do with us," but I can't shout at Enid, not now. "We must find out whether she really goes out to see him at night," I said.

"What, and meet Dottie doing the same thing?" said Cissie. "She wasn't born yesterday. She'll have put two and two together by now."

"All the more reason why we should warn Beatie," said Meg.

"Arthur as well," I said.

"They won't get rid of him," said Meg. "He drives the car. That's why it's so unfair. What's Beatie but a humble housemaid?"

Then Enid spoke, and I was pleased that she was taking an interest again. "How does she get out at night without being seen?"

"I'll find out. I'll stay awake tonight," I said. "Beatie's room's next to mine. The walls are so thin that I can hear if she opens her door. Then I'll come and wake you."

"Good," said Meg. "We'll try tonight."

The Launtons had guests, and we were kept busy late. At last we all went up the stairs. "Good night," said Beatie, and went into her room.

My candle guttered out before I heard Beatie's latch click softly. I put a new candle in the holder, waited a moment, then tiptoed outside and knocked on Cissie's door. Soon we gathered at the top of the stairs. "You've got the candle, Ellen," said Meg. "You lead the way." The seventy-four steps seemed like seven hundred, but at last we were in the kitchen. The table was scrubbed and the kitchen ranges were still warm. The bolts on the door were open. "That's how she got out," Cissie whispered.

"It can't be," said Enid. "You need a key, and Beatie hasn't got one."

"Dottie has," said Meg. "She must have opened it."

My stomach turned over and so, I should imagine, did everybody else's. "Then she's bound to have seen her," said Cissie.

Enid went into the big pantry. When she came out, she said, "The window's open. That's how Beatie got out."

"We can't help her now," said Cissie.

"Yes, we can," said Enid. Her eyes glittered in the candlelight. She looked a different person from the quiet creature she'd been before her brother was killed. "If we don't and Beatie's dismissed, our lives will be a misery. We'll climb through the window, catch up to her, and stop her."

"It's easier to go out through the kitchen door," said Cissie.

"Better not," said Enid. "We could be seen."

She was right, of course. We scrambled through the window and crept round to the stables, where the garage and Arthur's flat were. The stables formed a courtyard. Once they were full of coach horses and hunters, but since the army came requisitioning everything, the only two left were those that Lord and Lady Launton rode. The clock over the archway leading into the courtyard struck midnight. Cissie was sidling under the archway when Enid said, "No. Dottie would go that way."

There was a dormitory for stable lads over the stables, though only Sam and Ben slept there now. There was also a flat where the head groom and his family used to live, but he'd joined the army and his wife and children had gone to live with relatives. Arthur had the flat now.

"Arthur doesn't do too badly," said Meg, looking up at his window. At that very moment, there was a flickering glow from inside, as if a candle had been lit. "Beatie's only just gotten there," whispered Enid.

Cissie suddenly gasped, "There's Dottie."

We looked toward where she was pointing. I couldn't see anything. Then a bush opposite moved. But it wasn't a bush—it was Dottie. When she straightened up, nobody could mistake that long, thin figure.

"She only has to wait to catch Beatie coming back," said Enid.

"She might catch us as well," said Meg.

"Not if we warn them first," said Enid. She really was taking the lead.

"How can we do that?" I asked.

"There's a way into the courtyard from the other side," said Enid. "Two of us can go round there. The other two stay and watch Dottie."

"I'll go with you, Enid," I said.

We crept around the side of the stables to the other end. "There's the garage," said Enid, pointing to big double doors. "There must be stairs inside to Arthur's flat. We'll go up and knock on his door."

"What's he going to think if Beatie's not there?" I asked.

"She's there, all right," said Enid.

The garage doors weren't locked, and I eased them open. The car was a great shadow in the darkness. There was a strong smell of gasoline. Stairs? No more than a wooden ladder with a door at the top. "I'll go," I said. I cautiously climbed the ladder and knocked softly at the door. "Go away," Arthur said, and I heard Beatie giggle.

"It's Ellen," I called. "Open the door. This is important."

There was a muttered curse, then whispering and a scuffling noise. The door opened slightly, and Arthur's head poked through. "What the hell do you want?" he almost snarled.

"Dottie knows Beatie's here," I said. "She's outside waiting."

Arthur opened the door wider. Beatie stood there looking flustered, disheveled, and frightened. "What shall I do?" she gasped.

"Did Dottie see you?" Arthur asked me.

"I don't think so," I replied.

"You'll have to go back, Beatie," said Arthur. "I can't have you getting into trouble. Blast the woman."

"What about tomorrow night?" asked Beatie.

"Best lay off for a while," Arthur replied. "Wait till it blows over."

Beatie tidied herself up, they kissed, and then we went out of the garage and back to the others. "Is Dottie still there?" Enid asked.

"I'm pretty sure I saw her creeping off," said Meg.

We sidled carefully back to the pantry window, climbed through, closed it behind us, and tiptoed upstairs, well pleased because we'd managed to do what we'd set out to. But at the top, Meg said, "I'm sure I shut my door before I went out."

"So am I," said Cissie.

"I know I did," said Enid.

But now they were wide open, all five of them, including mine. "Dottie," said Beatie. "She's letting us know she saw us. There'll be hell to pay tomorrow."

CHAPTER TWELVE

I don't think any of us slept that night. But all too soon I heard the thin sound of the stable clock striking six. Once again, I was out of bed knocking on all the doors, and we gathered in Beatie's room. There was nothing defiant about her now. "Well, what are we going to do?" I said.

"I'll be dismissed and never see Arthur again," Beatie wailed.

"We're in as much trouble as you," I said. "Dottie knows we were out when we shouldn't be, and she knows why too. We'll all be sacked."

"There'll be no servants left," said Beatie. "They'll get no more now."

"If you go, we'll all hand our notices in," said Meg. "Mrs. Pardew won't like telling Lady Launton she's managed to lose all her housemaids."

"That's cutting off your nose to spite your face," said Beatie.

"If we don't get what we want, we'll go on strike like Beatie said," said Enid. "Unless she stays and there's a dance in Hartcross Park for ordinary soldiers, and we're their partners."

"They'd laugh at us," said Cissie.

"Then we'll hand in our notice," said Enid. "We'd win both ways."

"It's too good to be true," said Meg. "There must be a catch in it."

We made ourselves smart and went down to the kitchen for the morning inspection. Mr. Gudgeon, Mrs. Pardew, and Dottie, with an unpleasant smirk on her face, came in. Mr. Gudgeon, looking grave, stood to one side. Mrs. Pardew's face was white with rage as she spoke. "I have never known such a flagrant breach of discipline as the one that occurred last night, which was only discovered by the timely intervention of Miss Langley. One of you is dismissed now, this moment, with no references. You know who I mean. The rest of you had better give a convincing account of why you were outside after your permitted hour. I'm waiting."

Beatie was crying into her apron. The rest of us looked wildly at each other. Then Enid—who else?—spoke. "We were only doing what was right for our friend," she said.

"Right? What do you know of what's right?" Mrs. Pardew shouted.

"If you get rid of Beatie, then we go on strike."

There, Enid had said it. Mrs. Pardew was so angry that she couldn't speak. Mr. Gudgeon stepped forward. "Young ladies," he said. Nobody had ever called us young ladies before. "I little thought I would see the rule of the mob at Hartcross Park. I'll give you five minutes to think better of it. We'll retire to Mrs. Pardew's parlor while you reconsider."

After they left, nobody said anything for a long time.

Then Enid said, "I'm really stupid. I said too much. Now there's no chance that we'll have the dance."

"Enid," I said. "You used to be so quiet; I thought you were really timid. But you've changed."

"I know," she said in a calm, level voice. "I loved my brother. But he was the boy in the family, and I was expected to be seen and not heard, and I got used to it. When he was killed, I almost wished it had been me. Then I thought, he's not here anymore to do all my thinking for me, so it's time I started fending for myself. I said to myself, 'Right, Enid, just come out of your shell.' So I tried and I felt good, and that's why I'm taking over from Tom now."

"I wish I was like you," said Cissie.

"You wouldn't want to lose a brother first," said Enid.

"We won't waver now, will we?" asked Meg.

"No," we all said together, and Beatie smiled again.

They were coming back in. The smirk was wiped off Dottie's face, and she looked really angry. I suddenly realized something had changed.

Mr. Gudgeon spoke. "What I have to say does not imply any relaxation in the discipline and standards demanded of servants in this house," he said. "But in the circumstances in which the war has placed us, we are for the moment prepared to overlook last night's escapades. Beatie's notice is rescinded on condition that she does not see Arthur unless another person is present. Now, can we hear no more of this talk of strikes?"

It had worked. Enid was right: we had them where we wanted them. I couldn't help it—it was now or never. "Mr. Gudgeon," I said. "We've been talking. We all loved

the ball that Lady Launton gave for the officers. We were
wondering if we could have a dance here as well, just for
the ordinary soldiers. We could invite housemaids from
other houses as well to make up the numbers. . . ."

I could hear the others breathing in sharply. They all
turned to look at me, but I couldn't tell whether they were
pleased or not. For a moment I thought I might be dismissed
on the spot. Mr. Gudgeon looked at me; then he smiled. "I
don't see why I shouldn't ask Lady Launton," he said. "I'll
think about it."

We worked really hard and extra carefully for the rest of
the day so as to give Mrs. Pardew no cause to complain.
I've decided I really like Mr. Gudgeon. He's a fair-minded
man. It's not for him to say if we can have a dance, but before the day was out, he'd gotten us all together to say he'd
arranged for us to make a deputation to Lady Launton
herself tomorrow. Even though she will say no, at least
we'll have tried and gotten further than we ever thought
we would, and that makes us happy.

Meg, Cissie, Enid, and I are just going in to see Lady
Launton. Not Beatie; she's keeping well out of the way. We
drew lots to see who'd do the talking, and it fell to me. Mr.
Gudgeon is coming with us. Mrs. Pardew is trying hard not
to let us see she's angry with him, but it sticks out a mile.

We made sure we were extra neat and got all our chores
done before breakfast. Now it's time to face Lady Launton
in the morning room.

I've swept, dusted, and polished the morning room scores
of times since I've been here, but I've never stopped to look
at it before. Today I can see it properly. The fire I lit in the

marble fireplace this morning is burning well. There are comfortable armchairs and newspapers on the table, which Mr. Gudgeon ironed before he laid them out. The wallpaper is crimson and gold. I've been here four months and have waited on Lady Launton at breakfast, lunch, and dinner, and I've never really looked carefully at her before either. All I can think of now is that she looks like what I imagine Queen Alexandra, King George's wife, is like. Before we go in, Mr. Gudgeon says, "Don't expect this to be easy. I have spoken to her ladyship, but I have no idea what she will say. She may dismiss you all on the spot."

Enid speaks for us. "We understand that, sir. We'll risk it." I suddenly wish she were doing the talking instead of me.

Mr. Gudgeon nods approvingly. "You have spirit, all of you. I like that," he says. "However, remember that as far as her ladyship is concerned, you are only asking for a dance. She knows nothing of the events of the other night. You have Mrs. Pardew to thank for that, even though she says it's against her better judgment. I trust you not to give her reason to change her mind."

He leads us into the presence of Lady Launton. "These are the girls I told you of, my lady," he says. "They are grateful to you for consenting to see them."

Lady Launton is sitting on a chair at one end of the room, so she is looking up slightly when I stand before her to speak, yet I get the impression that she's on a raised throne and looking down on me. She's a tall lady, about fifty I should think, and peers at me through her lorgnette as though I'm a strange specimen.

"Wilkins here is to speak for them," says Mr. Gudgeon.

"Well, Wilkins, what do you have to say?"

"Your ladyship," I begin, and then my tongue seems to freeze.

"I'm waiting, Wilkins."

I can't do it. The others are looking at me. I'm going to let them down. I think how disappointed Pa will be if he hears that I had my chance and couldn't take it. No, I have to be strong. I must speak.

I start again. "Your ladyship, we, the housemaids, are being so bold as to ask if you would consider allowing a dance to take place in the house to which we might invite soldiers from Pembury Camp and servant girls from other houses."

"A servants' party, I presume. But you have them at Christmas."

"We thought more on the lines of the ball, ma'am," I say.

"Why do you think I would allow such a thing?" she says.

"Because the soldiers are leaving, and they might be killed," I answer.

"I am well aware of the risks soldiers run," she says. "I have already given hospitality to such soldiers."

"But they were officers, your ladyship."

"I'm aware of that too, girl. Do you seriously expect me to let ordinary soldiers of the working class make free with the contents of this house? Do you expect it as some sort of reward for doing the job you are paid for, as well as being given generous board and lodging?" She looks at me piercingly and then says, "The answer is no. It would not do; it would not do at all." Then she stands and sweeps out of the morning room.

We look at each other, aghast. Mr. Gudgeon says, "I'm

sorry, girls. You did your best. It's back to work now." We walk, silent and dejected, back to the kitchen.

Dottie knows what's happened. "That's taken you down a peg or two, Wilkins," she says. "Now perhaps you'll know your place here."

Mrs. Pardew snaps, "We'll have no more of this nonsense."

What upsets me most is that it's my job this morning to make Lady Launton's bed, tidy her dressing table, polish the furniture, and shine up the mirrors. I want to tear those smooth silk sheets into shreds, rip up the mattress, break the mirrors. I've never known just how weak, powerless, and insignificant I really am. What's the point of it all?

At last the day is over, and I can't quite take in how it's turned out. I'm excited again, trembling with the daring of it all.

This afternoon none of us spoke or even looked at each other. Beatie never asked what happened; she could see just by looking at our faces. I went up to my room. The others had the same idea, including Beatie, so we were a silent procession up the stairs. Enid was last, and as we got to the landing, she panted, "Come on, all of you. Surely we've got a bit more about us than this?"

"You heard what she said," Cissie replied. "We're just dirt to her."

"We can go on strike, like we said we would," said Enid.

"I'm not listening to you," Beatie shouted, then stormed into her room and slammed the door.

Enid hammered on it and called, "It was your idea in

the first place." No answer. "And we did all this for you," Enid added.

"She's still upset about not seeing Arthur," said Cissie.

"That's no reason to go back on what she said," replied Enid.

I thought Enid was talking sense, and it made me feel a bit better. "Do you think we could strike?" I said.

"Why shouldn't we? Things can't be worse."

Beatie shouted through the door. "We'd all be sacked."

"Oh, Beatie," said Enid disappointedly. "You had a different tale before. We won't be dismissed, you said, because they won't get new servants and, anyway, you didn't care because you'd work in a factory."

The door opened and Beatie came out. "That was then," she said. "I'm allowed to change my mind, aren't I?"

"It's Arthur, isn't it?" said Enid. "Don't let him rule your life."

"He doesn't," said Beatie indignantly. "I haven't seen him since the other night."

"If you had gotten the sack, you'd never have seen him again," Enid replied.

Beatie clamped her mouth shut and looked out the window.

"Nothing's changed," said Enid. "Lady Launton's just as likely to get rid of us now as she was before, and that's not very."

"Why are you so sure?" Cissie asked.

"She'd have done it yesterday," Enid replied.

How I admired Enid. She'd convinced me and made me feel a lot better. "If we did strike," I said, "we might get our dance after all."

"Is it worth the trouble?" said Beatie.

"Even more," said Enid. "We've been trampled on long enough."

"Come on, Beatie," I said. "Arthur would be proud of you."

"Arthur won't care," Beatie replied, and started to cry. "He wants to join the army. That's why he said we should lie low for a while."

Somehow I couldn't see Arthur in the army, and I told her so.

"The army needs men who can drive cars," said Beatie. "He says he could be a general's chauffeur."

"Oh, that makes me so angry," said Enid. "He'll only join if he can do something that will save his precious skin. I reckon you're more likely to get blown up than he is, Beatie."

"That's not fair," Beatie cried. "You know nothing about him."

"That's more like it, Beatie," said Cissie. "You have a good shout."

"If you join us, Arthur will think a lot more of you," said Meg.

"If he's a general's chauffeur, he'll have a better chance of coming back. You can wait for him in a factory just as well as here," said Cissie.

That seemed to settle it, so I'm lying here full of hope again.

We were all downstairs this morning, especially neat and smart. We had our usual bread and butter and cup of tea, and then Dottie, as always, said, "Go about your work now."

None of us moved.

"Are you deaf? Get to your work."

"No," said Enid. "We're on strike."

"What?" said Dottie. "We'll see about this."

She bustled off and came back with Mrs. Pardew, who shouted, "What's this nonsense?"

"It's not nonsense," said Enid. "We're not working."

"How dare you speak to me like that? Take your notice and go."

"If she goes, we all go," I said. "Then who's going to do your work?"

"Silence, girl. Miss Langley, fetch Mr. Gudgeon," said Mrs. Pardew.

When Mr. Gudgeon arrived, he looked at us sadly. "I thought you might have learned a lesson yesterday," he said. We were stubborn and didn't say a word. "There will be no dance. That is her ladyship's last word on the subject." Still none of us spoke. Mr. Gudgeon shook his head. "Well, since you so blatantly refuse to go to your duties, here is what I will do. Mrs. Pardew and I will go to her ladyship and put the situation to her, though I doubt it will serve any purpose. If you still refuse to work when we tell you she will not change her mind, there will be no alternative to dismissal and we shall make shift as best we can."

I suddenly found myself saying, "Thank you, sir," and then the others murmured, "Thank you, Mr. Gudgeon."

"Good. Can I take it that your little strike is over?"

"Yes, Mr. Gudgeon," we chorused, and Enid muttered, "For now."

If looks could kill, Mrs. Pardew's would have skewered

Mr. Gudgeon to the floor. "Now, about your business," he said. "I shall see you at the end of the morning."

We worked enthusiastically, partly because we'd won a little victory and partly because we'd probably lose in the end and this might be our last morning here. The hours whisked by until we gathered in the servants' hall. Mr. Gudgeon was waiting. Mrs. Pardew stood beside him looking as though she'd sat on a nail, which I thought was a good sign.

Mr. Gudgeon cleared his throat. "Well, girls, we spoke to her ladyship as we promised. You'll be pleased to hear that her ladyship has changed her mind. You may have your dance."

We gasped with a noise like air being let out of a balloon.

"Her ladyship will make certain conditions, which I shall tell you when I know them. Now, enjoy your free time."

Afterward, Cissie said, "There's a catch in it somewhere."

"We won—that's all that matters," said Enid.

"There'll be so many rules, it won't be worth having," said Beatie.

"I don't care what conditions there are," I said. "We made her change her mind."

It's Sunday afternoon, and I'm going home. The sun is shining, the air is crisp now that autumn is merging into winter, and we've done something we never thought possible. So I feel very happy as I lean the bike against the wall in the backyard and go into the kitchen. Once again, everyone is in the front room, Ma, Pa, Madge, and Betty. I'm bursting to tell them my news, but then I see their faces. "Something's happened to Jack, hasn't it?" I say. "Is he dead?"

"No, not dead," says Ma. She's been crying.

"We had news this morning," says Pa. "He's been wounded. He had to have his right leg amputated. He's been discharged from the army, and he'll be home for good when they let him out of the hospital."

"At least he's safe," says Ma.

Yes, he is, and I'm thankful for that. But it's awful to think of our Jack with only one leg, hobbling around leaning on a crutch.

"What use is he going to be to anyone?" says Pa. "Working men need two good arms and two good legs. He can't go back to the building trade; he can't come on the railways with me—what else can he do?"

"He'll find something; I know he will," says Ma.

"There'll be thousands like him after the war," says Pa. "There aren't too many jobs for one-legged men."

I came home happy, and I'm going back sad. It's little comfort to me that it was worse for Enid. When I'm alone in my room, I can cry as much as I like, with nobody to stop me.

CHAPTER THIRTEEN

We'd been so busy getting our dance that we never thought how to organize it. So I felt angry when Mr. Gudgeon told us that Lady Launton was limiting it to twenty soldiers. But if Enid, Cissie, and Meg—I didn't count Beatie because she'd cling to Arthur—and perhaps Effie the scullery maid were the only girls besides me, even twenty seemed too many. We needed fifteen more girls, seventeen if you added Sam and Ben to the soldiers.

Mr. Gudgeon brought unexpected news. "Her ladyship is anxious to help," he said. "She has arranged with the commanding officer to provide the twenty soldiers. She will also ask other householders to permit some younger female servants to attend, suitably chaperoned, of course. Her ladyship and his lordship will be away for the weekend. Mrs. Pardew and I will be responsible to her for the conduct of the evening, and the men will have their noncommissioned officers here."

Dottie sniffed. "While the cat's away the mice will play," she said. "Her ladyship will live to regret this dance."

"It's not a dance," I retorted. "It's a ball as much as the other was."

"Take back all I said about Lady Launton," said Meg afterward.

"I hope you're right," Enid replied.

The ball is over. When I look back, it's just a wonderful blur, but I think it may have changed my life.

Lady Launton had forbidden us to use the ballroom. "The soldiers will wear boots and ruin the floor," said Mr. Gudgeon. "Dancing will be in the servants' hall." Sam and Ben shifted the big table and put chairs round the walls. Mr. Crabtree and Mr. Cox built a raised platform at one end, and Sam and Ben lifted the old piano onto it.

We were allowed a tent on the lawn, and the men came to put it up. Mrs. Cox and Effie prepared the food, and we housemaids decorated the servants' hall and tent with colored paper streamers and a few flowers. By Saturday everything was ready. First to come were the other girls— maids from nearby houses, chaperoned by older women. The soldiers arrived soon after, in their best uniforms and shiny boots. I thought they might march here, but they came in the back of an army truck with a sergeant major and two sergeants. They also brought a drummer, a trumpeter, two flute players, two clarinet players, and a pianist. A real band.

We dressed in our best clothes to welcome the soldiers. I felt quite afraid, because, apart from Jack, I'd hardly spoken to a man that age before. The girls stood on one side and the soldiers on the other, and there was an awkward silence. The soldiers were as shy as we were. Then the band struck up a waltz, and suddenly the ball had started.

Arthur and Beatie were the first couple to take the floor, and then—how amazing—Mr. Gudgeon and Mrs. Pardew followed. Some of the soldiers must have felt bold then, because first one, then another, crossed the floor. One asked Cissie to dance, another asked Meg, and soon nine couples were dancing. The music played and the dancers swirled round the hall and I looked on, feeling out of it all. Then another soldier crossed the room and—was he?—yes, he was, he was coming toward me.

"May I have the pleasure of this dance, miss?" he asked. He was quite small, with dark hair, and he had a funny way of talking.

"Oh, yes," I gasped.

I'm no good at dancing. He wasn't very good either, and he trod on my toes a few times. I was quite glad when the waltz ended and I could go back to my seat. A few dances later, he asked me again, and this time we did better. By the time we went to the tent for supper, we'd danced six times, and though I danced with some others and so did he, I liked him best.

In the tent it was just like it had been before, except that this time Mr. Gudgeon was carving ham for me. The NCOs who had brought the soldiers were also behind the trestle tables. My soldier accompanied me, and as our plates were filled, we started talking. His name is Archibald Braithwaite, but he asked me to call him Archie. He comes from Barnsley, and when I said I'd never heard of it, he told me it was in Yorkshire. "The soldiers here are all in t'Barnsley Pals, and we stick together like fish glue. We go to France on Wednesday."

"Aren't you afraid?" I asked.

"What, me?" he said loudly. Then he muttered so only I could hear, "Yes, I am, lass. I'm scared witless."

"Oh, I do wish you luck, Archie," I replied.

Archie wasn't nearly as tall as Jack; he was small and wiry, and so were the others. We talked and talked, because with him it seemed so easy. He told me all about Barnsley and the coal mines. "Black Barnsley, that's what they call it, because of all t'coal dust." When I asked him if he was a miner, he said, "Aye, lass, I'm from down t'pit. So's us all in t'Pals. You'll have to put up wi' old 'uns and little boys to dig your coal now." I spent all my time with Archie and hardly talked to anyone else. When the sergeant major ordered the soldiers to line up and get back on the truck, Archie said to me, "Good night, Ellen; you've made it a reet good evening for me."

"So have you, Archie," I said.

Then, as if he'd been plucking up the courage, he said, "Would'st let me write to thee, lass?"

"Yes, Archie," I answered, and felt really happy. "But don't write to here." I told him my home address, and he said, "I'll remember that."

"Good luck in France, Archie," I said.

He said nothing, but suddenly he leaned forward and gave me a kiss. It was gone so quickly that I couldn't kiss him back. Then he said, "I'll write. I'll not forget."

"Fall in, you men," roared the sergeant major, and Archie was gone.

I couldn't sleep much; I was too excited. Archie. I kept hearing his unfamiliar northern voice, telling me softly about life in Barnsley. Pembury Camp, so near yet so far. I could be there in half an hour on my bike. In three days' time he'd be in France, and I might never see him again, might not even get a letter—not because he didn't want to write, but because he'd be dead. I had a feeling I'd never had before. I found a name for it from a story I'd read. Yearning. Yes, that's what I was doing: yearning.

It's Sunday morning. No sleeping in for us: we're up at six o'clock as always. Mr. Gudgeon isn't here this morning, and Mrs. Pardew inspects us on her own. Dottie is with her, smiling as if at some secret joke. We have our usual bread and butter and cup of tea, then it's chores for the rest of the morning. When we've finished and it's time for our midday meal, Mr. Gudgeon is in the servants' hall, looking grave. "I'll leave the talking to you, Mrs. Pardew," he says.

"You girls, you've had your fun now," says Mrs. Pardew. "Her ladyship did all in her power to give you a pleasant night. Well, everything has to be paid for. Her ladyship has decided that you are to take three days' notice. You will be off these premises with your belongings by midday Wednesday. I need hardly add that you'll get no references." Dottie splutters with laughter and clamps her hand over her mouth to drown it.

When we're together later, Beatie says, "The two-faced cow."

"Which one?" I ask. "Lady Launton, Mrs. Pardew, Dottie?"

"All of them," says Beatie.

"We might have known it," says Enid. "We shouldn't have trusted them."

"Even Mr. Gudgeon?" I say. "I've always thought he was fair."

"Did you see his face when Mrs. Pardew was talking?" says Cissie. "I don't think he liked it."

"They won't get anyone to take our places," says Meg.

"Yes, they will," says Enid. "Mrs. Pardew has three days to find them, and I bet a few girls were got at last night. They planned this from the start, and I don't believe Mr. Gudgeon knew until it was too late. Lady Launton's had her revenge all right."

"What are we going to do about it?" says Meg.

"Nothing," says Enid. "We'll go with our heads held high. We don't have to be other people's servants."

"There's nothing for me here now, anyhow," says Beatie. "Arthur's handed in his notice, and he's joining the army next week. I'll work in a factory."

"Who'll drive the car?" says Cissie.

"Arthur's been teaching Sam in the afternoons," Beatie replies. So that's what he was doing when I thought he was with some other woman.

"I wish I could learn to drive," says Cissie. "I'd drive an ambulance."

"What about you, Ellen?" asks Enid.

"I don't know," I answer. "I'll think of something."

Suddenly I feel free. I've learned a lot here, and now I definitely know what I don't want out of life. Roll on Wednesday, when I can be out of here.

But Wednesday, when it came, was a tearful time. We promised to keep in touch. Who knows, we might all meet again one day. But, in spite of feeling sad at saying good-bye, I wasn't sorry to close the door of my room for the last time and hand the key in.

Jem Medley the carrier came to take me home. He heaved my bike and the tin trunk on his cart, his old horse plodded down the drive between the poplar trees, and Hartcross Park disappeared behind me. As we came into Lambsfield, we crossed over the railway bridge. A train passed underneath, and for a moment we were smothered in steam. When it cleared, I watched the train moving slowly toward the sea. Even from here I could see that the carriages were packed with men in khaki. The soldiers were going to the war, and somewhere among them was Archie. When we stopped outside our cottage, Archie was all I could think of.

PART 3

·1916·

JACK AND ARCHIE

CHAPTER FOURTEEN

Christmas came, and a bittersweet time it was. We'd hoped Jack might be home, but he was in a hospital somewhere up north. He wrote us cheerful letters, and when he did come home it would be for good, but nobody could be happy with how the war was going. Twenty-seven joined up on the recruiting day so long ago. Eight were wounded, including Jack, and five killed.

Since I left Hartcross Park, I've stayed at home. In January I celebrated my seventeenth birthday. The railway company gave Pa a pay raise, an extra five shillings a week. "They want to make sure their skilled men don't join up, the unpatriotic lot." Betty and Madge work so hard and are so good around the house that I almost feel I'm not needed. My seven shillings and sixpence a week isn't missed.

Pa thought it was wonderful that I'd been sacked. "I'm proud of you, Ellen," he said. "As for that woman, I've always said you can't trust her sort."

I've heard from all the girls. Beatie is making munitions, like she said she would. She's in a factory in London. It's hard work, but she gets a lot of freedom—a lot of drinking too, which worries me. She didn't mention Arthur. Cissie and Meg are at home, while Enid wants to go to London and be a nurse. I do miss them.

Archie wrote as well. He's in a huge camp near Boulogne—Etaples it's called—learning what to do when he faces the Germans. I wrote back right away.

It's March now, and Jack's coming home tomorrow. I'm happy and fearful at the same time.

As the train came in, Jack was leaning out the window trying to open the door. Billy Fawkes ran up, opened it for him, and took his arm. Jack shook him off, said "I can do it myself," stepped out on his crutches, and nearly fell over. "I'm not very good at it yet," he said with a little grin. He was thin and pale, not the sturdy lad who left us. His right leg was taken off above the knee, and he wore a blue hospital suit, which hung off him in folds. He was unsteady and his face was gray with effort, but he made it to the cottage. Pa opened the door and Jack stepped through, tears pouring down his face. "I never thought I'd see this room again," he gulped. Ma made him a cup of tea, and he said, "I often dreamed of sitting here by the fire with a good cup of tea." But he didn't want anything to eat.

It grew dark, and we'd still hardly spoken a word. Then Pa said, "Fancy a pint down at the Plough, son?" Jack smiled for the first time and replied, "I've dreamed about that too."

So off they went. "Those men," said Ma, and I knew what she meant.

*   *   *

Jack's been home three weeks now, and we're not so shy of each other, though he won't talk about France. Sometimes I catch him looking as though he sees ghosts, but then he grins and says, "It's all in a day's work, Ellie. I'll make out, you'll see."

I got two letters this morning. One was from Enid. She's at a big hospital in London as a probationer nurse. The other was from Beatie. She doesn't like the munitions factory as much as she thought she would. The work is boring and the hours are long. Also her skin is going a strange color; she thinks it's something to do with the explosives. She noticed other women with the same trouble but never thought it would happen to her. "If Arthur could see me now, he wouldn't even speak to me," she wrote.

The letters make me restless. I'd almost put up with skin like Beatie's if it meant I was doing something worthwhile.

Jack had a nightmare last night. I woke up and heard him screaming—terrible howls that ripped through the house. We rushed into his room. His sheets and blankets were all over the floor, and he was covered in sweat and writhing on the bare mattress. He was still asleep, though cries like someone tortured in hell were coming out of his mouth. Ma gasped, "Oh, Jack," and reached out to touch him, but without waking he screamed, "Get away!" and pushed her so hard that she fell against the wall.

Pa picked her up and said, "Easy, love. He'll be all right." Madge and Betty stood by the door, holding hands and frightened out of their wits.

Suddenly Jack went limp and opened his eyes. He stared as if he saw something horrible a long way off. Then he sat up and said, "It's all right, I'm safe, I'm home." Oh, Jack. What terrible things have you gone through?

Another letter from Archie. His regiment is moving up to the front. Jack asked me who the letter was from, and I told him about Archie. "Here, see it if you like," I said. "There's nothing in it."

He took it from me, read it, looked at me strangely, and said, "Don't get to like him too much, Ellie."

I nearly answered, "What's it got to do with you?" but bit my tongue just in time because I knew what he meant. But I can't help how I feel.

Much as I like being at home, if it goes on too long, I'll be dead of boredom. But what's there to do near Lambsfield? I'd have to go a long way off to get work, to the town or to London. The thought of going on a train so far away that I couldn't come home on Sunday afternoons makes me nervous. Jack's nightmares keep coming. We'll never get used to them, but we're getting less afraid of them. One day he might tell us what they're about.

It's Sunday night. What has just happened was not good. Ma went to the evening service. I said I'd go with her, and the girls came too. Pa never goes near the church, but to our surprise Jack said he'd come as well. Two months home and now he takes it into his head that it's a good thing to do. "Oh, lovely, Jack," said Ma. "I knew you'd want to sooner or later."

We walked together up the street, him clacking along on his crutches like a three-legged spider. He thinks it's quite funny now and doesn't care when people turn to look. He was given a false leg but won't wear it because he says it makes the stump sore. The church was quite full. People like Dr. Pettigrew and Colonel Cripps always sit at the front. Even Lord and Lady Launton sometimes come to their reserved pew, though not tonight. Colonel Cripps shook Jack's hand before we went in and said, "Welcome home."

Ma sat near the back, and Jack tapped his way after her. She knelt and Jack tried to copy her, but he couldn't manage with the crutches. When he tried to put them to one side, they poked people. He muttered, "Sorry," and said, "I can't get the hang of these blasted things," so loudly that everyone turned round to look. In the end he stacked the crutches up at the end of the pew.

The organ played softly as the little choir, six boys, Mr. Phelps the butcher, and Pa's boss the stationmaster came in, followed by Mr. Brayfield the vicar. Jack stood, sat, and did his best to kneel when everyone else did, though he was always a tiny bit late. He sang the hymns lustily but out of tune. In "The Church's One Foundation" he sang, "We are Fred Karno's army, the ragtime infantry, we cannot fight, we cannot shoot, what bleeding use are we?" When people looked at him, he stared straight back at them and said out loud, "I know this one: we sang it on church parade and these are the army words."

Ma looked flustered, and Madge and Betty sniggered behind their hymnbooks. Some people tut-tutted to each other. I heard a snooty voice say, "It shouldn't be allowed; the vicar should do something."

Then Mr. Brayfield stepped up into the pulpit, cleared his throat, and started his sermon. "Soon we shall sing our last hymn for tonight," he said, "'Fight the Good Fight with All Thy Might.'" I saw the choirboys sniggering as well, and I knew they'd sing their own different words— "Fight the good fight with all thy might. Sit on a stick of dynamite, light the fuse, and you will fly, right through France and German-y. . . ." The vicar paused and shuffled his notes. Then on he went, about the war being God's crusade against the devil, and how right was on our side and that our banners were carried by clean-limbed young warriors happy to die for king and country. I glanced at Jack. He was listening hard, taking in every word. Then the vicar said, "I see one such brave young man, gladly bearing the scars of battle, who is by God's grace returned to us."

To my horror Jack stood up, swaying slightly on one leg and grasping the top of the pew in front. "Do you mean me?" he shouted. Nervous whispering rustled round the nave. "Do you think I'm pleased I lost a leg? What do you know, you old twerp? Bloody hypocrites, the lot of you." He gathered up his crutches, clacked his way down the aisle, and disappeared through the west door. I heard mutters of "disgraceful" and "doing the Hun's work for him." Ma started crying. "Look after her," I whispered to Madge and Betty, and followed Jack. He was hobbling through the churchyard, and I caught up to him at the church gate. "Don't talk to me, Ellie," he said. "I've had enough."

"I know," I replied, and tried to take his arm. He shook me off and hobbled on. I followed, but as we passed the Plough, he said, "I'm going in here. I won't be back till late."

When I got home, Pa was smoking his pipe and reading the paper. "Pa," I said, "Jack shouted at the vicar and walked out of the church."

"Good for him," he answered.

"He's gone to the Plough. I think you should go and look after him."

"He's a big lad," said Pa. "I can't drag him home if he don't want to come."

"I don't want you to drag him home," I said. "Just calm him down so he doesn't do anything silly."

"You know Jack as well as I do," said Pa.

"Yes, Pa," I replied. "He's like you."

Pa stood up, tapped his pipe out on the mantelpiece, and put it in his top pocket. "You're right, there," he said, just as Ma and the girls arrived.

"Where are you off to?" said Ma.

"Plough," Pa answered.

"That you're not," said Ma. "Jack's in trouble."

"That's why I'm going," said Pa, and stalked out.

"Oh, Ellen," said Ma. "What are we going to do?"

It was after eleven when Pa brought Jack home. He'd drunk too much and could hardly stand. "I couldn't stop him short of punching him," Pa said, helping him into his chair. "Easy, lad."

Jack tried to speak, but it came out slurred. There was spit on his face.

"I wasn't there a minute too soon," said Pa. "The likes of Straker and Pinkney had lined up pints for him, and he'd got through four already. I tried to get him out, but they shouted at me to leave him alone, he only wanted a drink, and what sort of a father was I to stop him from having a good time after all he'd been through. I nearly hit Fred Straker."

"You'd have been in trouble if you had," said Ma.

"Anyway, they got tired of it, and by then Jack was too drunk to stop me from bringing him home."

"Oh, Jack," said Ma. "What are we going to do with you?"

CHAPTER FIFTEEN

Jack didn't get up until the afternoon. When he came into the living room, he was unshaven and his eyes were staring. "You must have something to eat," said Ma.

He flopped into his chair like a half-empty sandbag, threw his crutches on the floor, and stared into the fire. There was a knock on the door, and I opened it. Mr. Brayfield stood there. "May I come in, Ellen?" he said.

"Of course, sir," I answered. I couldn't say no, but I wished he didn't have to see Jack the way he was. Ma was horrified. "Oh, vicar, I'm so sorry. I've not had a chance to tidy up."

"It's no matter, Mrs. Wilkins," said Mr. Brayfield. "It was Jack I wanted to see. How are you, Jack?" Jack didn't even look up.

"I can't tell you how sorry we are about yesterday, and in front of all those people too," said Ma. "So is Jack. He wouldn't have let it happen for the world, would you, Jack? You'll say sorry to the vicar, won't you?"

Jack shot them both a look of pure hate. Mr. Brayfield tried to look him in the eye. "Let's talk man-to-man about this," he said. Jack pointedly looked the other way. "Jack," said Mr. Brayfield. "You said I know nothing about what it's like in the war. Well, I don't, and I freely admit it."

Jack muttered, "Then don't talk all that bloody nonsense."

"If I thought it was nonsense, I wouldn't say it."

"You're paid to," Jack replied.

"I have nephews," said Mr. Brayfield. "One was killed at the Marne."

"He's not the only one," said Jack.

"Jack, we could go round in circles like this all morning. I see this isn't the time to talk to you. I shall remember you in my prayers."

"Don't bother," said Jack.

"I'll see myself out, Mrs. Wilkins. Perhaps better days will come, and he will listen. I'm so sorry to have bothered you." Mr. Brayfield closed the door silently behind him.

Ma sat down despondently. "I can never show my face in the church again," she moaned.

Jack stood up. "I won't have him pray for me," he said. "I'm off."

"Jack, don't go to the Plough again," Ma pleaded.

"I'll go where I like," he growled. And out he went.

"Don't worry, Ma; he's got no money," I said.

"I wish your father would come home," Ma replied. "He's never here when we need him."

"He's at work," I reminded her. "If only Jack could get a job."

"Your father's right, I suppose," said Ma. "If a working man hasn't got two good arms and two good legs, he's nothing."

"Ma, don't say that. Jack's not nothing, and he never will be."

"He'll end up being a drunkard in that dreadful pub," said Ma.

"Not tonight he won't, not without any money."

"If your father's to be believed, all the ragtag and bob-tail of Lambsfield will buy him drinks."

"Then I'll have to stop them," I said.

"I can never go to church again," Ma wailed again as I left.

The street was empty. I ran to the Plough and looked in, but Jack wasn't in the public bar, and I knew he'd never dream of drinking in the saloon. Where might he go? One way seemed as good as another. So I kept on walking, past the Plough and along the road where it climbs through Hangar Wood and comes out where you can see the bare slopes of the Downs hiding the sea. Nothing moved over all that wide landscape. Jack seemed as far away now as he was at the Battle of Loos.

It was no use looking. I trailed home feeling sad and powerless.

Jack was still missing when Pa came home. "Why can't you keep an eye on him?" he demanded angrily.

We told him about how Mr. Brayfield's visit had set him off. "I was so embarrassed," said Ma.

"Anything could happen to him, and all you are is em-barrassed?" Pa roared. "Don't be so bloody stupid, woman."

I'd never heard Pa talk like that before. I know some husbands shout at their wives and worse, but I never thought to hear it in our house. The war's nearly ruined Jack, but please, God, don't let it ruin the family as well.

When Jack finally came home, he wasn't drunk. His one boot was muddy, and his crutches looked as though they'd been pulled across plowed fields. "Are you all right, lad?" asked Pa.

"Why shouldn't I be?" Jack answered.

"We've been so worried," said Ma.

"No, you haven't. You wish the Hun had done the job properly and I'd been killed so you needn't be ashamed of me. I'm going to bed."

How could he say that?

It's midnight now and everything's deathly quiet. I heard Ma's and Pa's voices for a long time, but they weren't shouting. Then they stopped, so now I'm the only wakeful one in the house. Unpleasant thoughts keep coming. What happened to those great promises to myself? I said I'd stand on my two feet and make my own life, and look at me now. I'm trapped and everything's going wrong. I want to be anywhere but here. I want to be with Beatie in the factory or Enid in the hospital. I feel I'm at the bottom of a well with sides too slimy to climb up and escape.

What's that? A crash as if something's fallen to the floor. Now there's a cry, no, not just a cry, it's a dreadful, dreadful howl. A shuffling sound, then another crash. I light the candle, get up, burst through the door, and blunder to where Jack sleeps. He's crouched on the floor in the corner of the room, his eyes bulging out of his head, strange gobbling noises coming from deep inside his throat. I force myself to sit on the floor beside him, take his head, and cradle it. He thrashes his arms and hits me in the eye, but I don't care; I cling on until he goes limp, his eyelids drop gently, and he is calm.

Suddenly, the room is bright with more candles and everyone's there. The bedclothes are scattered over the floor, and the mattress is wet with sweat. Ma is hysterical; Pa is silent. They don't look at each other. They're like two trees, an aspen shaken by the wind, an elm solidly standing apart, with nothing to do with each other. It saddens me as much as Jack's plight does.

Now he breathes, soft and steady. Things have to be done, and there's only me to sort them out. "Madge and Betty, strip the sheets off. Ma, get clean ones." Ma shuffles out of the room. "Pa," I say. "Turn the mattress over."

Now Jack has a dry, cool bed. We help him back in and cover him up. The even breathing never stops; he's sleeping soundly and deeply. I signal to the others to leave him in darkness and peace, take Madge and Betty back to our room, and sit on the side of my bed. The girls keep quiet, as if they're afraid of me. What if I hadn't been here— what if I really were with Beatie or Enid? Ma and Pa can't cope. My family is collapsing, and it looks like it's only me who can keep it going.

I hoped that once Jack was quiet and settled I would be as well, but I'm not, and when daylight comes, I haven't had a wink of sleep.

Today was torture. Ma didn't make any dinner for Pa to take to work, and he muttered, "I wouldn't eat it anyway." It was a murky, gray day as he set off, and I thought of that day over a year ago when the sun was shining and the signal box was a happy place, and we ate bacon and eggs together. I watched him go. For the first time in his life, he looked like an old man.

The girls were cowed and silent. Ma said nothing either, but her eyes had a sort of pleading in them every time she looked at me.

The postman went past the window, then an envelope came through the mailbox. The girls scrambled to pick it up first. Madge won the race. "Ellen, it's for you," she said. "I bet it's from Archie," said Betty.

She was wrong. It was from Meg and Cissie. "Dear Ellen," they wrote. "You'll never guess where we are. In a college learning to be land girls. We have uniforms and smocks and are being taught to milk cows and herd sheep and churn butter and all things like that. When we finish here, we'll work on a farm. We hope we can stick together like at Hartcross Park. Why not come with us, Ellen? We got on so well together, and you would like it here. Being in the fresh air is better than those old kitchens, and the people here are nice, not like Dottie and Mrs. Pardew. Please say you will join us." They signed it, "Cissie and Meg."

How I wished I could just pack the tin trunk and be off to a carefree life with my friends. Then I felt guilty that the thought of deserting my family had even crossed my mind. Even so, their letter was like a visit when you're in prison.

"Who's your letter from, Ellen?" Betty asked.

"No one you know," I replied.

"Ooh, it's Archie, and you're too shy to tell us," said Madge.

Their happy, rosy faces beamed, and their giggles were

like a cool fountain. Last night they were scared out of
their wits, yet today they'd forgotten about it. They are
good girls, and they were a great help to Ma while I was at
Hartcross Park. But things are worse now, and they're only
twelve, too young to take on the burden I'd leave with
them if I went.

A week has passed. Ma and Pa haven't shouted since, but
they've hardly spoken to each other, and that's worse.
There's an uneasy, tense feeling in the house, and I don't
like it.

Mr. Brayfield hasn't called again, which is just as well,
and Ma hasn't gone to church. Most of the housework has
fallen to me, and I've had to tell Ma what needs doing,
which doesn't seem right. Nobody has any go in them anymore. It's like shifting boulders.

I had another letter this morning, and this time it really
was from Archie. He says there'll be a big push soon,
they've been training for it for weeks, and they've been
given a week's leave before it starts. He's going home to
Barnsley, but he'll go through London on the way back
and perhaps we could meet there. Oh, how I'd love to.
The thought of seeing Archie again is wonderful. But I
can't leave Ma and Pa in the state they're in, even if it's
only for the day. I'll have to forget it.

I found some notepaper and a pen and started the letter
to say I couldn't. "Dear Archie," I wrote, and then sucked
the penholder while I thought what to put next. "Thank
you for asking me to London. I would love to come. But I
don't think I . . ." Then I felt a lump in my throat. Archie

wanted to see me, and I wanted to see him; it might be the only time. I put the pen down and rested my forehead on my hands.

"What's the matter, Ellie?" said Jack. He was looking over my shoulder at what I'd written. "A letter to your soldier boy?"

"Yes, Jack," I answered.

"It's not making you very happy, is it?" he said.

"It's all right," I replied.

"No, it's not, Ellie. I'm not blind. Something's up."

"He's asked me to meet him in London," I said.

"Do you want to?" asked Jack. "What sort of a bloke is he?"

"He's nice. He's quiet and respectful, and I do want to go, Jack."

"Then why don't you?"

"It's Ma and Pa. They can't cope anymore, and Madge and Betty are too young to do it on their own."

"I don't know what you mean," said Jack. "What's this about Ma and Pa not coping? Coping with what? And Madge and Betty aren't that far off from leaving school. You forget people get older, Ellie."

I didn't know how to answer, and, anyway, Jack got in first. "Cope with me, that's what you mean, isn't it? It's me who spoils everything for you all—it's me who's too much trouble."

"Jack, don't talk like that, please."

"Why shouldn't I? It's true, and don't pretend it's not." I couldn't bear it if he said "I wish I'd been killed" again. But he didn't. "You needn't worry about me, Ellie. Nobody's got to worry about me again."

"What do you mean?" I said.

"What I say. I'm a trial to you."

"It's not your fault; we all know that."

He suddenly changed the subject. "You've got to meet Archie," he said. "He deserves it. I know what he's going into."

"I can't, Jack."

"Don't take everything on yourself," he said. "They can do without you."

"I won't know how to tell them," I said.

"Easy. Just say, 'My soldier friend has asked me to see him in London and I'm going.'"

"I've never been to London."

"All the more reason. If you won't tell them, I will."

"No. If anyone does, it has to be me."

"The last few days before there's a push might be the last he'll ever have for a good time, and he needs something to look back on. Archie matters more than us back here now."

He was right, of course. "I'll go somehow," I said. "Thanks, Jack."

So, later that day, Jack and I told Ma and Pa, which was hard.

"What do you know about him?" Pa demanded.

"He's nice, Pa. I know you'd like him if you saw him."

"You can't go off with strangers," said Ma.

"He might be dead in a few days," Jack said angrily. "That's all you need to know. And he's no stranger to Ellie."

"Well, if he's good enough for Ellie, he's good enough for me. You go, girl, and good luck to you," said Pa, and I looked at him gratefully. But I knew Ma would be the difficult one.

"You're too young to go all that way on your own," she said.

"I'm seventeen," I replied.

"London's a big place, and it's got bad people in it."

"Archie isn't from London. He's only passing through."

"Let her go, for God's sake," said Pa. "It's only for a day."

Ma was stubborn. "She stays here. It's what daughters are supposed to do. It's their duty."

"Not anymore," said Jack.

"There's so much more to do now," said Ma.

"Now that I'm home. Is that it? Don't use me as an excuse." Jack was really angry, and this made Pa angry too. "You have a care how you talk to your mother," he shouted, though I noticed he didn't look straight at Ma.

"Ellie's going, whether you like it or not," Jack retorted.

Ma sat down and wiped her eyes with her apron. "Oh, Jack," she said. "Why are you turning against me?"

"I'm not, Ma," he replied. "I just want fair play for Ellie. She's the only one keeping us going, and I know it's all because of me."

Ma covered her face with her apron so we wouldn't see she was still crying. "Ellie, write to Archie and tell him you're going," said Jack.

There's no turning back now, even if I wanted to.

Over the next few days, Jack tried hard to be no bother. He had a couple of nightmares, but not like the night we found him curled up in the corner. But the more I thought about how he talked Ma into letting me go, the less happy I felt. Some of the time it seemed as though losing a leg was something he'd get over, like a cold in the head. Other times it was a curse that would never be lifted. He often went out, and we wouldn't see him for hours. He wouldn't let me go with him, though I asked him often enough. He seemed miles away, as if only his body were here and his mind were in a place where we couldn't reach him.

As the week went on, all I could think of was going to London. I worked harder than ever. Ma and Pa had always been rocks in my life, but now they had as good as disappeared. Sometimes I thought this must be like being in a trench before the battle starts.

Saturday's nearly here. Archie will meet me off the train, and we'll spend the afternoon looking at the London sights. In the evening we might go to the music hall and perhaps see George Robey or Marie Lloyd. Then he'll take me back to the station and put me on the train, and I'll wave to him through the window and he'll wave back, and then he'll turn round and walk away, and soon he'll be back at the war again.

Chapter Sixteen

My big day out in London is over, but now everything's worse than ever.

This morning the sun shone as I waited on the platform. Ten minutes to wait: they seemed more like ten hours. When the train was signaled, I looked to where the rails seemed to meet in a point, where it's blue with distance, and bridges over the line look smaller one by one, like the layers of an onion. I saw the tiniest dot where the rails met and watched it grow larger and larger and sprout a little white plume of steam.

However hard I willed it to go faster, it was an age before the train clanked and panted past me and stopped. The engine was painted a sort of yellowy-brown color, which Pa told me was called, for some reason, Stroudley's Improved Engine Green. It gleamed in the sunshine. I opened a door and stepped in. I'd never been on a journey this long, and now that I was on my way, doubts poured in. Would we recognize each other? Was I only imagining how much I'd liked him? I couldn't picture his face. Was this a big mistake? When we came to the great, echoing

London terminus, he was there waiting. I knew him at once, and he knew me. He looked very smart in his uniform and shiny boots. He helped me off the train and said, "Here we are then, Ellen, and won't it be a wonderful day?" Then I knew that it really would be.

First he took me to a café, where he ordered sausage and mash and a pot of tea. I'd never been in such a place and had food bought for me. Then we got on a motor bus and climbed up the steps to the open top. The motor bus took us down Victoria Street, and we saw the Houses of Parliament and Big Ben. Archie said "Buckingham Palace is near here—shall we get off and look for it?" I said, "Yes, please, Archie. We might see King George." But when we got there, we only saw the sentry in his bearskin helmet, and King George wasn't there at all.

"Ever been to a picture show?" Archie asked, and I told him I never had, though I'd heard about them. Soon we were in a picture palace watching the screen with people moving on it as if they were really there. I'd never seen such marvels. There was a film with Charlie Chaplin in it, and I never laughed so much in my life. When we came out again, the sunlight made me blink, but then we went on an underground railway and I was in the dark again. We got off at Charing Cross, went to Trafalgar Square, and then walked up the Strand. There was so much traffic—all those motor buses and horses and carts—the noise nearly deafened me. Then we went to a tea shop and had another pot of tea and some cakes. I asked him when he was going back to France, and he answered, "As soon as I've put thee on t'train home."

"Did you enjoy your leave?" I asked.

"Aye, I did that. I went to church wi' me mam and down t'pub wi' me da' and laikin' football wi' me brother and his mates and then I went to Oakwell and watched t'lads wallop the Wednesday. It were a reet good leave, Ellen." He looked so happy, and I was about to ask him what walloping the Wednesday meant, when he said, "There'll be a big fight soon. We've trained so hard that we know what to do, down to t'very second. It can't go wrong. We'll win t'war next month and then we can all come home."

"Oh, that's wonderful," I replied. "Yes, it is," he said. "Drink that tea up, Ellen, and we'll go to t'theater while there are still tickets."

We went to the Shaftesbury Theatre to see a show called *Three Cheers*. The theater was even better than the picture palace, much bigger, with red plush seats and lots of gold paint. Somewhere below me I could hear the band tuning up, and when I asked Archie where the noise was coming from, he replied, "They call it t'orchestra pit, just in front of t'stage." The lights went down, the band struck up, and the show started. There was a man who juggled with flaming torches, another walking a tightrope, and a woman who tied herself up in all sorts of knots, with her legs behind her head and her whole body twisted round in a circle so that I felt quite ill just looking at her. The program said she was a contortionist. Then two men called a double act told a lot of jokes, including the very one Arthur Dunhill told about the man whose wife was coughing and his friend thought he meant her coffin, and now I knew where Arthur had got it from. Then on came a lady dressed as Britannia, with a helmet, spear, and shield painted with the Union Jack, who sang songs about our soldiers and sailors. Lots of people joined in, but Archie didn't, until she sang "It's a Long Way to Tipperary," and then he sang as loudly as the rest. That ended the first part.

The person everybody had come to see was in the second part. Harry Lauder, with his kilt and his curly walking stick, singing:

"Roamin' in the gloamin' by the bonnie banks o' Clyde,
Roamin' in the gloamin' with ma lassie by ma side."

Archie took my hand and held it then, and I felt my heart beating very fast. Harry Lauder told lots of jokes, and I laughed even more than I did at the Charlie Chaplin film.

The show finished with a big surprise. Harry Lauder sang his last song for the night, "The Laddies Who Fought and Won," and suddenly there was a skirl of bagpipes and on marched a bagpiper in his plaid kilt and sporran. Marching after him came a troop of soldiers in red tunics, with black trousers and huge black bearskin helmets on their heads. "Scots Guards," Archie whispered to me. They marched and countermarched across the stage to the tune of the pipes, and everybody stood up and cheered and cheered and cheered. Archie, though, didn't cheer. We rose from our seats with everyone else. He kept hold of my hand as he stood ramrod straight to attention, biting his lip slightly. Then it was all over, the lights came up, and we made for the exit. "Did you like it, Ellen?" Archie asked, and I answered, "Oh, Archie, it was wonderful," because that's what it was.

Outside, the streetlamps shone, the traffic was noisy, and the pavement was wet because it had rained while we were inside. Archie asked if I'd like to go to a public house, but I said no because I'd heard that women got drunk on gin in London pubs. We went into a café instead and had a cup of tea. Then we got on a motor bus, though we went inside this time.

Soon we were at Victoria Station, where I'd catch the last train home. Archie found an empty compartment, opened the door for me, came in as well, and sat beside me until it was time for the train to leave. He was still holding my hand.

"There'll be big things happening when I get back," he said. I didn't say anything. "But I might not come back," he continued.

I couldn't make out his face very well in the carriage's weak gaslight, and, anyway, tears were misting my eyes. I'd never liked anyone who wasn't in my family as much as I liked Archie. So I said something I really meant. "But you must come back, Archie. I want to be with you all the time."

"I want to be with you," he said.

The guard blew his whistle, and Archie said, "I've got to go." Just like at Hartcross Park, he gave me a little kiss, then another one, so long that I couldn't breathe. The train started; he opened the door and jumped out. I leaned through the window and waved, and he waved back and shouted, "Wish me luck, Ellen." I answered, "Good luck, dear Archie. Good-bye." Then we were steaming out of the station and Archie was gone.

The train was nearly empty and nobody got into my

compartment, even though we stopped at station after station, so for two whole hours I could cry to my heart's content. Every time the train stopped, I looked out the window and seemed to see Archie striding away up the platform toward places I couldn't imagine. A sad end to the happiest day of my life.

It was past one o'clock when I let myself in through the front door. Everything was deathly quiet. The gaslight in the front room was so low as to be almost out. The fire's last embers glowed in the fireplace. Then I heard breathing, and a voice said, "Is that you, Ellen?" Ma was sitting in a chair by the fire. "Ah, you're home," she said in a dead voice. She didn't ask what my day had been like.

I turned the gas up and said, "Is something wrong?"

"No more than it ever is," she replied. I knelt down beside her and took her hand. "Ma, it's all right. I'm home now."

"I know you are," she said. "I don't begrudge you your day out."

"You managed all right, didn't you?"

"Yes," she said. "I managed." We were silent for a moment. Then she said, "Ellen, I know you'll go away and leave us one day. It's just . . ."

"What, Ma?"

"You were so happy this morning, and I should have been happy for you. But I thought of Jack and then of that young man you were seeing and wondered if he might come back like Jack or perhaps not at all."

"So did I, Ma," I answered, because all the way home I'd thought of nothing else. "But whatever happens, he's had a lovely day to look back on, and so have I. I'm very fond of him, Ma, but that doesn't mean I'm looking any further forward than today."

"Ellen," said Ma. "That's very grown-up of you."

"I know what the war means now," I replied.

She nodded and said, "Jack's not been well today." She wouldn't say any more. As I climbed up the stairs, I heard regular breathing from the girls, Pa's deafening snores, and those same odd gobbling noises Jack had made on that dreadful night. Still, at least he was asleep now.

Chapter Seventeen

The day before I went to London, Jack had seemed almost himself again. This morning his eyes were sunk deep into his head, his skin had a troubling bluish tinge, and his face was haggard. Pa was on early shift even though it was Sunday, and he had already gone when I got up. Madge and Betty were quiet, and Ma's eyes were red-rimmed. Something more than Jack's not being well must have happened yesterday, and I felt guilty for not being here. I could never leave this house again. When we were in the scullery together, I whispered to Ma, "Tell me what happened."

"Oh, Ellen, he depends on you. He doesn't want us. I tried to talk to him about you and your soldier friend, and he turned on me. 'What do you know about it?' he shouted. 'It was you old ones that sent us out there.' He said Pa made him go when he said that being a soldier is what all men should want and if he had the chance he'd go himself. 'Don't say you didn't,' he shouted at your pa. 'I remember every word.'"

"That wasn't fair of Jack," I said. "He was just as keen as Pa was."

"Please talk to him," said Ma. "If you don't, what are we to do?"

I felt a weight on me too heavy to shift. Two days ago he'd been so good, making sure I went to London easy in my mind. I'd thought I understood. But I didn't. When Archie had walked away, I'd feared what he was going to, but I couldn't really imagine what it was like. If only Jack could tell me.

"I'll try, Ma," I said. "But not yet. When I'm ready."

I didn't know how to start, and when I looked at Jack, miles away in his own world, I knew this was the hardest thing I'd ever have to do.

The rain that had started in London last night came back today, and it was cold and gray outside. Jack slumped in his chair, his crutches on the floor beside him. He hardly moved all morning. The afternoon wore on, and the silence roared in my ears. Evening came, Pa was still at work, and Ma took Betty and Madge to church with her. Jack and I were on our own. I had to speak now or I never would.

I took a deep breath and knelt by his chair. "Jack," I said. He stared sightlessly at me. I took his hand but couldn't speak. Thankfully he did first. "Did you have a good day, Ellie? How was your Archie?"

"The day was lovely. Archie's very well." It was now or never. "Jack," I said. "What was it really like in France?"

It was a long time before he answered. "Nothing special."

"Jack, don't fob me off. I want to know what Archie's going into. I want to know properly, not what people keep telling us."

"The training's hard," he said.

"I want to know," I repeated. His hand was cold. I tried to warm it, but he took it away.

An hour passed in awful silence. Then the front door opened, and Ma and the girls came in. I didn't have to say a word; Ma could see what was going on. Half an hour later, Pa came home, muttering about something that happened at the station. When nobody answered, he said, "What's up?" Still there was no answer, and he shouted at Ma, "What have you done behind my back?"

"She's done nothing, Pa," I said.

"Keep out of this, Ellen." I never thought that he would speak so to me. "It's your mother's fault he's like he is."

Ma sat down and seemed to curl up into herself as though he'd hit her.

"You've no right to say that, Pa," I said. "It's not true."

"I've every right to say what I like in my own house. And remember who you're talking to, young Ellen." That really hurt me. "I'll not stay here watching you women killing the lad." He stormed outside, slamming the door behind him.

"Oh, Ellen," said Ma. "What's happening to us?" We must have stayed in the front room for hours without speaking. Ma wept silently and so did I. Jack sat unmoving, a dark statue. At last Ma roused herself. "I'm going to bed," she said.

After half an hour, I said, "Shouldn't you go to bed as well, Jack?"

He still didn't answer. More time passed, great oceans of it. The clock struck eleven. "Jack, you must go to bed," I said.

At last he spoke. "You go yourself, Ellie. I'm better on my own."

So I crept upstairs. Half an hour later, the front door opened and Pa's voice, slightly slurred, said, "Why are you still downstairs?" I heard nothing from Jack, and Pa roared, "I asked you a question." Nothing again. "She's ruined you," he snorted, and stalked up the stairs.

In all my life, I'd not felt so unhappy, nor so tired. I hadn't slept much last night, and today had been a wearying one. My eyes were closing. I don't know how long I slept, but suddenly I was awake. The only sound was breathing: the others were asleep. What woke me?

A tapping noise. Jack's crutches. He was out of his chair. Door bolts moved and a latch clicked. Perhaps he'd gone into the yard to get water from the pump. I looked out the back window, but nobody was there. Surely he hadn't gone through the front door?

I got out of bed and tiptoed downstairs to the front room. The front door was ajar. I found a coat, went outside, and looked up and down the street. Toward the Plough it was empty. But the other way, toward the church, I saw Jack's ungainly figure swinging along on his crutches. I followed him to the gate into the churchyard, then lost him. Was he hiding among the gravestones? Perhaps he'd gone into the church.

The big west door was closed. I opened it and felt its weight swing on the hinges. The church was cold and smelled of old hymnbooks and mildew. At first there was no sound. Then came the clack of crutches on the tile floor, echoing under the high roof. I still couldn't see him. Another door opened and closed. I'd disturbed him and now he'd escaped. Why had he come here? Why didn't he stay? Didn't he know it was me? He must have gone out through the south door or I would have seen him. Perhaps he was making for the gate on the other side. I ran there, in time to see him vanishing up the path that led to Oldwood Mere.

When we were little, the children of Lambsfield used to splash around in it. It was our swimming place, and some of us even learned to swim, or at least doggy-paddle. But then the youngest Gaylor boy went out to the middle where it was deep and he drowned. Nobody ever went there again. The place where we swam was called the Planks, because there was a little wooden jetty we jumped off. It was rotting away now, but I saw Jack standing on the end looking into the water and swaying to and fro. He'd neither seen nor heard me. I came nearer and whispered, "Jack."

He jumped, as if woken from a trance. "Go away, Ellie," he said.

"No, I won't," I replied.

"You can't stop me." He stood on the jetty facing the side where the water was deep and dark and the Gaylor boy had disappeared.

"Stop you from what?" I answered. There was a splash. He'd thrown one of his crutches in the water, and it floated away back to the shore. Giddy with fear, I ran up the jetty. Three steps away from him, my foot caught in a rotting patch in the boards, a shooting pain ran up my leg, and I fell.

"Don't pretend you're hurt, it won't wash with me," he said.

I tried to stand but the pain was too much, and I was down again. "Jack!" I screamed. "Please."

Perhaps my fall stopped him from jumping. He must have seen I really was in pain, and he knelt awkwardly on his good leg. "Ellie, what have you done?" He touched my ankle and again the pain seared through me. "You've only sprained it," he said. "Keep still. I'll get help."

"Jack," I replied, "stay here."

"Not with you like that," he said.

"My ankle can wait. What were you going to do when I found you?"

He didn't answer the question, but he didn't need to.

"Jack," I said, "nothing's worth that."

"What do you know about it?"

"I know what's right."

"You know nothing," he said. He clumsily shifted his position so he was half sitting. "I'll come back here sometime when you don't know. I'll not be stopped."

"Jack, why?"

"Look at me. What can I do? I can't work again—they wouldn't have me back at Crispin and Thacker with one leg—there's not a job in the world I could do now. I'm useless."

"No, you're not."

"And what's it doing to you? Ever since I came back, I've been tearing my family apart and you're better off without me."

"That's not true. We'll try, we'll learn, we will."

"You can't."

"Jack, we love you."

He stopped, as if thinking about that. Then he said, "You don't understand, any of you."

"You never tell us," I answered.

The sky had cleared, and the moon was beginning to rise. Now I saw his face, frowning as if he were trying to work something out.

"You've never told us what happened to you out there," I said. He went on frowning. "I have to know, so I'll understand what's waiting for Archie."

Jack's whole body shook. I took his hand. It was deathly cold. "Can you tell me?" I whispered.

He trembled, and his mouth was open. I waited, still holding his hand. He muttered, words I couldn't make out. "What did you say, Jack?" I asked.

His voice was a breathy croak. "You're right. I've got to tell somebody or I'll go mad. Ellie, you're the only one I can speak to." Another long pause. His trembling eased. He took a deep breath, and it seemed to me that his whole body gathered strength. "People don't know," he said. "I don't think they want to. I don't think they'd listen."

"I would," I said.

He sucked through his teeth. It sounded like air escaping. "I dream most nights," he said. "I keep seeing them."

"Who?" I asked. A slight breeze ruffled the water and sighed through the reeds. Far away a fox yelped. Jack looked away and went on speaking in a flat, expressionless voice.

"They told us we were to relieve a Scottish regiment in the line, and we all cheered, because we thought we knew all about being in the trenches after the little skirmishes we'd had, trench raids and the like, though they scared me quite enough, thank you very much. But now we were really going to make our mark at last. And we marched, five nights on the move, bedding down in farmers' barns at night. We had full packs on our backs—it's like carrying a sack of potatoes everywhere. We were worn out long before we reached the front. As we got nearer, we kept having to dive into old shell holes to dodge German shells, and we lost men even before we got there." His eyes glittered in the darkness. "We got the order to fix bayonets ready for a charge. Ellie, that really frightened me. I'd only bayoneted sacks full of straw before, I'd never thought what bayoneting a living man would be like. Waiting for the order to go over the top was terrible. When it came we rushed out, well, when I say rushed, we had all that load. For the first fifty yards, nothing happened. I was beginning to think it was easy. Then the Jerries opened up, machine guns, hundreds of them, all aimed at us, and the men in front of me fell like a line of trees being chopped down. All we had to fight with were rifles, bayonets, and a few Mills bombs. We only had three machine guns for the battalion because the generals don't believe in them, so they tell us." His eyes filled with tears and so did mine. He took a deep breath and continued.

"My mates were falling all round me. There was a lad from London, Fred Lane his name was, and he'd given me a Woodbine while we waited in the trench. He was hit in the head and I watched his head explode, and his blood spattered all over me and I trod on him before I could stop myself. I kept going because I had to, I wasn't going to stand there and get hit—keep moving, that's the thing, it gives you a chance. Then it was like a horse kicked me in the leg and I was down, fallen into a shell hole. If I hadn't, I wouldn't be here now. I lay there and wished I'd died like the rest. Then another man rolled into the shell hole right on top of me.

He wasn't dead, and he kept groaning and moaning until he was quiet and I knew he'd gone. I shifted him off me a bit so I could reach down to see what was wrong with my leg and then I knew it was smashed up and my trousers were soaked with blood. Then I must have passed out because the next I knew it was dusk and everything was quiet. I heard a voice say, 'Here's one still alive,' and I was lifted onto a stretcher. One of the stretcher bearers said, 'Look over there,' and I saw German soldiers standing in front of their trenches and not firing while our dead and wounded were picked up. Some of them had their helmets off as if they were showing respect for the dead, and that was the last I saw before I got to the dressing station."

I let this sink in, and Jack said, "There, I've told you. Now you know and there's a weight off my shoulders."

"Thank you, Jack," I replied.

"Fred Lane, that's who I dream about, his head blown off right in front of me, and then that poor devil who fell on me, moaning his heart out until he died. Over and over again I see them. I'll always see them."

"Perhaps you won't anymore," I said. "Not now that you've told me."

"Yes, I will," he answered. Then, "Ellie, can you fish my crutch out of the water?" His voice sounded more like it usually did.

"I can't stand up," I said. "My ankle really hurts."

"You're as bad as me in the shell hole," said Jack, and I thought he nearly laughed.

"No, I'm not, Jack," I said. "Nothing could be like that."

"Ah, well, I'll have to get it myself," he said, and hobbled off on one crutch back to the bank. When he returned, he said, "Come on, Ellie, let me give you a hand up. I wish we had stretcher bearers here."

Somehow I scrambled up as he held me with one hand, both his crutches tucked under his other arm. "If we cling together and have one crutch each, I reckon we could get along pretty well," he said.

We moved slowly off the jetty and, once on the bank, tried to time our steps so we could move forward. We couldn't get the hang of it and nearly fell several times. Now Jack really did laugh. At last we managed it and started the long hike home, two crutches and two legs between us. It took a long time, and we were worn out with effort and laughing when we got home. I hadn't heard Jack laugh since he joined the army nearly two years before. I thought we'd wake up all Lambsfield and the family would be waiting in the front room. But no, the house was quiet and in darkness. I wanted to wake everyone so they could see this new Jack, but he said, "No, Ellie, let them sleep. Time enough tomorrow. Let's look at that ankle."

He felt it and the pain made me wince, although he tried to be gentle. "You'll live," he said. "I reckon you've only bruised it. It'll be nearly gone in a couple of days."

So I hobbled upstairs and only then realized how tired I was. But I didn't sleep at once for thinking over all that Jack had said. A chill came to my heart. What happened to Jack could happen to Archie.

I got to sleep but was soon awake again. That same howl from Jack and then the gobbling noises. I nearly got up to see if I could help him, but once they stopped, they didn't come again and nobody else stirred.

Chapter Eighteen

It didn't matter how tired I was, I still woke early. I got up to do some chores, even though my ankle hurt badly and I could barely hobble downstairs. It was Pa's day off and he always slept late. The front-room fireplace was full of cold gray ash, so I cleaned it out and got newspaper and kindling to start a new fire. When I lit it, all I got was choking smoke, which made me cough. The chimney needed sweeping and the fire couldn't draw. I took a double sheet of newspaper to hold over the fireplace to get a draft going. The air roared behind it, the kindling flared, and I smelled paper scorching. Then I saw the headline. It was yesterday's paper.

BIG PUSH ON THE WAY
GREAT ADVANCE BY BRITISH ARMY PLANNED
"THIS CAMPAIGN WILL WIN THE WAR"

I heard Archie's voice. *We've trained so hard. . . . It can't go wrong.*

The fire was going well now, so I put on lumps of coal from the coal scuttle and went outside to get more. All the time I saw Archie, like Jack, lying in a shell hole with a dying man tumbling down on top of him. And what if Archie didn't just lose a leg? What if he was killed? By the time I put the filled scuttle in the fireplace, I was crying my eyes out.

Ma came downstairs. "Ellen, what's the matter?"

"It's Archie," I answered.

"Why, nothing's happened to him, has it?"

"I don't know. Jack told me what he went through, and I keep thinking of Archie in Jack's place."

"Ellen, you mustn't go on like this. You hardly know the boy."

"I know what it's like in the war now. And Jack seemed happier after he'd got it off his chest."

"It's about time," she answered. "He's put us through a lot too."

"Ma!" That made me really indignant.

"He doesn't help himself. He's not as badly off as some. At least he's home, not like those poor Carter and Pinkney boys."

I couldn't believe this. "Ma, what's happened to you? He'd help himself if he could, but who'd give him work? It's not even worth asking."

"Then there's your father. He's no help either. He's been a different man since Jack came home."

"You should thank God Jack's back," I replied.

"Oh, Ellen," she said. "May God forgive me. I don't know what I'm saying lately, I really don't. I just don't know what to do next, and your father blames me for everything."

"I don't think he does, Ma," I replied.

"Then why is he like he is?"

"He's as frightened as we are." Then I thought—*I'm not frightened anymore,* not for Jack anyway. "Things will be all right; you'll see."

But when Pa came downstairs, eyes bleary, unshaven, no collar, and a stud hanging loose from the buttonhole, I began to wonder. "Don't stir yourselves on my behalf; I'll look after myself," he grunted, and slouched into the scullery. A moment later he came back into the living room. "Why couldn't you light the stove? A man can't even have a cup of tea in his own house now. If you want anything done, do it yourself."

I heard him blundering around in the kitchen as he got the stove lit and then the sound of the bread knife sawing through a loaf and the larder door opening. He'd be at the bowl of drippings again. Ma sat, her mouth tight shut. I hated it, and when I heard Jack clacking his awkward way down the stairs, my heart sank even further. Yet he seemed almost jaunty. "Morning, all," he said. "Weather's better today."

He was right, and I hadn't even noticed. June was here: sunlight poured in through the windows, and the summer would be a good one. He smiled, and we hadn't seen that for a while. "Cheer up, Ma," he said. "Worse things happen at sea. Don't fret yourself, I'll get myself something to eat." He went into the scullery. "Any tea left in that pot, Pa?" he said. "Bread and drippings? Is that all you've got? I'll have a look in the chicken shed. Perhaps there'll be an egg or two."

Two minutes later he came back. "The hens have done well. Four eggs, that's one each. I'll fry them and fry some bread up as well."

"I've had me breakfast," Pa grunted.

"Then have another. Something good and hot. Put a

lining on your stomach." He poked his head round the door. "Fancy some, Ma?"

"I couldn't eat," said Ma.

"Yes, you can. Get it down you—it'll do you a power of good. Ellie, I don't have to ask you, do I?"

Seeing him so different today made me feel hungry. Eating eggs and bread fried by Jack was a wonderful thing. He chivied us round the table and doled out knives, forks, and plates while the eggs and bread crackled and spat in the frying pan and tea steeped in the teapot. "Eat up," he said. It was the best meal I'd ever had. Jack was trying so hard, and I loved him for it.

At first Ma picked at her food, and I thought she'd push the plate away. But then she began to eat as if she enjoyed it too. Pa muttered, "I told you, I've had me breakfast," but he ate it just the same. Jack hovered round watching us, like I used to in the breakfast room at Hartcross Park.

When we'd finished, he said, "Ma, you've left some," as if she were a little girl, and she ate it at once. Then he gathered up knives, forks, cups, and plates, shoved them in the sink, and looked round happily. "Now then," he said. "What have you got to say about that?"

"Jack, it was lovely," Betty exclaimed, and Madge added, "I'm glad they taught you something useful in the army."

Pa kept his head down and stared gloomily at the table. Ma burst into tears. "Oh, Jack, I'm so sorry."

"You don't have to be," said Jack. "What about you, Pa?"

Pa grunted. "Pa," said Jack, "I'm trying my best. Why can't you?"

Pa looked up and I saw something I didn't think I ever would. There were tears in his eyes. "Son," he said, "I never thought to see you the way you are. What are you good for now? What's going to happen to you?"

"Whatever it is," said Jack, "you're not to blame Ma for it."

Pa slumped in his chair. "I can't help you," he said. "It's beyond me."

"Yes, you can," said Jack. "You can get us back to where we were before I went away."

"Easier said than done," Pa replied.

There was still strain in Jack's face, and then I knew you didn't get over something just by being able to talk about it.

"I'll wash up," said Ma.

"No, you won't," said Jack. "I will."

I thought Ma would argue, but she said, "Of course, Jack."

"You sit down," said Jack, and Ma obediently went into the living room. I offered to wipe, but he said, "You go with her, Ellie."

"It's not right he does it on his own," said Ma.

"Let him do what he wants, Ma," I said. "He needs to."

Pa stood in front of the fire and said, "Well, well, how about that."

"If we can help him now, he might be all right," I said.

"Yes," Pa replied gruffly, and then spoke to Ma. "Sorry, old girl," and Ma smiled for the first time in months.

The day is over. We've made a start. It will take a long time, and Pa's got to swallow some pride before he and Ma are back like they used to be. There will be bad days. What happened won't leave Jack; it will come back in his dreams. And then he'll look to where his leg used to be and wonder how he'll spend the rest of his life.

CHAPTER NINETEEN

Two weeks have gone by. Slowly things have become almost normal. But I fear that it will start again, because Jack won't be content with such a life. We sometimes go on long walks together now that he's getting quite agile on his crutches. He never talks about his worries, but I know them and spend hours wondering what I could do to help.

Yesterday I met Colonel Cripps in the street. "Why haven't you been down to see us?" he asked. "We've been worried about you. How's that brave brother of yours? I haven't seen him since his outburst in church."

"We're sorry about that, sir," I said.

"Then you shouldn't be. Such things need to be said where people can hear them. I admire Jack for it." He stopped, and it seemed to me that he was making his mind up about something. Then he said, "Forgive me for asking, Ellen, but what will Jack do with his life?"

"He doesn't know," I answered. "He says there's nothing for him round here; he can't go back to the building trade the way he is."

"That will be true for many young lads, I fear," he said. "It will be a big problem when the war is over. If only there were a simple answer."

He left me then and walked away down the street. I went home wishing there were a simple answer as well.

Enid wrote this morning. Her nursing training in London is going well. I'd envied Cissie and Meg before, but this really made me jealous. Nursing. What a wonderful thing to do. Looking after wounded soldiers. As long as Archie wasn't one of them.

I decided to ask Jack if he'd tell me about the nurses in France. "Jack," I said. "What happened after you were wounded?"

His face seemed to screw up in pain. "You can't imagine," he said.

"It can't be worse than what you told me before."

"It can," he replied. Then: "No, it can't. Parts of it were good. All right, I'll tell you. After I was picked up by the stretcher bearers, I must have been taken behind the lines to the field dressing station. I don't know, because I kept passing out, but I do know they stopped the bleeding somehow and dressed my leg. When I was awake, I saw hundreds of men round me—dreadful sights I can't bear to talk about—and I remember thinking, you lucky sod, Jack Wilkins, you've hardly got a scratch compared to them. I don't know who looked after me or who did the dressings, but I do know I was woken up by this terrible jolting up and down, and for a moment I didn't know where I was. But then I knew it was the ambulance train, and I was still on the stretcher, lying on a shelf. They told me afterward it was an old milk train, and the shelves used to be for stacking milk churns. It must have had square wheels—the jolting made my leg hurt something cruel—and I must have shouted out, because a voice said, 'Steady, old chap,' and that was that, because I went out like a light. They told me afterward that the MO stuck a pad of chloroform over my face. I don't know how long I was on that train, but I was awake enough to know that I was picked up and taken out in bright sunlight. The next I knew I was lying in clean sheets, and I've never felt anything so marvelous in my whole life. A nurse stood over me with her hand on my forehead. 'Everything's all right now, soldier boy,' she said, and it was the loveliest voice I've ever heard. Miss Bakewell was her name. She was from the Volunteer Aid Detachment—a VAD—and she was wonderful, they all were.

"Anyway, I caught a whiff of this terrible smell—I can't describe it—and I asked Miss Bakewell, 'What's that stink, miss?' 'I'm sorry, Lance Corporal Wilkins,' she said, 'but it's you. Your leg's got gangrene. We just can't stop it coming, I'm afraid, and then we can't get rid of it.' I tried to sit up, but she pushed me down and said, 'Don't look.' Well, the MO, Dr. McFadden, came along and said, 'Wilkins, I'm afraid that leg's got to come off, and I can assure you you'll be better without it. I'm afraid I can't wait, because there's a few other chaps' limbs to saw off before I go off duty.' 'What does he mean, better without it?' I whispered to Miss Bakewell, and she took my hand and said, 'He means that if he doesn't amputate, you'll die.' The next I knew the chloroform was over my face, and when I came round, I could feel the leg not there, if you see what I mean. The pain was unbearable and Miss Bakewell still held my hand, and while she was there, I could put up with it." He looked at me hard. "I reckon I would have died if that woman hadn't been there, but after that I never saw her again, and sometimes I wonder if I dreamed her." I didn't answer. "Ellie," he said. "Never tell Ma and Pa or anyone else about the gangrene. Let them go on thinking it was a clean break and came off because it wouldn't be any good to me anymore. Promise."

"Of course I promise," I replied.

"Well, they shipped me home, and I spent months in this hospital in the country—well, it was a big house, really—getting better, and the nurses were very good, but I never met one like Miss Bakewell."

"I'd like to be like Miss Bakewell," I said.

"Yes, Ellie," he answered. "Yes, you could. You would."

This morning there was a knock on the front door. Pa was at work, Jack was in the garden weeding, and Ma and I were making a pie. "Go and see who it is," said Ma. "My arms are covered in flour."

I opened the door and there stood Colonel Cripps, his left sleeve pinned up over his coat. He and Jack had something in common now. "May I come in, Ellen?" he said.

"Of course, sir," I answered. I remembered his son at the ball and asked, "How is Major Cripps?"

"He was well the last time I heard. Edmund is a survivor, like me."

Ma came out of the kitchen, red-faced and flustered. She gave a little curtsy and said, "Oh, Colonel Cripps, please excuse this pigsty. If I'd known you were coming, I would have made it all so neat."

"It's no matter," he said. "It's Jack I want to see."

"He's out the back. I'll call him in," said Ma.

"Please don't. I'd like to talk to him outside."

Ma was even more flustered when he entered the kitchen, but he passed through without a word. Jack was kneeling on his good leg, pulling at weeds among the pea sticks. He stood up, a puzzled look on his face.

"Oh, Ellen," said Ma. "To think a gentleman like him should see us in this mess. Whatever will he think?"

"Colonel Cripps isn't like that," I replied. "I don't expect he noticed, and it wouldn't bother him if he had." I watched them through the window. Colonel Cripps was doing the talking, and Jack listened hard. Once or twice he spoke, and I wondered if he was asking questions. This lasted nearly ten minutes. Then they shook hands, and Colonel Cripps came back.

"Thank you, Mrs. Wilkins," he said. "I'm glad to have had a word."

I went with him to the front door. "I know you're bursting to know what we were talking about," he said. "But I'll leave it to Jack to tell you."

When he had gone, Jack came in. I didn't expect what he said. "Ellen, do you mind if I take your bike apart and put it together again like I used to?"

"You can if you want, but don't ruin it. Why?"

"The colonel's opening a business. He wants me to run it for him."

"What do you know about running a business?" asked Ma.

"I'll learn," he said. "Old Joe Long the cobbler is giving up at last, and the colonel's renting his shop. The colonel says that what's needed round here is a bicycle repairer, so he's setting one up. He's putting me in charge, and I keep everything I earn while he pays the rent. What do you think of that, then?"

"Well, there are a lot of bikes in Lambsfield, I suppose," I said.

"He says the only condition is that if I take on new people, they have to be war-wounded like me."

"Oh, Jack," said Ma. "Did you say you would?"

He grinned and said, "What do you think, Ma?"

"Wait till your father hears this," said Ma.

But Pa wasn't a bit pleased. "Since when did our family accept charity from toffs?" he said angrily. "First Ellen serves in the big house, then my own son has to take scraps from Cripps's table. I won't have it."

"That's not true," I said. "The colonel's getting nothing out of it."

"Ellie's right," said Jack. "He pays the rent, I take the money."

"Well, if that's not charity, what is?" said Pa.

"All right, you suggest something," Jack answered angrily. "You're a right old curmudgeon. You've done precious little so far but make everyone's lives a misery."

Pa was furious. "If you hadn't only one leg, I'd give you a good hiding," he roared.

"The colonel's only doing this because he knows what it's like for me," said Jack. "That's a lot more than you do, Pa."

"Pa, listen to Jack, please," I said.

"You keep out of this," Pa shouted. "Nobody speaks to me like that in my own house. I'm off. You can give my dinner to the pigs." The door slammed behind him; he hadn't even changed out of his railway uniform.

Ma was in the kitchen wiping her eyes on her apron. "And I'd made such a lovely shepherd's pie for him," she said. "We're back where we started."

"I'll go after him," said Jack. "I'll make him see sense."

"You'll only make it worse," I replied. "He'll be in the Plough, and wouldn't Fred Straker love to hear you two arguing. I'll go, and don't try to stop me." And I was out the door before anyone could say a word.

Pa was already in the Plough. I saw him through a blue haze of tobacco smoke, standing gloomily in a corner with a pint tankard in his hand. "Why are you here, Ellen?" he said. "Go home. This is no place for you."

"I must talk to you, Pa," I said.

"If it's about Cripps and his crack-brained charity, I don't want to know. I'll not have my son doing it and that's it."

"Pa," I said. "Remember last year, before I went off to Hartcross Park, when I came down to the signal box and the engine men fried bacon and eggs on the shovel?"

His face softened. "Yes, I do," he said. "That was a good day."

"You told me something I'll never forget," I said. "You said, 'I'd rather stand straight and be beholden to no man.'"

"And I meant it," said Pa.

"But that's all Jack wants—to be his own master."

"Ellen, that's the whole point. He won't be. He'll be beholden to a toff; he'll be at his beck and call; he'll never call his life his own."

"But he's not a servant—he's not like me at Hartcross Park."

"It's a toff's money behind him, and they don't lay out for nothing; they want something back."

"That's wrong. Colonel Cripps just pays the rent and buys the tools."

"I don't trust toffs."

"I thought you liked Colonel Cripps."

"That's nothing to do with it. I've had no proper dealings with him. When it comes down to it, these big people are all the same."

If I'd been strong enough, I'd have wrung Pa's neck. "I don't think you want to see. You've got a silly idea in your head, and you won't get rid of it." I tried again. "What have Jack and the colonel got in common, Pa?"

"Search me."

"They've both lost limbs in war."

"Yes, but I've no time to worry about the colonel's when it's happened to my own flesh and blood."

"Pa!" I was angry now. "That's why the colonel's doing it. It's not through greed; it's not through pity. I bet you don't remember something else you said in the signal box."

"What was that, then?"

"You said it's a terrible time, and we've got to sink our differences and all pull together."

"I'll say this for you, Ellen, you've got a good memory."

"It's a pity you haven't, Pa." I'd never have dared speak to him like this last year. "Why don't you practice what you preach? This is Colonel Cripps's way of all pulling together."

"I don't believe that," said Pa.

So I said something really dangerous. "Look at you in your signal box."

"What's that got to do with it? I'm my own boss there. I make the decisions, and if I'm wrong, people can die. Nobody tells me what to do."

"What about the railway company? Don't they rule your life? They tell you when to come and when to go, when you can take time off and when you can't, and they can sack you as well. All for two pounds ten a week."

"We can go on strike if we don't like it."

"And probably be locked out," I said. "We went on strike at Hartcross Park, and we were all sacked."

"It's like I said," Pa replied. "These people have us at their mercy."

"Then stop being so stubborn and let Jack have his chance."

I almost thought I'd won, until he said, "I'm your father, Ellen, and you're a girl still, so don't you forget it. I've given you enough rope already. Tell your mother not to wait up for me."

He turned away from me as if I weren't there, and I trailed miserably back home.

That night I dreamed I was a nurse in a hospital near the front line and the soldiers kept being brought in on stretchers. One looked up at me, and I took his hand and said, "You'll be all right now," and when I looked, it was Archie. But he couldn't have been too bad at all, because he jumped off the stretcher and said, 'I'm going home to Barnsley now. Are you coming with me, Ellen?' Before I could say anything, another soldier was brought in. It was Archie again, and this time he was dead.

I woke up, still feeling tired. The sun shone, but the air

struck cold and made me shiver. The house was silent. Pa
must have gotten himself off to work without waking anybody. The chickens hadn't laid, so it was bread and drippings again.

Nobody talked much throughout the long day. I didn't
mention last night, and nobody asked me. Jack wasn't bub-
bly like he was yesterday. "I don't care what he thinks," he
said. "He can't stop me."

Ma's face was troubled, and I thought of the years
ahead if Pa thought we'd gone against his will. I knew families who dreaded the time the husband came home from
work. We'd been a bit like that ourselves these last months,
and I wanted it changed to how it used to be.

Afternoon came, and I made up my mind. I didn't care
what he said or how angry he was, I'd go to the signal box
again.

"Why are you here, Ellen?" said Billy Fawkes when I got
to the station.

"To see Pa," I answered.

"I warn you, I don't know what's got into him today,
he's in a foul temper," said Billy.

"I know," I replied, and carried on down the platform,
climbed the steps to the signal box, and opened the door.
Pa had his back to me, looking through the window up the
line.

"May I come in?" I said.

"Suit yourself," he replied, not even looking round. I felt
so tense I hardly dared breathe. "Pa . . .," I said.

Only then did he turn round. His face wasn't angry. He
was pale, hollow-eyed, unshaven. I'd never seen him

anything but as smart as a sergeant major when he went to work. "What do you want?" he said. His voice was flat, surly.

"I'm sorry," I replied, "I'd better go," and I opened the door again.

"No, Ellen," he said. "I want you to stay." He pulled out the two chairs in the box, and we sat facing each other. "We've got a few minutes. There's no train due yet. I've been thinking. I might have got things wrong. Seeing Jack come home like that knocked me all of a heap."

"It was the same for us all, Pa."

"I tried to tell myself it hadn't happened, that it didn't matter, that we'd go on in the same way now that he was home for good. After all, he wasn't dead. He'd only lost a leg. That's what I thought, God help me."

"But it couldn't be the same anymore, could it, Pa?"

"I know. But I started blaming your ma for how he was. I thought she wasn't even trying to cope. He's not a baby; he should be able to look after himself and get on with things properly."

"But he can't, Pa, not on his own. You're always saying a working man without his two arms and two legs is no use to anyone."

"I know I am, but I expected our Jack to show me I was wrong."

"Pa, how could he? You heard him at night, shrieking and howling, and that terrible gobbling noise. All those nightmares, how could he?"

"I wanted him to try harder. I didn't want your ma stopping him, or you, for that matter."

"Pa, that was very wrong. You've been horrible to Ma."

"I'll make it up to her, Ellen. I will, honestly."

"But what about Jack's shop? You know what it could mean to him."

"I should be the one to do all that for him. I would have if I could. How do you think it makes me feel to see someone else coming along and taking on what's my responsibility?"

I felt so sad for him then. His pride was gone, the most valuable thing he had. "Pa," I said, "Colonel Cripps is only thinking of Jack and men like him. He's not doing it to make you feel bad."

"It's not right, Ellen. It should be me."

"Just be thankful that Jack's happy. He must go into this with a good heart, not worrying about what happens at home."

"I suppose so," he said. The telegraph tinkled and he said, "I've got to do some work. The down London's due." He stood up, heaved back the lever for the distant signal, then for the home signal, and pinged the telegraph to show he'd got the message and accepted the train. "I'll just have to put up with it, won't I, Ellen?" he said. "I'll try to get used to the idea, you'll see."

"That's wonderful, Pa," I replied.

He caught me by the hand before I left. "You're a good daughter, Ellen," he said. "A man should be proud to have one like you."

I had a real lump in my throat as I ran down the steps outside.

Chapter Twenty

Neither Ma nor Jack said a word when I got back. But when Pa came home, Jack spoke to him at once. "I've been thinking," he said. "If I do well and make money, as soon as I can afford it, I'll start paying the rent, not the colonel. I couldn't start this without him, but I aim to make it all mine."

For the first time in months, Pa sat down in his chair by the fire, lit his pipe, leaned back, looking comfortable, and said, "Good for you, son. That's what I wanted to hear." It really seemed that the atmosphere in the cottage was something like it used to be, especially when Ma brought in one of her famous pies and Pa said, "No one makes them like you, old girl."

Everyone's talking about a huge battle at the river Somme, so Archie was right. The papers say that we'll break through and then the war will be won. Oh, how I hope so. Two weeks have passed since Pa and I talked in the signal box. Yesterday Ma said to me, "Isn't it grand how much nicer it is now? Oh, Ellen, I wonder where we'd be if it wasn't for you."

"It would have happened by itself sooner or later," I replied. "But, Ma, I was so frightened."

"Me, too," said Ma. "And look at Jack now."

The colonel did all he said he would. He paid the rent, bought new tools and spare parts, a workbench, a till, and even a safe to keep the money in. Pa gave the walls a coat of whitewash and painted the doors. The old signboard outside—J. LONG SHOE REPAIRS AT REASONABLE PRICES—went and J. WILKINS, BICYCLE REPAIRER was put up in its place. The colonel had posters printed and put up all over Lambsfield and the villages nearby. Tomorrow Jack will open the shop.

I was waiting with Jack in the shop, sniffing the new paint and looking at the shiny new tools. We waited . . . and waited . . . and waited. Two hours passed. Jack was agitated. "Nobody's interested. What a stupid idea this was."

"They'll come," I said.

Ten more minutes went by. "No, they won't," said Jack.

Just then, someone did, and my heart sank. Fred Straker. "Careful—he's out to make trouble," Jack muttered. Straker wheeled in a black bike and looked embarrassed. "It's completely seized up," he said. He cleared his throat. "I know your family and mine haven't always seen eye to eye, but I'd be grateful if you'd take a look at it. I need it to get to work."

"That's what I'm here for," said Jack. He pushed at the pedals with his hand, and they didn't move.

"About how much might you charge?" asked Straker.

Jack stepped back and surveyed the bike. I could almost see his mind working, as if he'd really make Straker pay. At last he said, "I reckon one shilling and sixpence will do it."

Straker looked surprised. "That's very fair," he said. "Thank you."

"Come back about one o'clock," said Jack. "I'll have it done."

When Straker had gone, I said, "You could have charged him half a crown, and he'd still have been pleased."

"I'm not daft," he answered. "I need everyone's goodwill. I want the Strakers and the Pinkneys and the Langleys on my side."

"I reckon you'll do all right, Jack," I said.

"This one's an easy job," he said. "I'll strip the crankcase down, pack it with grease, put the ball bearings back in, and Bob's your uncle. The bike's a dirty old rust bucket anyway; I'll give it a good cleanup as well."

I watched him work, so neat and tidy. "I've never seen Straker on a bike," he said. "I bet he only came to test me out."

When he'd finished on the crankcase, he tested it, and it worked perfectly. Then he polished the handlebars and wheel rims until they shone. By one o'clock the bike looked almost new. When Straker came back, dead on the dot, he couldn't do anything but say, "I have to admit, that's a real good job you've done," and produced the shilling and sixpence, which Jack put straight in the till.

"That'll be all over Lambsfield in an hour," said Jack when he'd gone. "I reckon I'm made."

Ten minutes later Mr. Brayfield came in. "I'm so pleased to see you working, Jack, and doing such an important job," he said. "My bicycle needs a complete overhaul. Visiting is so hard without a bicycle I can depend on."

"No trouble, vicar," said Jack. Mr. Spendlove was next with his, and by six o'clock four more jobs had come in, two so big that he had to promise them for the next day, and ten shillings and threepence was nestling in the till. "At this rate, I'll clear three quid in the first week," he said. "The colonel will see his money's being well spent."

At six o'clock he pulled the blind down over the front door, and we went home. "Best day I've had in years," he said.

Chapter Twenty-one

A letter from Archie arrived this morning, though it was posted three weeks ago. He said he was keeping well and tomorrow they'd be over the top in the big push. "We can't lose now," he wrote. "The noise as the shells from our big guns go over scares us enough, so I don't know what it does to the Germans. We're told that they will all be dead and everything destroyed, so taking the trenches will be easy. Let's hope so."

That was three weeks ago. What if something happens to him? I might never know—the army would tell his family but never think of telling me. What can I do? Just wait, that's all. But waiting is a terrible thing.

I take out all of Archie's letters, from the time I met him at Hartcross Park until now, and read them. Then I look at the letter from Cissie and Meg about the Land Army. I wonder how they're getting on. I suppose I could join them now that things are better here, though I don't think I want to. But if Archie is spared, I'm determined to get away and do something useful. Like Enid, learning to be a nurse in London.

*   *   *

July is two weeks old. The sun shines out of a cloudless sky, and the morning air is warm. Jack sits at the kitchen table, drinking tea out of a mug. He's telling Ma about something at the shop. "Anyway, I'd gotten all these spare bits and bobs—wheels, a frame, things like that—and I thought I'd see if I could put them together and make a bike out of them. When I'd finished it, Jem Medley the carrier came round and bought it off me for ten shillings. I'll make myself a fortune at this rate." There's a broad grin on his face. I've seen a miracle happen.

There's a knock at the door. It's the postman, George Gilmore. "Letter for you, Ellen," he says, and hands me a brown army envelope. "It's your favorite soldier boy." It's not Archie's handwriting. I tear it open. It is dated eighteen days ago, though it was postmarked in Dover yesterday. For a moment my heart leaps. Then I read it.

Dear Miss Wilkins,

You don't know me, but my name's Harry Swain, Archie's best mate. I am afraid I have bad news. Archie was killed in our big push at the Somme. Our lieutenant wrote to Archie's mother and father, but I thought that nobody would tell you and you would never know. He thought such a lot about you, miss, and was always talking about you. I found your address among his things, so I thought I would write. He told me you were a tough lass, so I will tell you how it happened because I think you would want to know.

We came into the line on June 29 and waited in the trench for two days and nights while the big guns

softened up the German lines. The noise fair tore your
eardrums out. Then, early next morning, we waited. The
day was beautiful, the sky was blue, the sun shone, and
when the big guns suddenly stopped firing, all we
could hear was birdsong. The wait seemed endless, and
I think we were all trembling with funk. Archie stood
next to me, and when the whistle blew and it was time
to go over the top, he touched my shoulder and
winked, and then we were away. At first everything was
quiet. I could see the enemy's barbed wire in front of
us, but it wasn't as chewed up as they told us it would
be. But I still thought we would be all right until suddenly the Germans started firing, and it was like walking into steel rain. We'd been told a pack of lies; our big
guns hadn't even touched them. I saw men go down all
round me, dead and wounded, and I just kept going and
nothing hit me. I turned to look at Archie and he
grinned back at me, and then suddenly he wasn't beside
me anymore. He'd been caught full-on by machine-gun
bullets and I knew he was dead. I thought it was time to
get down, because we'd be taking no trenches that day,
so I dived into a shell hole and stayed there until the
bearers came out after dark to pick us up. Now me, I
wasn't scratched, praise God Almighty, but Archie had
bought it and so had most other of us Barnsley lads.
There weren't many left of those who'd joined back at
the beginning in 1914.

Anyway, miss, I thought I'd better let you know, and
if I should have kept my mouth shut, then I'm sorry,
but from what Archie said about you, I think I was
right. God speed, Miss Wilkins.

Yours truly,
Harry Swain
(Pte, 13th Battalion, York and Lancaster Regiment)

P.S. I'm giving this to a mate coming home on leave, and I've told him to post it as soon as he gets to Blighty, because I don't want the censors cutting bits out of it.

Jack watches me and knows. "He's gone, hasn't he, Ellie," he says.

I can't speak; I just hold the letter out to him, and he reads it. Then he folds it up, puts it back in its envelope, places it carefully on the table, and then hugs me while I lean on his shoulder and cry my heart out.

"That's the way, weep it out of your system," he says. "Don't worry, Ellie, I'll help you through this, just the same as you helped me."

PART 4

·1916–1917·

LONDON FIELDS

CHAPTER TWENTY-TWO

Last night I dreamed of Archie. I was with him on his last leave in Barnsley. In my dream, Barnsley was a warm, sunlit place, but all round it, like black crows brooding, were coal mines swallowing long lines of men and spewing them out again. Archie was just as I knew him, dark and wiry, with his soft Yorkshire voice. I watched him go with his dad to the pub and thought how much like Pa his father was. The pub was just like the Plough, and I was surprised to see Straker and Pinkney and all the regulars in there. Then Archie played football with his mates, and one of them was Jack, with his lost leg back again. It was wonderful, I thought, to see what great friends those two were. When the game was finished, Archie told me we were going to Oakwell to watch the lads wallop the Wednesday, and I was so pleased because at last I'd find out what he meant. Before we got there, he said, "Eh, Ellen, thou'rt a tough lass, and I do like you," and I answered, "And I like you, Archie, and I always will." But just as I was going to find out what walloping the Wednesday was, I woke up.

For a moment it still seemed true, and that the footsteps outside the room were Archie's, but it was Jack clacking downstairs on his crutches. The morning was gray, Archie was gone forever, and I sat up and cried.

Harry Swain's letter came a month ago, and since then I've thought of nothing else. Jack has been so good to me. He understands, but Ma and Pa, though they try, don't, and I know they're losing patience with me. This morning Ma said, "Your father and I have been talking, Ellen. It's time you snapped out of this." I nearly answered, "How dare you, Ma? How do you know how I feel?" but bit my tongue because I didn't want to upset her. "After all," she went on, "it's not as if you were engaged or anything. It's not even as if you knew him that well. How many times did you see him?"

"You know how many. Two."

"Well, there you are. There's no use crying over spilt milk. Your father thinks it's time you stopped mooning around like a sick calf, and so do I."

At that moment, Jack came in from the shop for a bite to eat. His first weeks of work had gone well, and he always had a smile on his face—yet only two months ago he was threatening to drown himself in Oldwood Mere. The first thing he said was, "Now then, you two. What's going on?"

"I've been telling Ellen it's no good her carrying on the way she's been. People will think she's a fool."

"Don't talk about my sister like that," he replied.

"I'll talk about my daughter the way I see fit," said Ma.

"You and Pa don't understand," said Jack. "Everything's different now, especially for us young ones."

"Why?" said Ma. "It's us parents who see our children maimed and killed."

"And it's us who get killed. You only watch, it's us it happens to."

"It doesn't happen to Ellen," said Ma.

Jack answered, "It's our generation, Ma, not yours. You sent us into this; you never asked if we wanted to go; you just told us we had to and we believed you. Never again."

Ma flinched as if he'd slapped her face. "Oh, Jack," she cried. "I never told you to go. I wanted you to stay at home."

"Jack, that's not fair," I said. "It's nothing to do with Ma. It was men who started it all."

"Old men, not the likes of me," said Jack.

"Anyway, Ma," I said. "I'm past mourning what happened. I'm mourning what might have happened and never will now."

"You've no idea what might have happened," said Ma.

"Yes, I do," I replied, and meant it.

That's what the last month has told me. I can relive every moment of the servants' ball at Hartcross, of the wonderful day in London. I can see and hear Archie as if he's standing with me on the landing at the top of a flight of stairs with an open door in front of us. "Let's go in there, lass," he says. A bright golden light pours out, but just as we're stepping through, the door slams in our faces and the key turns from the inside. There are no other doors leading off the landing.

CHAPTER TWENTY-THREE

It's the next morning, and a letter from Enid has arrived. Cissie and Beatie had passed on news about her when they wrote, but I hadn't heard from her for months, and I was sorry, because we have something in common now. I remember how quiet and reserved—timid almost—she'd seemed when I first met her. We'd thought there was nothing to her, but she changed completely after her brother was killed. That's why she'd gone to be a nurse. I hated to think what it would have been like for me if Jack had been killed. I wondered whether I would have had the courage to get out straightaway as she did. I don't think I would; I'd have stayed for the sake of Ma and Pa. But Jack hadn't been killed—he'd had his bad time and now he's through it, and I helped him. And he'd told me what it was like in the hospital in France, and I kept thinking about his Miss Bakewell, and how good—above all other things—it was to be doing what she did. Now Jack's taken his chance and found his place, and nobody deserves it more. Is it like that for other wounded soldiers? Somehow I don't think so. Jack was lucky; not many have a Colonel Cripps to sort things out. But while some might have gone on sponging off him, Jack wanted to stand alone. When he told Colonel Cripps that he'd pay the rent as soon as he earned enough, the colonel said, "I would have been happy to go on paying, Jack, but I know you well enough now to be sure you'd say that sooner or later. I'm very pleased for you. I'll take steps to transfer the tenancy to you the moment you tell me."

It was just as well that he did. As soon as Straker and his friends had shown they supported Jack, someone started whispering. Dottie Langley's father was my chief suspect. Why should the colonel favor Jack? What was so special about us Wilkinses? Jealousy, that's all it was. When it got around that Jack was landlord now, and taking on Willy Doughty, who was wounded at Gallipoli, to work with him, the jealousy seemed to be forgotten. But it left a nasty taste in my mouth.

Anyway, things seem quiet now. It's back to normal between Ma and Pa. Madge and Betty are still little treasures about the house. They leave me hardly anything to do, and I almost feel not needed anymore. Nobody wants me to go away, and I often feel I don't either. But something tells me I must if I want to be true to myself. I'm eighteen in January, and time is slipping by. So I'm reading Enid's letter very carefully because I want to do what she's done.

She's at London Fields Hospital in the East End. She isn't working with wounded soldiers. It's all sick children, old folks with TB, ordinary people with ordinary illnesses. She works so hard that she's always tired and that's why she never writes. But she loves it in spite of the long hours. She shares a room with another probationer nurse in the nurses' hostel. She says a lot of girls go to military hospitals when they've got their certificates.

A nurse in the war. That's what I want to be. I sat down at once to write back and ask how I can become a probationer nurse.

After posting the letter, I went to see Jack in his workshop. He was working on a bicycle clamped upside down in a vise. He looked up as I entered. "Hullo, Ellie. Madge and Betty doing all the work this morning?"

"I want your advice," I said.

"Go, girl. Don't stop to think, just go and be a nurse," he replied.

"I haven't asked you yet."

"You don't have to. I can see it a mile off. If you want to go, go."

"It's not so simple."

"Of course it is. Ma might cut up a bit rough, I suppose. I don't know about Pa."

"It's strange, Jack. I used to talk to Pa about things a lot once. But since you took this place on, he's hardly said a word to me."

"You know what?" said Jack. "I think it's all getting too much for him." He turned the pedals round to make sure they ran smoothly. "There," he said. "Sweet as a nut. Another satisfied customer." He took the bicycle out of the vise and stood it in a corner. "You must tell them, you know."

"How can I? They wouldn't understand. I must wait until I'm sure about this." I told him that I'd written to ask Enid how I should go about getting into the same hospital.

"Why can't you go somewhere near home?" he said.

"I don't know if there is anywhere, not if I want to be

qualified. Wherever I go it won't be like Hartcross Park, where I could ride home once a week. Besides, I want to go to London."

"They'll say you're too young."

"I'm eighteen in January."

"They'll say a girl can't live alone in a place like London."

"Enid says there's a nurses' hostel. I'd never be alone."

"Ha! That's what she says."

"You don't know Enid. I do, and I believe her."

"I'm only saying what Ma and Pa might say."

"Enid would show me the ropes. She'll watch out for me."

Jack laughed. "You've got all the answers, Ellie."

"I'll need them," I said.

That was three days ago, and Enid's answer is here already.

"You have to come to the hospital so the matron can interview you," she wrote. "Write to her and she'll tell you when to come and what to bring. Here's what I was told, and I expect it will be the same for you. You must bring two testimonials, one from a minister of religion and one from your previous employer. I told the matron I'd been at home helping to look after my grandmother but now she was dead, so I was free to come without needing a reference from an employer. That was true, except that grandma died before I came to Hartcross."

I wondered why she did that. Then my heart sank. It was no use asking Mrs. Pardew for a testimonial because we were dismissed without references. I didn't want to lie and say I'd never worked, but I couldn't get a testimonial from an employer. There must be some way round this.

I wrote to the matron right away in my best copperplate handwriting. Ma saw me and said, "You're always writing letters lately. Who's your new friend?"

"Just one of the girls from Hartcross Park," I replied, crossing my fingers under the table as I spoke. When she'd gone away, I finished it off and read through it.

Dear Matron,

My name is Ellen Wilkins. I am eighteen in January.

I wish to train to be a nurse at London Fields Hospital and would be very grateful if you would kindly furnish me with details about how I should go about it.

Yours truly,

Ellen Wilkins (Miss)

I addressed the envelope:

THE MATRON

LONDON FIELDS HOSPITAL

BETHNAL GREEN

LONDON

I was just about to seal the envelope when I had another thought and added:

P.S. I enclose a stamped and addressed envelope for your reply.

I found an envelope and put our address on it. Then I saw we had no more stamps. I'd have to go to the post office.

Well, it's not a proper post office, just a counter in Daines the Grocer's, with Mrs. Daines behind the counter. A man was already there sending a parcel, and when he turned round, I saw it was Mr. Randall.

"Why, it's you, Ellen," he said. "We haven't seen you for months."

When I'd posted my letter, we walked down the street together.

"I'm pleased to hear about Jack," said Mr. Randall. "Thank God there's still good news to be had."

"It only happened because of the colonel," I replied.

"I know," he answered. "He's a good man." We walked a little farther. Then he spoke again. "I was lucky. Some soldiers I knew were servants to brutes. The army's a hard place, you know."

Our ways parted here. "I'm sure the colonel would like to see you again," said Mr. Randall as we said good-bye.

When Jack came back from the shop, I told him what Mr. Randall had said. "What did he mean by brutes?" I asked.

"He's right," he replied. "Things went on that I don't want to think of, let alone talk about."

"You told me bad things before," I said.

"Yes," he said. "And you have to expect that in war. But some things shouldn't happen anywhere, and you won't see them in the papers. Soldiers were shot," he said.

"Of course they were," I said. "It's a war."

"I don't mean by the Germans. By us."

"I don't understand," I said.

"You can get put in front of a firing squad for cowardice.

They've got a funny way of deciding who's a coward. Some of the higher-ups don't seem to understand that those trenches can drive men mad."

"I don't believe we shot our own soldiers," I said.

"You'll have to." He looked down at the floor frowning and then said, "I knew a man who was shot."

"Tell me," I said.

He didn't speak for a whole minute. Then he said, "Lenny Doble, that was his name—a scrawny little bloke, from the East End of London. He looked as if he could hardly pick up his rifle, as if a full pack on his shoulders would make his body break in two. But he was tough in his own way, and he stayed that way too. Ellie, it's hard in the trenches; you never know each minute whether you'll still be alive the next, and sometimes it drives you over the edge. Little Lenny, though, he kept going—life and soul of the party he seemed, and he wasn't afraid of going out into no-man's-land on a raiding party. But one day he just broke, suddenly, crying his eyes out. And that night he ran away. When we were all getting a couple of hours' sleep, he must have slipped off down the communications trench. God knows how nobody saw him. They picked him up three days later; he'd been hiding in a French farmer's barn. The farmer found him there and turned him in."

"That was horrible of him," I said.

"Yes," said Jack. "But I've been thinking about that too. What if that farmer had seen his sons go off and they'd gotten killed? Why should he help a soldier trying to get away when he'd lost his own? It's very likely. The French have lost more men than we have. It's not all black-and-white in war. Anyway, they dragged little Lenny off to a court-martial, sentenced him to death, and shot him the next morning. They picked soldiers from another regiment to do it. If they'd asked us, there'd have been a mutiny. It's bad enough having to shoot a stranger, never mind one of your own mates. Well, that was Lenny, and now that I've told you, I want to forget about him."

"I know, Jack," I said.

"It could have been me," he said. "It could have been anyone. These things don't happen often, but they happen all the same, and you won't hear about them. Everybody dies a hero's death, that's what you read in the papers. Ellen, some of the people put over us are bastards, and others I'd follow to the ends of the earth. It's pure luck which you get."

"Mr. Randall thinks that Colonel Cripps is one you'd follow," I said.

"I reckon he's right," said Jack. "Most of those I got were somewhere in between, the best of a bad bunch." He turned back indoors. "Ah, well, it's all over for me now," he said. "There's not much I haven't told you, and now that you know it all, I feel I can forget about it." As we walked into the kitchen, he said, "I wonder how your Archie found the officers."

I wished he hadn't said that. Archie might have had a bastard in charge. I didn't sleep much last night.

Next day I thought I'd take Mr. Randall at his word and go and see the colonel, so after breakfast I walked to Fieldfare House.

The colonel was in the garden with Mr. Randall. After a few words about how pleased he was about Jack, he said,

"And what about you, Ellen? I heard that you had another shock in your life." He must mean Archie. "I was sad to hear of it. Such things are inevitable in these terrible times." His voice trailed away, but then he seemed to brace himself. "Do you intend to stay at home from now on?"

I told him how I would like to go to London and be a nurse, and he said, "What a good idea. You would be excellent."

"I don't think I can go. They want testimonials from a minister of religion and my previous employer. I could get a new one from the vicar, but I can't ask the people at Hartcross Park because they gave us all the sack."

"Ah," he said. "That is a difficulty. If only I could have taken you on as a maid here when you asked me. What have you told them?"

"Nothing, only that I want to apply and how should I go about it."

"And you need a reference from your employer saying whether you would be suitable," he said musingly.

"Yes, sir. But I can't have one, and if I said I'd not done any work, I'd be telling a lie, and, besides, they'd say I was only a girl with no experience and not suitable, and send me straight home."

"You have a problem," he said. "But don't give up hope. I'll see if I can think of something."

"Thank you, Colonel Cripps," I said.

"Edmund's in a hospital now, you know," he said. "He had some sort of breakdown. They sent him home, and he's now in some curious establishment near Edinburgh—Craiglockhart it's called. I don't know if he'll ever go back to the front. It would be strange if you ended up nursing him."

I went home soon afterward. As I walked through Lambsfield, I thought what a tiny little place it seemed. I'd always love it. But there were some old people here who'd never gone more than three miles away all their lives. How could they stand it? It wouldn't do for me.

Yesterday a letter came from London Fields. They want to see me for an interview in a week's time and, sure enough, they want testimonials from a minister of religion and my previous employer. Well, that settles it. I can't go. My big ideas are all dreams. Lady Launton's had her revenge.

Ma was in the washhouse putting wet clothes through the mangle. Madge was sweeping the living room, and Betty was peeling potatoes. Jack and Pa were at work. I was just thinking that I wasn't needed here anymore when there was a knock at the door. It was Mr. Randall holding an envelope. "The colonel asked me to deliver this, Ellen," he said.

When he was gone, I opened it. There was a note inside from the colonel and another envelope marked "Confidential" and addressed to "The Matron, London Fields Hospital. By hand." This envelope wasn't sealed. The note said, "Dear Ellen, I hope you will find the enclosed testimonial suitable. You have my permission to read it before you go."

In the other envelope was a sheet of thick cream writing paper covered in the colonel's neat, orderly copperplate.

TO WHOM IT MAY CONCERN:

I am very pleased to testify to the character and abilities of Miss Ellen Wilkins. Miss Wilkins worked in service as a housemaid for several months until she left to help at home after her brother returned severely wounded from active service in France. During that time I was able to see her admirable qualities to good advantage. She has shown herself to be conscientious, hardworking, entirely dependable, honest, and trustworthy.

She is a responsible person with a caring attitude to people, amply illustrated by the way in which she helped her brother through his convalescence. In my opinion, she has every quality necessary to become a good nurse, and I recommend her without reservation. I am willing to answer any other queries you may have.

H. C. StJ. Cripps,
MC, DSO, Colonel (retd.) Grenadier Guards

I read it three times, and by the end my ears were burning. Did he really mean all that? How could he, when he hadn't been my employer? Then I read it a fourth time. He talked about being in service but hadn't actually said who for. The matron would assume it was for him. The colonel hadn't lied; he just hadn't told all the truth. I had to thank him. "Not at all," he said. "I write what is true but choose what not to write. Sometimes you have to be— how shall I put it—a bit canny."

That evening I told Ma I'd been asked to the interview.

"Well," she said, "go if you must. But don't blame me if you come home with your tail between your legs."

Chapter Twenty-four

Today was the day of the interview. It was cold and gray, and rain spit in the air as I waited for the London train. I wore my best dress—dark blue, freshly ironed, and stitched up in a few places where it was torn. Mrs. Randall had lent me a hat, so I looked quite the young working lady. Now that the time had come, I didn't want to go.

When I got to the station, Pa was beckoning through the signal-box window, and I climbed the steps to see him. "So you've really made up your mind," he said.

"They might not want me."

"They'd be daft not to."

"I bet there are thousands of girls better than me trying to be nurses," I said. "Why should they choose me?"

"Because they will," he replied. "You give it to 'em, girl." The telegraph tinged. "Your train's due. You'd better go."

"I'll be back tonight," I said.

"Not for long, Ellen," he answered gruffly, and bent to the levers. The signal arm went down, and I ran down the steps as the train came in.

On the day I'd gone to meet Archie, the engine had gleamed, its paint had shone, and its brasswork had glistened.

The engine today was soot-stained and grimy, and the carriages dirty and shabby. As we slowly moved off, there was
a sudden deafening flurry of blasts from the chimney, the
train jolted and jerked, and I felt quite shaken. Pa once
told me that this was when wet rails made the engine
wheels slip. I shivered and wondered whether this was how
the day would go, nothing but slipping and jolting.

Without Archie, London was not a pleasant place. The
steps down to the Underground were dingy and smelly,
and a weird, unnatural wind blew through the dark tun-
nels. I had to get to Liverpool Street station and catch a
train to London Fields. Liverpool Street was even more
smoky and choking than Victoria. The board at the end of
the platform said: BETHNAL GREEN, CAMBRIDGE HEATH,
LONDON FIELDS, and HACKNEY DOWNS. This made me feel
happier, because with such names, we must be going back
out into the country.

But we weren't. The train chugged slowly along, and there
was no countryside—just lines of streets and factories—and
there were no fields in London Fields either. The hospital
was a huge building of stained brick, which reminded me
of the old poorhouse back home, though twenty times as
big. I'd never seen anything quite as depressing in my life.
But there was no going back. This was what I wanted to
do, and I had testimonials from a colonel and a vicar to
show I could.

I waited in a cheerless room outside the matron's office
with six other girls. The walls were painted a dull brown
to the height of my shoulders, with a washed-out yellow
above it. None of us spoke. After ten minutes the matron's
door opened, and another girl came out and walked away

without a word. I heard a woman's voice call, "Barker, next, if you please." The girl beside me said, "That's me," stood up, and walked in. She came out fifteen minutes later. "Snooty cow," she said, and left.

My turn came an hour later. "Wilkins," the voice called. I somehow expected another skinny Mrs. Pardew behind the desk, but the matron looked very large—though not in a roly-poly, comforting way.

"You have your references?" she said.

"Yes, ma'am."

"Matron. You call me Matron at all times. I address you by your surname. Give them to me."

I did so and she opened them. "Sit," she commanded.

The chair was so hard and straight-backed that I couldn't really sit and had to perch on the edge. The matron put on a pair of glasses and read the testimonials, now and again looking up at me. "Well, Wilkins," she said. "It seems you are highly thought of by not only a gentleman of the cloth and, I notice, an Oxford man, but a colonel of the Grenadier Guards."

I didn't answer, but I could see she was reading Colonel Cripps's reference again. Then she said, "I presume that you were in the colonel's employ. He does not specifically say so, although he gives that impression."

My heart sank. This woman didn't miss a trick. I couldn't say I wasn't because she'd send me packing, but anything else would be lying. I made up my mind to lie. "I was Colonel Cripps's maid for two months," I said, and a weight lifted from my shoulders. I'd told an untruth to get what I wanted, but I'd asked to be his maid and I'm sure that if he could have afforded it, I would have been, so perhaps it wasn't really such a lie. I didn't feel guilty because I might have to tell a few more lies before the war was over.

"Ah, yes," she said, and sounded satisfied.

Then she asked me was I strong, did I have any illnesses, any conditions like rickets or TB, was I afraid of hard work and long hours, was I squeamish at the sight of blood and other such horrors as I might encounter. Then she said, "I expect that, like most girls who come here, you want to nurse young men brought in from the trenches."

I shouldn't have said, "Yes, Matron," because she glared at me over her glasses and said, "Should you be accepted as a new probationer, you most certainly will not. Soldiers are the preserve of senior nurses with experience and lady volunteers. We have two hundred extra beds for wounded servicemen, but your concern would be the care of the local population, young and old and with every imaginable complaint. Besides, you are only seventeen. You must be twenty-one to nurse soldiers."

"My brother was wounded at Loos," I said. "He told me what happened and how he was treated, and that's why I want to be a nurse."

"And go out to France one day, I presume." I bowed my head. "Wilkins, there is one thing you must get firmly into your head. Nurses such as yourself will not be allowed away from these shores. Ladies whom the War Office accepts for overseas duty are either experienced sisters or volunteers of good family: VADs who, without certified training such as you may receive, have learned such skills as they possess through assisting at military hospitals here in England. Whether this is a sensible course is the business of the War Office. However, you must forget such fantasies. Your work is here. You would be a probationer nurse. You would no doubt see lady nurses, VADs and the like, in the military wards, but you will have no contact with them unless ordered by a staff nurse or sister. Your probation would normally last for two years. However, because of the needs of wartime and because so many young girls follow the lure of easy money and work in the factories, we at London Fields have shortened our course to eighteen months, although our standards, I assure you, have not been lowered, and you will have to work all the harder. Perhaps when the war is over, some government busybody will insist that all hospitals take the same course. Until then we shall train nurses as we think fit. At the end of that time, if you have proved satisfactory, you would be given your certificate. I trust that is clear."

"Yes, Matron," I said.

"Wilkins, you are vouched for by an Oxford man and a high-ranking officer from one of our best regiments. Not many girls coming here bring recommendations from such people." I remembered the other would-be nurse saying "Snooty cow," and saw what she meant.

"The interview is over," said Matron. "You will hear in due course. Do not build up your hopes. In peacetime, for every girl we accept, we turn away a hundred. It is little better in war. Shut the door as you leave."

Two more girls had arrived for an interview. "What's she like?" said one. I could say a bit more than "snooty cow." "She's a snob," I said. As I walked back to the station, I thought more about it. Matron was a snob because she thought more of my references just because of who wrote them. Was I a snob for bringing them? It was pure accident who I got to write references for me. I didn't ask Colonel Cripps to be a higher-up officer, nor could I help where Mr. Brayfield went to university. But if it got me what I wanted, then so be it, and the same went for telling lies when I had to. I wondered if life away from Lambsfield would change me for the worse. Yes, it probably would. London would make me hard.

A week has passed since the interview, and this morning a letter came from the hospital. I'm in, to start as soon as possible. Now I can't wait, even though there'll be tears in this house before I go.

I told Ma that day. I might have known that she would cry.
    "No, Ellen. You can't."
    I was right. London was making me hard already.
    "I'm sorry, Ma. I've made up my mind. I'm going."
    I felt awful and cried all night, but Ma didn't mention it again.

Chapter Twenty-five

November's here, and there's a thick dirty fog over London. If you go outside, you're choking and coughing in less than a minute, and if you put a scarf over your mouth it's soon black with the dirt, smoke, and coal dust in the air. What a hateful place. Sometimes I think of Meg and Cissie milking cows on the farm. Sunshine, fresh air to breathe, rain with no soot in it. But I soon forget. No matter what it's like, this is where I want to be.

I'm so tired. I'm run off my feet; the wards are hot and airless. They smell of disinfectant and the bodies of old, sick people. Feeble voices call "Nurse," wanting me to straighten their bedclothes, bring them water and bedpans or commodes, which I then have to empty. Then there are the doctors' rounds. They march in like lords, Mr. Scrivener-Green, the chief surgeon, leading, with young Dr. Pewsey, Matron, Sister, and a gaggle of students trailing behind. They stop a moment by each bed. Mr. Scrivener-Green and Dr. Pewsey talk in loud voices about patients' conditions as if they can't hear. Sister Agnew, who is in charge of our ward, really drives us on: everything's got to be just so, floor gleaming, beds made with the sheets squared off in hospital corners, and woe betide anyone who leaves a sheet not looking as if you could cut yourself at the edges. Sometimes I just want to drop and sleep on the floor. On top of that there are lectures, things to learn, exams to take. Yet for all that, I'm really happy.

I'm on one of the women's wards. I don't see much of Enid because she's on a men's ward and, besides, she's doing nights now. When I arrived she was really good, helping me get to know the place. She's just the same as she was when we left Hartcross. But she's not my only friend. I share a room in the nurses' hostel with Annie Smithers. She's older than me and has already got her certificate. "Now that I'm qualified, I want to get out of this place and try a military hospital," she said.

"Matron didn't seem to think the likes of us could go nursing soldiers," I replied.

"Fat lot she knows," said Annie. "I come from Cambridge way, and there's lots of army hospitals. They won't be too fussy to take me on. I'll get there; don't you worry." That cheered me up. If she could, so could I.

We get all sorts here. There are old ladies with pneumonia. We know they haven't got long for this world. Already I've helped to lay out four bodies, and if the weather goes on like this, there'll be a lot more before Christmas. We get young women beaten up by their husbands, men friends, fathers. They come in with arms and legs and noses broken, black eyes, and faces swollen with bruises and cuts, but they never say a word against the ones who did it to them. That really makes me angry. There are prostitutes racked with disease, some very old, others terribly young, younger than Madge and Betty. I see them all and wonder how people can bear to spend their whole lives in this city.

Then there are the munitions girls. They come in droves, hardly able to breathe, with yellow faces from working with high explosives. People call them "canaries." Some have TNT poisoning. Most get over it and go back to work, but some are too far gone, and we've had a couple of deaths already. I always look to see if Beatie's among them. The last I heard she was in a factory somewhere in London. I wonder how she's getting on. I must ask Enid if she's heard anything. I hope I never see Beatie come in here with a yellow face.

Enid knows where Beatie is. "She works in Silvertown, down by the river, like a lot of those who come in here," she said. "She's written saying we should get together. Now that you're here, we'll have to make the effort."

We managed to get away a week before Christmas. It was my day off. Enid was working nights and so was Beatie. By rights they both should have been sleeping. We caught an omnibus to Canning Town, where Beatie and two other girls lodged in a little two-up, two-down terrace house with a Mr. and Mrs. Higgins. When we knocked, the door was opened by a little shriveled-up woman. If this was Mrs. Higgins, I wondered how she had the strength to keep the house, a husband, and hungry women munitions workers going.

When we told her we'd come to see Beatie, she pointed up the narrow staircase and then disappeared somewhere out the back. There were two doors on the upstairs landing, but as we wondered which to knock on, one of them opened and there was Beatie all smiles. Her face wasn't yellow. It was redder than it used to be, and her skin was rougher.

Her room was even smaller than our old rooms at Hartcross Park, and the only furniture was a bed and a chair. Clothes were thrown over the back and littered the floor, though she was always very tidy at Hartcross. The window looked over the little backyard and straight into the back window of the house opposite.

"Where do the others live?" said Enid. "I only see two rooms."

"We all pig in this one," Beatie answered cheerfully.

"There's only one bed," I said.

"It's Cox and Box here," said Beatie. "We're on different shifts. As soon as one gets out, the next gets in. No wonder the sheets are filthy."

"Doesn't Mrs. Higgins ever wash them?" Enid asked.

Beatie laughed. "Her? She can hardly lift a broom, let alone turn a mangle. Mr. Higgins works on the docks, and when he comes home drunk, he knocks her about something cruel. I hear them all night. It's almost worth working the night shift to get out of the way."

"What time do you start?" I asked.

"Seven," she replied. "But only till January. There'll be no more night shifts after the New Year, not now that there's a new factory opened up near Barking. After that it's two shifts, days only, till quitting time at seven. I'll have to put up with the two old fools knocking each other about all night then, and it won't half be horrible in bed with all three of us in it."

Soon after that she took us down the narrow streets to a

little pub on a corner. "I'm not sure Matron would like us to go in there," said Enid.

"Oh, come on," said Beatie. "She's not here. What the eye don't see, the heart won't grieve over." We went in. "Gins all round," Beatie cried.

"I don't think I . . .," Enid started, but Beatie plunked it in front of her and said, "Get it down you. You don't know what living is, you two."

I thought the gin tasted horrible and didn't finish my glass, and Enid only took a couple of sips. But Beatie swallowed hers down like water, and when she saw we weren't drinking ours, she said, "Well, if you don't want them," and poured them down her throat as well. I looked at Enid and she looked at me, and I knew we were thinking the same thing. Beatie had changed since Hartcross, and we weren't sure we liked what we saw.

"Have you heard from Arthur?" Enid asked.

That wiped the smile off her face. "Not for months," she said. "He's a sergeant now, and he drives a general round in a big posh car, like he said he would. He hadn't even left England when I last heard, and then he told me he had a new lady friend and I could take a running jump. The bastard." She called for another gin and gulped it down. "Men!" she spat. "You'll find out for yourself soon enough."

"I always knew Arthur was no good," said Enid.

"But he was," said Beatie. "He was very, very good."

"You'll find someone else," I said.

Tears streamed down her face. "No, I won't," she wailed. "Just look at me. I feel like forty, and I'm sure I look fifty. A man would have to be blind and drunk to take any notice of me."

"I'm sure he wouldn't," Enid said faintly.

"Worst day's work we ever did, making that stuck-up cow at Hartcross give us the sack. At least I was a bit happier there."

"But you wanted to go," I said. "You wanted to work in a factory."

"I needed my head examined," she replied. "Having your freedom's not all it's cracked up to be. I'll have another gin."

"Do you think you ought to?" Enid said. "You'll be at work soon with all those explosives."

"I work better when I've had a few," Beatie answered.

We left soon after. Neither of us spoke on the way home. We were much too upset.

Christmas came and a lot of nurses went home. I wasn't allowed because I was new. I had a bit of a cry about it in my room, thinking of everyone at home celebrating without me, but I hadn't really expected anything else. Besides, Jack hadn't been home last Christmas, and that was a lot worse. I bought some cards and a few little presents—tobacco for Pa, that sort of thing—and mailed them. But when Christmas came, I wasn't prepared for how nice it turned out to be. Mr. Garner, the hospital superintendent, bought trees for every ward, and we decorated them on Christmas Eve. The grim old ward looked almost lovely with paper chains and holly. The tree at one end really topped it off. We wanted to put candles on it, but Matron wouldn't let us, so we contented ourselves with putting the presents that people sent the patients under it, and some for ourselves as well. On the night of Christmas Eve, we sang carols and some of the old ladies had tears in their eyes. On Christmas morning the hospital chaplain came round and gave a little service, and then Dr. Pewsey, dressed up as Father Christmas, came in and gave out the presents. He was young and very nice, and didn't seem to mind being on duty over Christmas. Then we served Christmas dinner from the kitchen. Everyone managed to eat something, though we had to mash the chicken and vegetables up for the ladies with no teeth. In the afternoon we led the old dears in a sing-along, and even the sickest managed a few tunes in their weak, quavery voices. And I felt really happy. When my turn on duty came to an end and I finally crept dead tired into bed, I was truly certain that coming here had been the right thing to do.

CHAPTER TWENTY-SIX

It was the dawn of 1917, and everyone prayed that this was the year the war would end. It was a cold winter, but not as cold as in France, or so the papers said. Streams of soldiers kept coming onto the military wards. Sometimes we were taken off our jobs and detailed to see them in. Their poor, pale, haunted faces as they lay on their stretchers stayed with me all night. I wished I could go into the military wards properly and work there, but Matron had said I couldn't, so I would have to be content with my old ladies after all.

January 17th and it's nearly seven o'clock in the evening. I'm on the ward helping old Mrs. Fossett get some beef tea down her. Matron swears by beef tea for frail patients. Suddenly the sky glows a lurid red, and the whole hospital shakes. "It's an earthquake," someone screams. A second later there's a huge noise, an ear-splitting roar, as if the whole world has opened up and we're all going to slide down into a gaping hole.

"The Germans have come!" one of the old women shrieks.

"They wouldn't dare to," says Annie Smithers.

Mrs. Fossett whispers to me, "Have they zeppy-what-you-call-its dropped another bomb on us, dear?"

"The explosion's too big for that, Mrs. Fossett," I reply. We'd had a few zeppelins flying over us, and their long silver bodies were frightening the first time I saw them. But their bombs don't do much damage unless you're standing right where they fall, and people seem to have gotten used to them.

Dr. Pewsey is making his last round of the day. "I read somewhere that the Germans have huge guns that can fire right across the Channel," he says. "Perhaps that's what it is." That doesn't make anyone feel better.

The news comes soon enough. There's been a fire and then an explosion at the Silvertown factory. A lot of people have been killed.

"Beatie!" I gasp. "She's just going to work." Then I remember. Day shifts only at Silvertown now. She'll be leaving, so she'll be all right. But she must still have been near the factory. I pray she will be safe.

The sky is still glowing red, but it's a darker red now, more like blood. Matron comes bustling into the ward. "Listen, everybody," she calls. "We expect to receive casualties from the explosion. Space has been made in two of the military wards to take them. The following two nurses about to go off duty are to report there at once: Smithers and Wilkins."

Now, ten minutes later, Annie and I are in the military ward making up beds, bringing bedpans, and generally getting ready. Our ward is detailed for women. There are three more nurses with us, and one of them is Enid.

We're hearing more news. The factory was nearly empty when the explosion came, and most workers were on their way home. What would have happened had they all been inside doesn't bear thinking about. Even so, a lot of people were killed and many more injured and taken to hospitals all over London. A few minutes later the first casualties are carried in, and we help them into bed. They don't seem too bad.

"Oh, it was terrible," an old lady says as I help her into bed and smooth her pillows. "There were chunks of red-hot metal flying around. I don't know how they missed me."

"Were you in the factory?" I ask her.

"Me? Lor' no, miss. I live down the next street. Or I did, because I reckon my house has been knocked flat. Still, mustn't grumble; at least I'm here. It was the fire that did it for most of us, not the big bang."

More casualties are brought in, much worse. Some are unconscious. We see terrible burns that turn my stomach over. Enid looks at me, and I nod without saying anything. We're both fearing the same thing.

The evening wears on, and still they come. Some who aren't too bad, like the lady who had been talking to me, are gotten out of bed and told to try and walk. A few, including the old lady, are quite happy to and are allowed to get dressed and go. Others can't, so they stay where they are. Most beds are still occupied, and it's nearly midnight.

"Surely there can't be many more," I say to Enid. "Won't they go to hospitals nearer Silvertown than us?"

There's a woman being wheeled in unconscious. Dr. Pewsey and Sister Agnew are with her. Her clothes have been cut away from her terribly burnt chest and arms. Half of her face is scorched livid red. But we recognize her at once. "Beatie!" Enid cries.

Sister notices. "Do you know this patient?" she says.

"Yes, Sister," we answer, expecting her to tell us to go away.

"Good," she says instead. "She's not expected to last the night, so if she comes round, it will be better for her to be among friends."

I can't speak. "We'll look after her, Sister," says Enid.

We begin the long night watch together, taking turns by her bed. The hours pass. Beatie breathes short, rasping breaths, as if it hurts to move her lungs. Toward five o'clock even these become faint. At half past five, her eyes open. She sees me but takes a few moments to recognize me. "I might have known it," she breathes.

"Enid," I call, and Enid tiptoes up the ward. "You as well," Beatie faintly manages. Then, "If Arthur should want us to get together again when the war's over, he'll be out of luck. He'll have to pig along without me after all." Her eyes close again, and the shallow breathing is now almost imperceptible. By six o'clock it has ceased completely. I feel for her pulse. Nothing. I call Sister, who comes at once. She, too, feels for Beatie's pulse, then shakes her head and covers her face. "I'll call Dr. Pewsey," she says.

Suddenly Enid wraps her arms round herself and sways to and fro. "Oh, God help me, God help me, God help me," she cries.

"Enid, what's the matter?" I ask.

"Don't you remember? When Beatie was so upset because Arthur said he'd join the army? I said not to worry about him; she'd get blown up before he would, and now she has been. I didn't mean it like that, Ellen; I didn't, I didn't—it was a joke. Oh, God help me."

"I know it was, Enid," I say, and try to put my arms round her. But she won't let me comfort her, and she cries alone until it's time to go off the ward. When I'm back in my room in the hostel, I cry too.

Chapter Twenty-seven

Beatie's funeral was in the church in Leytonstone, and Enid and I got the day off to go. It was a bitterly cold day, and snowflakes began to fall when we were in the churchyard. Beatie's mother came over to us after the coffin was lowered into the ground and said, "I'm so glad you were with her when she died. She thought a lot of her friends at Hartcross Park. She often talked about you. You'll come back to the house, I hope."

A lot of people—Beatie's aunts and uncles, cousins, neighbors, and friends—were packed into the tiny living room to eat sandwiches and drink sherry and talk about old times. Beatie's father was a small man who kept his cap on in the house and said little until we were about to leave. Then he whispered, "Thanks for being good to my little girl. When the war started, I told the missus, at least we haven't got a son to lose. But to lose our only daughter this way, it makes you weep, doesn't it?"

By the time we got back to the hospital, the snow was nearly six inches deep, and I hadn't felt so unhappy since Jack was at his lowest ebb.

*   *   *

I'm on my way home for the first time since I came to London Fields. Beatie's funeral was nearly four months ago, April has started, I'm nearly halfway through my time as a probationer nurse, and as the train nears Lambsfield, I feel six years, not six months, older than when it took me the other way. I've written home a lot and they've written to me, but even so I feel afraid that everyone's changed and we'll have nothing to say to each other.

I'm getting off the train now, and there's nobody to welcome me. Pa isn't in the signal box, so he must be working a different shift. Lambsfield station is strange without him. I have to lug my suitcase home on my own.

But once I'm there, it seems as though I've never been away. Pa's still just the same as when I left, and Ma bustles around and can't do enough to make me welcome. Madge and Betty, though, are regular young ladies, real little housewives. They're both fourteen now, and soon they'll be going out to work. Betty is going to be parlormaid at the vicarage, while Madge hopes to work for Dr. Pettigrew. "We're not as venturesome as you, Ellen," says Betty. "But wait till we're older," says Madge. "We'll do as well as you, you'll see. I won't be Dr. Pettigrew's servant for too long." I see that Betty is the homebody while Madge will be more like me, restless and impatient.

Jack came home from his shop just as Ma was serving up roast beef and vegetables, more like a Sunday dinner. "I could smell it cooking all the way down the road," he said. "I knew you must be home, Ellen; it's usually bread and scraps when I've finished work."

"Get on with you," said Ma. "You never go hungry in this house."

"How's the shop going?" I asked Jack.

"Mustn't grumble," he replied.

"He's doing really well," said Pa. "Lambsfield couldn't manage without him. Tell Ellen what you did last week."

"Dr. Pettigrew brought his car round to the shop. He said there was something wrong with it; it kept backfiring and could I do something about it. I said I'd have a go. All I did was retard the ignition a bit, and it worked a treat. He was so pleased, he gave me a sovereign and said I should give up bikes and take to cars instead. 'I might just do that one day, Doctor,' I said."

"But you won't, will you?" I said.

"I'll think about it. 'Wilkins Motors.' Doesn't sound bad, does it?"

I dug into my beef and vegetables and felt so happy to be back.

This morning I set off to see Colonel Cripps but met him before I reached his house, walking with a beautiful black-and-white collie. "Barney died nearly three years ago, and I've only now been able to bring myself to get another dog," he said. "Say hello to Ellen, Bonny."

Bonny was hardly more than a puppy, frisking round me and wagging her tail enthusiastically, and I remembered the night Barney was killed.

"And how's hospital life treating you?" he asked.

I told him all about it, and he asked a lot of questions. Then he said, "And when will they let you nurse wounded soldiers?"

"Matron says they won't," I replied. "She says only lady

nurses and VADs are allowed to do that, and I'm not old enough yet, anyway."

"I've no doubt she's right," he said. "But it's preposterous nonsense. Although the Volunteer Aid Detachment ladies do sterling work, I know for a fact that properly trained nurses would be more use."

"But I won't get my certificate until next April. The war will be over by then, won't it?"

"Ellen," he said. "There are those who say this war will only end when there's nobody left standing to fight it. Soldiers will need nursing long after April 1918. You'll be needed."

"I wish . . ." I started.

"Yes? What do you wish?"

"I wish they'd let me go out to France. Jack told me how a nurse looked after him, and it made me want to be there. But you've got to be a VAD and three years older than me."

"Things could change," said Colonel Cripps.

"I doubt it. I expect I'll have to stay with my old ladies," I replied.

"Old ladies, not to mention old men, need nursing just as much," he said. "But I know exactly what you mean, Ellen."

Walking back home, I made up my mind that I'd be content with what I had. After all, I'd really come to love my old ladies.

CHAPTER TWENTY-EIGHT

My few days at home are over, and I'm back at the hospital. I knew I'd be sad, but I wasn't prepared for just how empty I felt. I hoped that I'd see Annie and have somebody to talk to when I got back, but her bed was stripped and her closet empty. I wandered down to the canteen and found Enid drinking a cup of tea. "Annie's gone to an army hospital near where she lives," she said. "It came up very suddenly."

Lucky old Annie, I thought, and wondered who I'd share with now.

There's another change. They've taken me off my women's ward and put me on men's medical. So I'll be missing my old ladies as well as Annie. But it's Annie I'll miss most. You couldn't be sad with her around.

When I came back to my room, I saw a suitcase on the other bed, and a few minutes later its owner came in. She was small, about my age, with dark hair and a turned-down, serious face. She didn't look as if you'd get many laughs out of her. "Hello," I said. "I'm Ellen."

She didn't answer as she hung her clothes up. So I said, a bit louder this time, "I'm Ellen Wilkins. Welcome to our humble abode."

"Ivy," she muttered, as if it were a secret she shouldn't really tell anyone, and started making her bed. "Ivy Turner."

"Let me help you do that," I said. "Matron likes hospital corners in the hostel as much as in the wards."

"I'll do it myself, thank you very much," she replied. When it was done to her satisfaction, she sat primly in the wooden chair and stuck her nose in a Bible. She might as well have built a brick wall round herself.

I have to say that now that my first day is over, I'm going to enjoy working in the men's ward. At least they have a laugh and a joke, though they can get a bit saucy. Sometimes they go too far for Sister O'Leary's liking, and then she's down on them like a ton of bricks. Most of the patients are old, but neither that nor Sister O'Leary can stop them. I found it a bit off-putting to start with. "Nurse, I bet you've got a sailor on every ship," one called out as I passed his bed. It was daft answering, "I don't know any sailors," because quick as a flash he said, "Lucky soldiers, then."

Sister heard. "Now then, Mr. Jenkins, we'll have no more of that," she said, and then whispered to me, "Never answer them back. You'll only encourage them." She's a fine one to talk. I don't know what the man three beds down from Mr. Jenkins said to her, but she smiled and said, "Get away with you, Mr. Adams." Still, she's not old and motherly like Sister Agnew; she's young—not that much older than me.

The men must have thought I was fair game because as I was washing old Mr. Phelps, the men in the next four beds started singing very softly,

"Who were you with last night,
Out in the pale moonlight?
It wasn't your brother, it wasn't your Pa . . . "

Sister was down the ward in a flash. "I shan't tell you men again," she snapped, and Mr. Fenton said, "Oh, Sister, I love it when you're angry."

Ivy Turner was on the ward as well, making Mr. Granby's bed. "Oh, nurse," he said. "I'll be dreaming about you all night."

Even I could feel the chill of the freezing look she gave him. Poor Mr. Granby muttered, "Beg pardon, nurse," and I felt really sorry for him. I was making Mr. Bilton's bed, and he said, "That new one's a hard nut, make no mistake. I hope you're not like her." I tried to give him the same stare, but it didn't work, because he said, "No, you couldn't be, nurse."

When I had a moment, I watched Ivy. She's like an island sailors try to land on but give up because there are rocks all round it. The talking dies away when she passes. If it were me, I'd be really upset, because though I've been flustered a few times, it would be worse if they were afraid of me. She seems to like it that way.

"Those men are a handful," I said when we were back in our room.

"By their fruits shall ye know them," she snapped. Then she opened her Bible, and that was the last word spoken that night.

It's plain she doesn't think much of me. At least she

hasn't tried preaching yet, though she will sooner or later. To her I must seem a weak vessel, probably the flighty type and beyond trying to save. I almost wanted to tell her that I went to church most Sundays when I was at home and that the vicar had written me two testimonials. Besides, the school inspector once gave me a prize for Religious Knowledge when I was in Standard 4 at school. But she never gave me a chance, and if I had, she'd have sniffed, because that still didn't make me as good as she was. When I won my prize, Jack said, "Ellie, you're holier than my old socks," but if he'd said that to Ivy, he'd have really meant it.

How I wished Annie were back. I thought about her a lot over the next few weeks, especially after she sent me a letter saying how good it was to be at Eastern Military Hospital No. 26.

CHAPTER TWENTY-NINE

Most men on the ward are old because the young ones, except for those not fit to go or the conscientious objector we had in here until he was carted off by the police, are all at the war. When I wrote home saying most male patients are over fifty, Ma wrote back, "At least you'll be safe with them." Don't you believe it, Ma. They haven't changed since I came. In fact they get worse, and it's not just the ones who are on the mend. Poor Mr. Atkins was at it the day before he died.

Since Mr. Granby's sad experience a few weeks ago, nobody's tried it with Ivy again—not, that is, before this morning. Mr. Tompkins dared Mr. Walker to pinch her when she wasn't looking. She fixed him with her usual freezing glare and came out with some hellfire text from the Old Testament, which shut him up good and proper, and the rest of the ward as well, including Sister O'Leary. Well, that's what Ivy's like—always got a line from the Bible to shut them up and sometimes a religious tract to read. I've noticed that Reverend Parslow, the hospital chaplain, doesn't like her much, while she talks about him with contempt. She thinks the fire of the Lord doesn't burn brightly enough in him.

She's decorated her half of our room with Bible scenes, and there are some religious books between two bookends on her chest of drawers. Most nights she settles down with the Bible, though she must know it by heart by now. We hardly ever speak. I'm sure she thinks I'm not worth talking to.

Just as on the women's ward, most of the men talk about their sons and grandsons in the army. As time goes on, more and more get the news that they're dead, wounded, or missing. Sometimes they find out through letters, or the whole family comes to tell them the bad news. Everybody knows within two minutes, and then the whole ward, all forty beds, falls silent and a shared sadness descends. I think of Archie, and I share it with them. I wondered whether coming here would make me so busy that he wouldn't be on my mind so much, but it hasn't. At times like these, we tiptoe round trying not to make any noise.

We keep reading in the papers how we are winning the war: there's a big battle round Arras, British mines cause a huge explosion on Messines Ridge, thousands of Germans are killed, we're taking so many prisoners. One more push will do it, that's what they say, but it was one big push when Jack lost his leg and another big push when dear Archie was killed, and however many pushes there are, when we look at the maps the papers print, the war always seems to be in the same place. Now we're being told that we're winning the Battle of Arras, and yet even more families are coming in to tell of another death. It's April now;

next week it will be May. I often think of what Colonel Cripps told me: "There are those who say this war will only end when there's no one left standing to fight it."

Mr. Jenkins, the one who said "I bet you've got a sailor on every ship," has been in here for months now. We've watched him wasting away. Nobody, not even the highest doctors in the hospital, can fathom what's wrong with him. His daughter and her husband came to see him today. They stayed a long time. When they went, he didn't try to wave to them. When they were gone, tears streamed down his face. "What's the matter, Mr. Jenkins?" I asked.

"My Georgie's been killed at Arras," he sobbed. "I've lost both my grandsons now. They were fine boys, nurse. What are we all coming to?"

I tried to comfort him, but I wasn't any use. So I asked Sister O'Leary to give him something to stop him from lying awake all night thinking about it. "I'd rather nurse the soldiers than the ones who lose them," I said.

"I daresay you would, Nurse Wilkins," she replied. "But the men's medical ward is your place, and you must make up your mind to it."

When I told Ivy about poor Mr. Jenkins, she shouted at me. "Why should you be sorry for him? Why should he shed tears for his grandson, who girded his loins, put on the armor of light, and jousted with evil for the glory of the Lord? There's honor in making the supreme sacrifice. What is the loss of a mere earthly life when the true home of the warrior is in Heaven among the elect? I'm only a weak woman . . ."—I know she didn't believe that—". . . but if I were a man, I would feel privileged to have such an end."

For a moment I was amazed, then afraid, then puzzled.

After all the death and misery and heartache of the last three years, nobody speaks like that anymore. I felt almost sorry for Ivy, but really sorry for Mr. Jenkins. Anyway, I wasn't going to argue, so I let her get on with her Bible until it was time to put the lights out.

Ivy and I haven't spoken to each other for three days. Mr. Jenkins died last night. Oh, this hospital is such a sad place.

CHAPTER THIRTY

November's nearly gone, and it doesn't seem possible that I've been here a whole year. I still share a room with Ivy. She knows better than to try converting me. I go to the hospital chapel with the other nurses and sing the hymns and say the prayers. I like Reverend Parslow and love to listen to his sermons because they're funny and wise. I don't need converting.

There's been a really big battle, Passchendaele it's called. I had to copy that name from the *Daily Mirror* because when I first heard it, I thought it was "Passiondale," and it reminded me of Mr. Brayfield and Reverend Parslow speaking at Easter about Jesus's Passion. So many wounded came to the military wards that I thought my way of spelling it was better.

It's a dark autumn with thick, choking fog outside most days. Everyone says this will be a hard winter. People talk about a huge new weapon the Germans can't fight against, which will steamroller its way to Berlin. It's called the tank. Nobody knows what it looks like, though the *Daily Mail* and the *Daily Mirror* are full of it. The war doesn't seem to stop, though.

*   *   *

Christmas is two weeks away, and this year I'll be home for it. I can't wait. The wards are full of old people who can hardly breathe. We hear their poor lungs frothing away. A few have got pneumonia; most are too exhausted to talk and lie propped up on the pillows gasping for air. But there's one little old man who tries to be as lively as a cricket. It's inspiring, that's the only word I can think of, to listen to him laughing and joking, though every word is an effort. His name's Jim Doble, and I think he's the nicest old man ever to be on this ward, and that's saying a lot, because there haven't been many horrible ones.

Doble. I'm sure I know that name. It nags in the back of my mind and worries me. After I come off duty, I look for Enid and ask if she knows it. She thinks for a moment and then says, "I've never come across anyone called Doble. It's not a very common name, is it?"

Matron came into the ward this afternoon. This was a surprise. The only time we see her is in the procession up the ward every morning. She whispered to Sister O'Leary, who clapped her hands twice and said, "Pay attention, please. Finish the job you are doing and go to the sluice room. Matron wants a few words with you. I shall keep an eye on the patients."

We crowded into the sluice room, which wasn't a very suitable place for Matron to talk to us, so it had to be important. We were silent and respectful because we'd all been interviewed by her once, and it wasn't easily forgotten.

"I must remind you of the most sacred duty of the nurse beyond the welfare of the patients," she said. "There has been an occurrence in another ward in which a nurse broke a confidence given her by a patient. This breach of trust had serious consequences. Many of our patients have unfortunate personal circumstances, made worse by the war. Often they receive bad news. It is you they will confide in. I need not tell you that you must listen and give what comfort you can." I saw Ivy nod in agreement, and I thought it would take a strong person to be pleased with the comfort she would give. "What you will not do," Matron continued, "is let these confidences go outside the ward. This is an absolute rule, and anyone breaking it will suffer severe consequences. If you must tell someone, let it be the Reverend Parslow. He is a minister of religion, and any confidence will be safe with him. That will be all. Return to your duties." She nodded to Sister O'Leary and swept out of the sluice room and the ward.

"I wonder what brought that on," said Daisy Partridge.

Nobody knew, so we went back to work and soon forgot about it. But Ivy said, so we could all hear, "It's very sad that Reverend Parslow is the only one thought capable of bringing the comfort of the Lord."

Three more days and I go home. Christmas with the family and four days without Ivy. Mr. Doble's breathing is better this morning, so he can talk easier. "Have you lost anyone in the war, nurse?" he said.

"No," I said. "But my brother lost a leg at Loos."

"Ah," he said. "That's where my little lad went west. He were a little terrier and no mistake. Took after me, he did. Not afraid o' nothing. They picked on him at school something shocking because he was so small, but he gave back as good as he got. As soon as the speechifying about the war started and them posters with the finger pointing went up on every wall in the land, he was off. 'I never thought he'd have it in him,' said my Elsie. 'You don't know your own son, that's your trouble,' I told her. 'He's dead set on it. It's a chance to show what he's made of.' We're not much of what you might call a warlike family, nobody on my side has been in the army, and though Elsie's uncle Sid sailed on the *Cutty Sark* on the tea run, that wasn't navy, it was a merchant ship. Except for Sid we're a dockland family. When we'd loaded the ships, we didn't want to go off in them. But that palaver in 1914, well, it made you want to do your bit, didn't it, miss?"

"It was the same with our Jack," I said.

"Well, off he went," said Mr. Doble. "When he came home in his uniform, he said, 'Them bullies at school wouldn't pick on me now, Pa.' I've still got the letter from his officer. 'He faced his death like a man,' that's what it said, and it makes you proud to hear it, however sad you are."

I couldn't say a word, because I'd just remembered where I'd heard the name Doble before. "Leonard," said Mr. Doble. "Our little lad."

When my shift was over, I couldn't get out of the ward quick enough. I'd often wanted to cry since the war began, but never more than now. How could I look Mr. Doble in the face knowing what I did? I was really howling when Ivy came. She looked at me with disdain, sat on her bed, and started reading the Bible. Perhaps I'd slip outside and walk round the hospital grounds, even though the weather was horrible as usual.

I was just turning the doorknob when Ivy said, "What's up with you tonight?" I should have kept going, but suddenly I wanted to tell someone, even Ivy. I closed the door and said, "It's Mr. Doble."

"Yes?" she said, though she didn't sound very interested.

"He's so proud of his son."

"Why shouldn't he be? His son was killed in battle. He died a noble death in the service of the Lord."

"My brother told me about him. He wasn't killed fighting—he was shot for desertion." Only then did I realize that Ivy was the very worst person to tell. "So he was a coward," she said. It wasn't a question; she made it sound like a simple fact.

"He was frightened, that's all," I said. "Being frightened doesn't mean people are cowards. He didn't deserve to be shot by his own side."

"He who is not for us is against us. Those who strive for good are never afraid because the light of truth burns brightly in them. Truth could not have burned in Mr. Doble's son."

"That's an awful thing to say. Haven't you ever been afraid?"

"It is the devil who brings fear. God takes it away."

I thought Ivy was very hard and told her so. She smiled as if it were a great compliment. "Those enlisted in the army of the Lord must be hard. I shed no tears for Mr. Doble's son."

"But his father thinks he was a hero," I replied. "That's so sad."

"The scales will fall from his eyes," she said.

Talking to Ivy depressed me so much that I went out

after all and walked alone until the time came for lights-out, even though a bitter wind blew and snow flurries froze on my face.

I couldn't avoid Mr. Doble, but I didn't speak as I washed him and made his bed. His speech was clearer, and he was getting stronger. "I wish I had a picture of Leonard to show you," he said brightly. "You'd have liked him." I gritted my teeth. "Next time my old girl comes, she'll bring one in. We had some taken in his uniform before he went to France."

Thank heavens I'll be on my way home before the next visiting day.

CHAPTER THIRTY-ONE

The snow, which was so nasty in my face at London Fields, was soft and gentle in Lambsfield, but as I walked home from the station, I knew it wouldn't last over Christmas. Dark was falling fast as I stepped off the train. Pa watched for me through the lit signal-box window. I ran up the steps and opened the door. The heat from the stove hit me like a wall. He poured two mugs of strong tea and spooned sugar in them. We sat down in front of the window to drink them and watch my train steam away.

"Glad to be back, girl?" he said.

"You can't begin to guess," I replied.

"It's a big thing that you did, going away like that." I wished he hadn't said that: it made me feel bad. "I don't blame you," he continued. "I know you were aching to go. I'm proud of you. We all are."

"I want a Christmas just the same as it always used to be," I said.

"It will be," he answered. "As far as anything is like it used to be. Lambsfield's a sadder place now than ever. That Passchendaele thing has taken a few more away from round here. When's it going to end, Ellen?"

"I see the soldiers coming to the hospital," I said. "I wish I was looking after them instead of my old men. I do like them, but it's the soldiers who need us most."

"Anyway, you get on home, girl," said Pa. "I'll be back when my shift's over. Not too long now."

The walk home was so familiar, yet I felt I was seeing it for the first time. There was the Plough—I remembered the night when Mr. Straker and his crowd streamed out of it to the colonel's house. Farther on was the church, where I looked for Jack before following him to Oldwood Mere. And finally, round the corner was our cottage, with its welcoming yellow gaslight—so much gentler than the hard electric light of the hospital—shining through the window.

Betty came to the door. I was surprised. "Aren't you supposed to be at the vicarage now that you're Mr. Brayfield's parlormaid?" I asked.

"He's let me off tonight because you're home," she said. "He's given me Christmas Day off as well."

"So he should," I said.

"Madge isn't home from Dr. Pettigrew's yet," said Betty.

I remembered that last time I was here she'd said she wanted to work for him. "She's not a parlormaid too?" I said, feeling quite disappointed.

"Oh, no, she keeps his appointments in order and writes up all his notes so he can read them." I remembered that Dr. Pettigrew's handwriting was the joke of Lambsfield. "I don't think he could do without her now. Jack looks after his motorcar."

"It sounds like it's the Wilkinses who keep the doctor going," I said.

It was really good to see Jack. The bike business was still flourishing. "Colonel Cripps has bought a car now, so I get to look after his as well as the doctor's," he said. "Lord Launton's chauffeur came round the other day and said they were thinking of letting me loose on theirs too."

"Not Sam?" I cried.

"That's the one," he said. "Nice bloke."

It was so lovely to be home, especially when Ma came out of the kitchen with a plate of mince pies straight from the oven and said, "Here, have one, Ellen," as if I'd never been out of the house.

Christmas was all I'd hoped it would be. On Christmas Eve we went to the midnight service at St. Botolph's, even Pa. On Christmas Day itself, there was warmth, happiness, and a Christmas dinner from Ma as good as it ever was. Pa had bought a bottle of sherry at the Plough. Before we sat down to dinner, he put the stopper in the bottle of bitter he and Jack were sharing, opened the sherry, and poured everyone a glass. He ignored Ma's cry of "Charlie, you know it only takes one to make me feel all funny," and said, "Let's drink a few toasts."

So we drank to Jack's shop, to Madge and Betty and their new jobs, and to me, to welcome me home. Then Jack said, "My turn now. Let us young ones drink to Ma and Pa, because it's you two who keep us going."

"The other way round, more like," said Ma, wiping her eyes.

"My turn again," said Pa. He lifted his glass. "We'll drink to the hope that the war's going to end before next year's out and that we'll have won it."

"To the end of the war," we all said, but I don't think any of us really thought the end would be so close.

That evening I said to Jack, "Do you remember what you told me about Lenny Doble?"

"How can I forget?" said Jack.

"His father's a patient on my ward. He thinks Lenny died a hero's death."

"Poor sod," said Jack. "Don't tell him, will you?"

"Jack, I'd never, never do such a thing," I replied.

On Boxing Day morning, we went to the Hartcross Hunt meet in the market square. They met there every year, even when the war was on. "I won't go," said Pa. "I'm not cheering a lot of toffs on horses." That's what he said every year, so we weren't surprised. I didn't like the hunt much, and I always hoped they'd ride all day and never find a fox. But it was quite exciting all the same, the huntsmen and huntswomen in their red jackets and the dogs baying and the thin sound of the master of foxhounds' hunting horn. Although I partly agreed with Pa about the toffs— along, if truth be told, with most of the other people who'd come to watch—it was a brave sight, and Boxing Day in Lambsfield wouldn't be quite the same without it. I saw Lord and Lady Launton on their horses, but I don't suppose they noticed me, which hardly worried me. After the hunt had clopped its way out of the square and the people began to disperse, I saw Colonel Cripps standing watching. Bonny sat at his feet. She hadn't moved or made a sound, even with the hounds near her, though every other dog in Lambsfield had gone wild. I thought how well the colonel must have trained her.

There was someone standing with him. At first I thought it was his son, but then I saw that it was a woman, tall, with short dark hair. Something in her look told me that she and the colonel were related. "Ellen, come and meet my niece Daphne," he called.

I remembered the photograph in the colonel's sitting room. "A remarkable woman," he called her then.

"Daphne," he said. "Meet Ellen. Ellen is a nurse."

"Is she now?" said Daphne. "And where do you nurse?"

"London Fields Hospital. I get my certificate in April."

"Ah, a proper nurse. And are you good at it?"

"It's hard work, but I love it."

"I didn't ask you that. I asked if you were a good nurse." She was very direct, but somehow I didn't mind.

"That's for Matron to say," I replied.

"No, it isn't. It's for you to say. Are you a good nurse?"

"Yes," I said. "I am. I'm a very good nurse." I meant it too.

"That's what I like to hear," said Daphne. "Someone with confidence in herself. And who do you nurse?"

"I'm on the medical wards. Old people mostly. Bad chests, bronchitis, flu, pneumonia, TB. But we often do duty on the military wards when there's a lot of soldiers coming in."

"And I expect you'd prefer to be nursing the soldiers all the time."

"Well, yes, I would. But they tell me it's only lady nurses, VADs and people like them, who get to do that. Also, I'm not old enough. Besides, my old folks need me."

"Of course they do. Will you stay at London Fields when you have your certificate?"

I'd never thought about that before; I'd just assumed I would. "I suppose so," I said.

"Of course," said Daphne. "No hospital wishes to lose good nurses. Yet you'd prefer to be in a military hospital."

I thought of Annie's letters from Cambridge and said, "Yes, I would."

"And it's because you like young men better than old ladies?"

That annoyed me. "No," I replied. "I want to nurse soldiers because of what happened to my brother, Jack, after he was wounded. I want to nurse soldiers because my friend Beatie was killed in the Silvertown disaster and I watched her die from an explosion, just as the soldiers do. Then her father told me how, when the war started, they were so pleased they didn't have a son because at least they wouldn't have a child blown up in combat. Then there's Lenny Doble."

"Who is Lenny Doble?" asked Colonel Cripps.

I told them. Colonel Cripps looked both angry and sad. "The army can be a cruel and brutal place, and often needs to be," he said. "But it can be a supremely ignorant place as well. Edmund would tell you that."

"How is Major Cripps?" I asked.

"They say he's cured. The silly fool insists on going back to the front. I suppose I have to be proud of him; he could have sat on his backside in the War Ministry. But the people he met while he was at Craiglockhart made him think a lot. He even said he almost agreed with that poet fellow Sassoon who sent his Military Cross back, and I'm sure he has something to say about military executions. Few people are cowards by nature, and Doble doesn't sound one to me. It's just that you can stand so much and no more, and the army doesn't understand that yet, though it will soon have to."

"It sounds to me, Miss Wilkins, as if you don't just want to help the soldiers, you'd like to reform the entire armed services," said Daphne.

Was she laughing at me? I didn't see a flicker of a smile on her face. As I went to sleep that night, I thought of Daphne Cripps and almost felt I'd been interviewed.

CHAPTER THIRTY-TWO

Back at London Fields. When I entered our room, I saw that Ivy's bed had been stripped. Next morning on the ward, I had a terrible shock. Mr. Doble's bed was empty. "Where is he?" I whispered to Daisy Partridge.

"He died on Boxing Day," said Daisy.

"But he can't have. He was getting better."

"He had a shock. It killed him."

An icy fist seemed to close round my heart. "What sort of shock?"

"You'd have to ask Ivy."

"Where is she?"

"Gone. And don't ask where to. I don't know and don't care."

"Nurse Wilkins." It was Sister O'Leary. "A word if you please." I approached her nervously. "You're to report to Matron's office at once," she said. "Wait outside until she calls you."

Heart thumping, I walked down the corridor to the cheerless waiting room where we'd sat before our interviews. Matron's voice snapped, "Enter." I went in and stood before her desk. She was writing. When she put her pen down, she said, "You may sit."

She looked at me; her eyes narrowed. "You have heard that Mr. Doble is dead," she said.

"Yes, Matron. I'm so sorry."

"Do you know why he died?"

"Nurse Partridge said he'd had a shock."

"Nurse Partridge is right. Do you know what caused the shock?"

"I think I do."

"You think correctly. Well, let me see if I can apportion blame. On Christmas Day Nurse Turner told Mr. Doble that his son was not killed in battle as he had been told but had been shot for cowardice. Mr. Doble went into a steep decline and died on Boxing Day. I asked Nurse Turner what right she had to tell Mr. Doble such a monstrous thing, and she said it was her duty, that the truth should be known by all men, and that to conceal it was against the will of God. She further said that it was you who had told her. Is that true?"

"Yes, Matron."

"Before you say any more, you should know that I dismissed Turner on the spot. She had abused a confidence and told Mr. Doble something that she had absolutely no right to, thereby directly causing his death. I must warn you that unless your next answers are satisfactory, I shall not hesitate to mete out the same punishment to you. Did you tell Nurse Turner about Mr. Doble's son?"

"Yes, Matron."

"What grounds did you have for such a statement?"

"My brother, Jack, told me. He was at Loos, and

everybody in his regiment knew about Lenny Doble. He told me, like he told me a lot of things that had happened to him. When Mr. Doble spoke to me about his son, I realized at once it was Lenny. I was so upset, I had to confide in someone, and it happened to be Ivy—Nurse Turner. I never thought she'd spread it. If I had, I'd never have said a word."

"Why did you not wait until you could speak to Mr. Parslow?"

"It would have been better, Matron."

"It would, indeed." She fiddled with her pen for a moment. Then she said, "Nurse Wilkins, I shall not dismiss you out of hand because there are mitigating circumstances that did not apply to Nurse Turner. You will report to me here at ten o'clock tomorrow morning, and I will tell you my decision. Shut the door as you go out."

I walked back to the ward in a daze. *She's going to dismiss me,* I thought, *I know she is.* Ivy did this to me. It's the end of a long story. If someone hadn't shouted "Shame on you, Colonel," Colonel Cripps would be a distant figure like Lord Launton. If Jack hadn't been at Loos, he wouldn't have known Lenny Doble. If I hadn't worked at Hartcross Park, I wouldn't have met Archie. If Archie hadn't been killed at the Somme, I wouldn't have been so concerned about how brutal the army was. I'd never have spoken to Mr. Randall in the street, and Jack would never have told me about Lenny. If Mr. Doble hadn't caught pneumonia, he wouldn't have been in London Fields. If Annie Smithers hadn't left, I'd never have had to share a room with Ivy. If, if. Everything since the war began seemed to lead up to this moment. The night was long and sleepless.

*   *   *

Next day, the sight of all the familiar patients and Daisy
Partridge's friendly "Morning, Ellen" cheered me at first.
While I bustled round the ward as though everything were
normal, I began to think properly. Ivy didn't hate me. She
may think I'm a lost soul, but that's not the same. She
probably consigns us all—me, Matron, everybody—to
hellfire because she's right and we're all wrong. Sad but
true. No, I can't be too angry. That's her.

The time went dreadfully quickly, and my cheerfulness
disappeared. I dreaded the outcome awaiting me, and the
ward was a warm refuge hard to leave, though I was only
there in body, mechanically doing my duties. My mind was
hours ahead, packing my suitcase to leave.

Ten o'clock came, and when Sister O'Leary nodded, I
slipped out, hoping nobody noticed. Matron kept me waiting even longer than yesterday, and I was a quivering
wreck before she snapped, "Enter." I went in and stood in
front of her desk, looking at the floor, my hands clasped
behind my back. This time she seemed to write a whole
book before looking up.

"I have considered your case thoroughly, Wilkins," she
said. "I have consulted Mr. Garner the hospital superintendent and such governors as I could contact. I have spoken to Mr. Scrivener-Green. Sister O'Leary and Dr. Pewsey
have also given me the benefit of their experience with you.
There are many things to be taken into consideration, and
I have endeavored to weigh them fairly. The results of
what you have done have been most unfortunate. Mr.
Doble's relatives have overwhelming cause for complaint."

"I know, Matron. I'm truly sorry."

"I accept the fact that you did not yourself tell Mr. Doble about his son. I also accept the fact that you could not know your trust would be betrayed when you confided in Nurse Turner, nor would you have expected it to be. I understand your dilemma in having such knowledge and the feelings it engendered in you. All that is in your favor."

"Thank you, Matron," I said.

"On the other hand, it was extremely foolish to say anything to Turner. You know that the only person to speak to in confidence is Mr. Parslow, because he alone has that God-given responsibility. You have known Turner for some months and at close quarters. You should have realized the danger, both to yourself and to Mr. Doble. What happened seems entirely consistent with Turner's character."

I was amazed Matron seemed to know us so well. It was creepy to think there could be no secrets kept from her.

"You are culpable, Wilkins, though not as culpable as Turner. I cannot overlook the fact that you divulged confidential matters about a patient to an inappropriate person. You know the nurse's first rule, that everything you find out about patients is to be kept to yourself."

I hung my head, waiting for the damning verdict. Matron continued. "In other respects, you have proved yourself a capable nurse. Sister O'Leary and Dr. Pewsey speak highly of you. It would be unfortunate if, in these trying days, such a one as you were lost to the profession and left without the London Fields certificate."

I lifted my head again. Incredible. I was going to get away scot-free.

"Here is my decision. I will allow you to stay here and

complete your probation. But after that you must leave and seek employment elsewhere, because there will be no place for you at London Fields. That will be all, Wilkins. Shut the door behind you as you leave."

"Thank you, Matron," I said again, but she had already forgotten me and was busily writing again. I trailed back to the ward.

"Well?" said Sister O'Leary. I told her and she nodded. "That's fair," she said. "Don't worry. You'll find another place."

"That's not so bad," said Daisy when I told her. "I'm thinking of getting out of here myself."

"Yes, but it would be your choice," I replied.

That was what saddened me. True, I'd get my certificate. True, I'd be a proper qualified nurse. But it didn't seem to matter now. I'd tried so hard over the last three years to do the right thing, but it was all for nothing. As far as London Fields was concerned, I had failed.

PART 5

·1918·

DAPHNE

Chapter Thirty-three

The New Year came and went. I felt flat, as if London Fields meant nothing to me anymore. The news from France was bleak. Wounded soldiers kept coming in, but probationers still weren't allowed to help them, except when too many arrived at once. I was taken off men's medical and sent to the children's ward. Sister Jamieson there was nice enough, but I knew none of the nurses. I wrote home to tell the family what had happened and that I couldn't go back to London Fields after I'd gotten my certificate. Ma wrote back saying that she was sorry, especially as it wasn't my fault, and at least I'd come home for good in April. But I couldn't possibly stay in Lambsfield: that would be real failure. I would have to find another hospital. Wasn't there a navy hospital in Portsmouth? That wasn't so far away, and perhaps I might at least get to nurse wounded sailors.

I thought I should write to Mr. Brayfield and Colonel Cripps, as they'd written testimonials for me. Mr. Brayfield replied, saying that he was sure I was blameless for what had happened, but perhaps it was God's will. That didn't make me feel happier. Colonel Cripps said how sorry he was and that he'd written to Daphne about it, as he thought she might like to know. I couldn't imagine why. But a week later, I received a letter from her.

5 Cadogan Square
London
January 12, 1918

Dear Ellen,

So sorry to hear about your little contretemps. Still, it's an ill wind, as they say, so chin up, all's not lost. I've got a bit of time free soon and I intend to pop down for a few days with my uncle, so I wonder if you could go home as well and then we can have a chin-wag. Let Uncle Henry know the days you can manage, and I'll fall in with them. Really looking forward to seeing you again. By the way, if Matron gives you a hard time, just tell her Daphne Cripps says she's jolly well got to let you go.

Yours, as ever,
Daphne

How strange to put "as ever" when we'd hardly spoken. And why so keen to see me, even picking her days to suit mine? It was odd. I asked Sister Jamieson if I could see Matron, and she said she'd ask. "Is it about what you might do when you leave?" she asked, and I replied, "Sort of."

Amazingly, the summons came the next day. I thought she'd treat me like something the cat brought in, but no, she was really quite genial. "Well, Wilkins, what can I do for you?" she said.

"I wondered if I could go home for a few days," I replied.

Her tone changed. "I understood you wanted advice about what to do after you gained your certificate. I did not expect a request for days off."

"I'm seeing someone named Daphne Cripps," I said. "She wants to talk to me." It seemed a pretty weak excuse, so I didn't expect Matron's look of wonderment. "You're seeing who?" she exclaimed.

"Daphne Cripps."

"How do you know Daphne Cripps?"

"I met her on Boxing Day. Her uncle wrote one of my testimonials," I said. "Colonel Cripps."

"Cripps. Of course. I should have realized. So Daphne wants to talk to you. Well, well, well. You don't know what about, I suppose? But of course you wouldn't tell me if you did, because she would be most annoyed. Yes, of course you may go. Shall we say next weekend? Give Daphne my very best regards."

I left amazed. *Good old Daphne*, I thought. *You've made me shoot up in Matron's estimation.* And it meant I'd be home for my nineteenth birthday. Suddenly London Fields seemed a friendly place again.

CHAPTER THIRTY-FOUR

They were surprised to see me home so soon after Christmas. "They haven't sacked you already, have they?" said Jack.

When I told everyone that Matron had allowed me home because the colonel's niece wanted to speak to me, they were as mystified as I was. "She's not making you an honorary toff, is she?" said Pa, but he had a smile on his face.

That was last night. This morning I went to the colonel's house. Miss Cripps was waiting for me, sitting in an armchair in the sitting room. "Henry's taken Bonny for a long, long walk, so we can jaw away to our heart's content," she said. "There was no trouble with Cora, then?"

"Who?" I asked.

"Cora Watson. We've known each other for years." I must still have looked puzzled, because she repeated, "Cora. You know, your matron." I'd never thought of Matron having a first name. "Now then, Ellen, I expect you've been wondering why I've asked to see you."

"Yes, I have, Miss Cripps."

"Come on, Ellen. None of this Miss Cripps nonsense. We don't stand on ceremony here. Call me Daphne, please."

"I will, Miss Cri—Daphne." It didn't sound right.

"You see, I'm a nurse as well," she said.

Now that I looked back at how she'd almost interviewed me on Boxing Day, it was obvious. "As soon as I spoke to you, I knew you were exactly the sort of person we need," she said.

"We?" I said.

"Lavinia's Flying Circus," she replied.

"Who?"

"Surely you've heard of Lavinia, Duchess of Faringdon?"

"No, never."

"I'm amazed. Well, when the war started, Lavinia saw what nobody else seemed to understand—that Britain was in no state to fight a war, that this one would last a long time, and that there weren't enough medical services to deal with the thousands of casualties she knew would be coming. She saw further than any of those thick-headed generals. The thing about Lavinia is that she knows everybody and they're all afraid of her. She got hold of the prime minister and the foreign secretary and the War Office and bullied them into letting her put a band of nurses and doctors together to go out to help. Well, they let her, though they wouldn't give her any money, but that didn't matter because the duke's fabulously wealthy. She roped me in to find nurses and a couple of doctors and all the medical supplies I could get, while she bought two ambulances and learned to drive them. Then we dashed around Belgium doing sterling work, though the army didn't like us because they said we got in the way. But she put the fear of God into Sir John French, as well as the German fellow on the other side who was an old friend of the family, so they both let us roam the country looking after any soldiers we found wounded, no matter which side they were on. Oh, it was great fun. She even bought a run-down château near Abbeville and fixed it up as a hospital. All good things come to an end, though, and soon the War Office told us we were obstructing operations and had to stop it. Lavinia was furious, but this time they wouldn't budge. But at least they let us keep our hospital, and we still run it. Best hospital in France. You see, I'm a matron as well, like Cora."

"Why are you telling me this, Miss Cri—Daphne?"

"Because I want you to join us at Abbeville. Look here, Ellen, I'm sick of all these VADs who swan around like Lady Muck and don't know their ears from their elbows, if you'll pardon the phrase. I'm not saying that some of them aren't marvelous, but I don't want any of these 'France-seers' who only come so they can boast to people at home about where they've been. I want proper nurses with proper training, and believe me, they're not easy to find. When I spoke to you on Boxing Day, I knew at once that you'd be ideal, but just to check, I telephoned Cora and she told me all about you." This alarmed me slightly, but then she said, "She's sorry about what happened, and she really didn't want to let you go because she knows you're good at your job, but she couldn't let it go unpunished. Never think badly of dear Cora, Ellen."

I remembered what Matron said at the interview about working in military hospitals. "But I must be twenty-one to nurse soldiers," I said.

"Yes, and twenty-three to go abroad. Those are War Office rules, and we follow most of them because that's the deal we made. But Lavinia doesn't agree with some, and they're still too scared to make her. I'm matron at Abbeville, and if I say you're old enough, you're old enough."

"Is the duchess in Abbeville as well?"

"Oh, yes. She drives one of the ambulances. We have a tame Frenchman to drive the other." I must have looked doubtful, because then she said, "Look here, old thing, you mustn't be scared of Lavinia just because she's a duchess. Between you and me, she's a bit of a Red on the quiet—Bolshevik even—and she knows all the Labor people: Keir Hardie, Jimmy Maxton, the Webbs. She adores Lenin above all and opened a couple of bottles of Bollinger when the Russkies kicked the tsar out. Of course, she was a bit miffed when Lenin took Russia out of the war, but she doesn't blame him, because he's got bigger and better fish to fry now."

She stopped. There was silence in the room, and I knew I'd come without warning to the most critical moment of my life.

"Well, Ellen, what do you say?"

It was the answer to all my prayers, the granting of my dearest wish. But now that it had come, I couldn't say a word. I wanted to say, "Yes, yes, please. And thank you again and again." But I didn't dare. "My parents won't let me," I said. "Ma thinks I'm coming home for good when I leave London Fields. It would kill her."

"So there'd be family opposition. I don't want to split up families."

"Jack would say I should go. It's because he told me about what happened to him when he was wounded that I knew nursing was the right thing for me. I wanted to be like Miss Bakewell."

"And who's Miss Bakewell when she's at home?"

"The nurse who looked after him in the base hospital. It was her voice and her hands so cool on his forehead that he can't forget."

"VAD, I suppose. Well, as I said, some of them are wonderful."

"Miss Cri—Daphne," I said. "I want to go. If it's humanly possible to manage it without causing too much hurt, I will go."

"That's the spirit, Ellen. You leave your family to me. I'll talk 'em round. Expect me this evening."

CHAPTER THIRTY-FIVE

What was that all about?" said Pa when I got home.

"Nothing," I replied.

"You can't fool me, Ellen. There's something on your mind."

"Miss Cripps is coming round to speak to you this evening," I said.

"Oh, lor'," cried Ma. "I'll have to clean the house."

"Calm down," said Pa. "She'll take us as she finds us." They seemed more worried about what Daphne might think than what she might say, and I thought I'd better leave it like that.

Jack was out watching Lambsfield playing Greenhurst at football. Pa bought herring at the fishmongers to fry up for tea. Jack came in when they were cooking and said, "Have you got one for the colonel's niece?"

"She's not coming for tea, is she?" Ma nearly screamed with horror.

"How do you know about Miss Cripps coming here?" I said.

"Met the colonel and his new dog at the match. I've got a pretty good idea of why she's coming, and what I say is, you go, you'll never have another chance like it."

Ma put the plates down and looked at me. "What does he mean, Ellen?" she said.

"He doesn't mean anything," I replied.

"Yes, he does," she said.

"All right. Miss Cripps is matron of a hospital in France and wants me to go and nurse there."

"No," said Ma flatly.

"What if I want to go?"

"No," she said again. "I thought you were our daughter and your own home was good enough for you. But since the war started, you've drifted away from us, and if you go out there, you may as well cut yourself off altogether."

"That's not fair, Ma," I said. "I'll always come back. If I didn't have you all to come back to, I'd die."

"I came back, Ma," said Jack.

Ma rounded on him. "Yes, and look at you. Only one leg and you nearly didn't come back at all. What if Ellen's killed? She's only a nurse; she can't shoot back."

"I won't be killed, Ma," I replied. "I'd be working miles behind the lines. Jack was safe as soon as he was out of the trenches."

"You're not going. Tell her she can't go, Charlie."

"I'm not saying a word either way," said Pa. "Whatever I said would upset one of you."

"You coward," said Ma.

"I say Ellen should go," said Jack. "She's cut out for it."

"Please let me go, Ma," I said.

Ma looked at me, and I saw anger, sadness, and despair in her face. It was like recruiting day all over again. In another second she'd fetch me a stinging slap on the face. Except that there was a knock on the door.

Ma stepped back. Jack opened the door, and Daphne walked in. Pa got up out of his favorite chair and said, "Sit here, Miss Cripps."

"Ah," said Daphne. "I see you're expecting me, so you know why I'm here." She looked round. "And that you're not all happy with it. No, Mr. Wilkins, I wouldn't dream of taking your chair, though thank you for the offer."

There was an awkward silence. "Now, where shall I start?" she said.

"You can start by telling me what right you have to take my eldest daughter away," said Ma grimly.

"I'm sorry you see it like that," said Daphne. "I see it as a chance for Ellen to do a greater service to her country and the men called upon to fight for it, including your own son, than she could ever have imagined."

"Why Ellen?" said Ma. "There are millions of girls you could take."

"Not many like her," said Daphne. "I'm a good judge of character. I have to size people up at once, and I'm not usually wrong. Ellen is ideal. Mrs. Wilkins, if I believed in such things, I'd say it was her destiny."

"Do you hear that, Ma?" said Jack.

"This isn't fair," said Ma. "You're trying to put me in the wrong."

"I'm sorry, Mrs. Wilkins, but I'm doing no such thing," said Daphne.

Pa cleared his throat. "Excuse me, miss, but you ought to tell us just what Ellen would be getting herself into."

"Of course," said Daphne. "Thank you, Mr. Wilkins." She told them everything, about Lavinia's Flying Circus, the hospital at Abbeville, everything she'd told me, but quietly, without making it sound all a jolly joke. When she finished, she waited for their reaction and so did I.

"This duchess in charge," said Pa. "I suppose she sits at home in her castle telling you all what to do."

"Lavinia?" Daphne laughed. "That wouldn't do for Lavinia. She's out in France with the rest of us, just one of the ambulance drivers, along with Monsieur Sagnol, and she strips the engines down when they act up as well as any man."

"A toff like that?" exclaimed Pa. "Sorry, miss, I forgot myself there."

"Mr. Wilkins," said Daphne. "Lavinia's a friend of Keir Hardie. She goes to rallies in Hyde Park. If ever there's a British revolution, she'll be manning the barricades."

"But she's a duchess," said Pa.

"Only when it suits her," Daphne replied. "She's a duchess when she wants something out of the generals. When she's at the hospital, she drives the ambulance. I'm in charge at Abbeville, not Lavinia."

"Why aren't you there now, then?" said Ma.

"Ma, don't be so rude," said Jack.

"No, no, fair question," said Daphne. "I've been home over Christmas scouting round for medical supplies and hoping to find new nurses. The War Office doesn't help us, you know. We do everything ourselves. It's Lavinia's money I spend, or rather her husband's."

"Miss Cripps," said Pa awkwardly. "I daresay that you

do very good work. But I thought nurses in France were girls from rich families."

"I know, Mr. Wilkins. That's exactly why I want nurses like Ellen. The VADs do well enough, but most of them picked up what they know by coming out of their drawing rooms and just lending a hand. I want girls who are used to the rough side of life before they go out to France, who know suffering and hardship. I know where Ellen's been nursing and how she's been trained. If you don't know your job after training at London Fields, you never will. Ellen wouldn't turn a hair at what she might see in France; she'd go straight in and get on with it."

"Miss Cripps," I said. "I don't know anything about broken limbs or bullet wounds. I've only worked on medical wards."

"Care, Ellen. It's care I want. I want ordinary soldiers being cared for by the sort of women they know and won't feel afraid of. We have as many sick men as we have wounded. You've worked for a year in crowded wards with suffering people. You'll have nothing to get used to because you'll pick up the other side of the work quickly."

"She doesn't want to go," said Ma flatly.

"Yes, I do, Ma," I replied.

We all fell silent, as if there was no more to say. "Well," said Daphne at last, "I think I'll leave you to make up your minds." She sounded disappointed. "I'll bid you all good evening. Let me know what you decide." Then she slipped outside, closing the door quietly behind her.

"She had no right to come here turning your head," said Ma. "No right at all. Still, we sent her packing."

But I knew that if Daphne went away now, I'd regret it

as long as I lived. I rushed outside, shouted, "Miss Cripps! Wait!" and ran after her, catching up with her outside Mr. Daines's shop.

"I'm sorry, Ellen," she said. "I seem to have made an enemy of your mother. I never meant to do that."

"I'm coming to France," I panted.

"No, Ellen. It would destroy your family, and I see how much they mean to you."

"I want to go to France," I repeated.

Daphne looked at the ground as if thinking hard. Then she said, "Look, Ellen, I've finished my jobs in England, and I leave for France tomorrow. If you decide to come, let Uncle Henry know. He'll get word to me. If you decide not to, let him know anyway. We'll leave it at that, shall we?"

"Daphne," I said. "You know I want to go to France."

"I know you do, Ellen," she answered. "I know you do."

Back in the cottage, you could cut the atmosphere with a knife. Ma stood by the kitchen door, her mouth set in a hard straight line. Jack looked mutinous and angry. Pa sat sucking on his pipe, though he hadn't lit it.

"Did you speak to her?" Jack asked.

"She says I'm to write to her with my answer," I told him.

"She knows already," said Ma. "It's no."

"Ellen wants to go," said Jack quietly. "You shouldn't stop her."

Ma went in the kitchen, slamming the door. I heard her sobbing.

Pa said, "I don't know what you're to do, my girl. I've told you before that I know you could do anything you turn your hand to, but if you leave home again, it will kill your mother."

"No, it won't," said Jack. "Go and tell Miss Cripps now."

"Don't breathe another word about it tonight," said Pa. "I beg you."

All my life I'd never heard Pa beg anyone to do anything. "Don't worry, Pa," I said. "I won't." And in truth I couldn't even if I'd wanted to. It wasn't until I was in bed that I remembered it was my birthday tomorrow.

The birthday was a sad affair. Madge and Betty knew something had happened but didn't ask what. Perhaps Jack told them. I felt empty. Two weeks ago I thought things couldn't possibly be worse: Mr. Doble dead and Matron banishing me from London Fields. Then, out of the blue, I was lifted higher than I could ever have imagined. Now I was down again, lower even than before, because I'd caught a glimpse of what I now knew was my heart's desire. For three years and six months, since dear Barney lay dead and Colonel Cripps lay unconscious, I'd followed a road leading to this point. Now I wished I'd never stirred outside the house.

I had a few cards and presents, and Jack and the girls muttered "Happy birthday." Ma didn't speak. Pa looked embarrassed, as if whatever he did would be disloyal to one of us, though when Ma was out of earshot, he muttered, "I hope everything goes well now that you're nineteen." But for Ma not to talk to me on my birthday was more than I could bear. I spent the afternoon crying in my bedroom. Several times I nearly came downstairs to say, "It's all right, Ma, I won't go," but each time something held me back.

I came downstairs when Jack called, "There's tea on the

table, Ellie." Ma had made a birthday cake, iced just like when I was a little girl, with "Happy Birthday" on the top in pink and more candles than ever before. She must have worked so hard on it, yet here it was, just plunked on the table with no sign of her. The beautiful cake was like sawdust in my mouth.

We ate in silence, and then I cleared the tea things and took them to the kitchen. Ma sat in the kitchen chair, her elbows on the pine table, her face expressionless. "Thanks for the cake, Ma," I said. "It was lovely."

"Take what's left away with you, or I'll feed it to the birds," she said.

Jack came with me to the station. "Don't worry," he said as the train drew in. "She'll come round."

"No she won't, Jack, and you know it."

"I'll make her," he said. "I owe it to you."

So I left for my last months at London Fields, all my dreams in ruins.

CHAPTER THIRTY-SIX

Enid was the one I wanted to talk to. We'd been through a lot together. Since Beatie died, I hadn't seen much of her. I came back very late but was up early, hoping I'd catch her before she came off night duty. We only managed a few words, but it was enough. She was on days next week, and we had the same day off. So now it was back to the ward and little Billy Craddock's developing diphtheria.

This afternoon Enid and I caught the train to Liverpool Street and walked down past St. Paul's Cathedral to the river. The wind blew bitterly off the river, but we were wrapped up well. We bought roasted chestnuts from a stall, sat on a bench, and watched the ruffled gray waters of the Thames. London was full of soldiers and sailors, some in groups together, laughing, singing, and going from pub to pub, others with women leaning on their arms. There were several Americans among them. I had a piercing memory of Archie and our wonderful day in London. For many, this would be their last day here, their last happy time. I thought of their lady friends alone on the platform as the train steamed out on the journey to Dover. If I could only go on that train, some of those men might see England again because of me.

"It must have been a real disappointment for you," said Enid, as if she read my thoughts. "But you'll do as much good here in England with ordinary folks. It's a different sort of good, that's all."

"I know that," I said.

"I thought of being a nurse in France," said Enid. "But what hope did I have? You were lucky to get a chance at all."

"If Daphne had met you and not me, would you have gone?"

She thought for a moment. "No," she said. "Going out to France is not what I want."

"Nobody could have stopped you. You're twenty-one. When you said you wanted to be a nurse, I thought you'd be wanting to go there, especially after your brother was killed."

"Perhaps it was because he was dead that I didn't. If he'd come home wounded like your Jack, I might have felt different."

"What happened to our brothers changed us both completely," I said.

"I know," she replied. "It made me want to do things I never thought I could, things I decided for myself, not just because it was what girls like us were supposed to do. It made me think for myself. Can you imagine going to work at Hartcross Park now?"

I remembered how she changed from a shy, quiet girl to

the one who led us, who became Beatie's equal. Poor Beatie.

"I shall stay at London Fields," she said. "Perhaps I'll get to be a sister and then, who knows, even a matron. Unless I get married." She looked at the river and said, "Do you know what I'd really like to be? I'd like to be a doctor. But how can I? I left school at thirteen, I haven't got the education, and my parents could never pay for me. So I'll stay a nurse, meet a man I like, get married, have six children, and nobody will ever hear of me again. Deciding for yourself what you do only goes so far. If it hadn't been for the war, we might not have done nearly so much, but when it's over, things will be no better than before and we'll be back where we started."

"That's a hard thing to say," I replied.

"But it's true," she said. "I think you should go to France, by hook or by crook. You're right for it, and it's right for you. Who knows what wonderful thing it might bring you that you can't even imagine now?"

"I know I should," I replied. "But it's not easy."

We'd long ago finished the roasted chestnuts and were getting cold again. We left the river, went back to Liverpool Street, and had a cup of tea and a bun in the refreshment room while waiting for our train. We didn't say much; all we seemed to have done was depress ourselves even further. But I think we knew a lot more about each other, and perhaps a little more about ourselves as well.

Billy Craddock died. It was the first time I'd seen a dead child. "It's something you'll never get used to," said Sister

Jamieson. "But it's what we sign up for when we start this job, so you must just harden your heart."

Two weeks have gone by. I haven't written to Daphne, because whatever I write will make me unhappy. Except for Enid, I've had no close friend here since Annie Smithers left, nobody to go out for the day with. It's a surprise when I get a message saying Matron wants to see me.

So once again I wait outside that door. Matron calls, "Enter." When I go in, I get the shock of my life. There stands Ma. "Hello, Ellen," she says.

I'm too flabbergasted to speak. Matron says, "I suggest you go for a long walk together. I think you have a lot to talk about."

We sit together on a seat in the hospital grounds. "Is it bad news?" I ask.

"No, it's not bad news," she says. There is an awkward silence. I have no idea what to say next. Why is she here? But I know why, really, and the more I think about it, the more inevitable this visit becomes.

Ma speaks first. "I wrote to Matron saying that I wanted to see you, but that she wasn't to tell you. She said I must see her first. I told her it was family business but didn't say what. I think she guessed, though."

Matron has never inquired about my talk with Daphne. Perhaps she knows. Perhaps Daphne told her.

"It's about how you want to go to France," Ma goes on.

"It's all right, Ma," I say. "I won't go."

"You could have written to say that. I won't have you saying it just because I'm here."

I nearly say, "I would have anyway," but stop in time.

"Ellen," she says, "I've come all this way because it's time we talked about it without losing our tempers. We have to be on our own, without Jack and your father in the way. They'll never convince me, though God knows Jack keeps trying to, bless him. He's a good brother to you."

"I know," I say.

"So he should be, after the way you helped him. But he won't make me change my mind."

I nearly say, "What did you come here for, then?" but she answers the question for me. "Only you can do that."

"Ma, I've told you why I want to go."

"No, Ellen, you told me how much you want to, and Miss Cripps has told me why she wants you. They're not the same thing. Would you want to go if you were staying at London Fields?"

"I only met Daphne through Colonel Cripps. If I wasn't leaving London Fields, I'd have forgotten all about it."

"I sometimes think that man has too much of a hold over you children," Ma says. "I don't doubt that he's a good man. But most things that happen to you or Jack nowadays seem to be because of him."

"Perhaps he can size people up at once, like Daphne says she can."

"I take that with a pinch of salt, and so should you."

"Ma, if you're telling me you don't trust Daphne and the colonel, then there's no more to say, because I do trust them."

Ma hesitates, and then says, "If you hadn't met Daphne, would you have tried to go to France some other way?"

"I couldn't. I'm not old enough, and besides I'd have to be in the Red Cross or a VAD or a proper army nurse."

"I know, but if you were old enough, would you have tried?"

"Yes," I say. "I've only got this chance because the duchess can ignore what the War Office says. Daphne doesn't think I'm too young."

"Ellen, since you were last home, I've been trying to find out about this Flying Circus. I asked Mr. Brayfield, and he knows about them. He says they've done sterling work since the war started, and some people think their hospital is the best run in France. Then I met Mr. Randall in the street and asked him. He knows all about Daphne, and he said there couldn't be a better, more honest soul in the world. I asked him what he would think as a parent if his daughter, still a girl, wanted to go out there among the blood and bullets, seeing sights such as no person should, and he answered that he'd have to think about that one. Then I asked him what he would think if his nineteen-year-old daughter was miles away from home in a dangerous place surrounded by young men. And he laughed. He said that the state that daughter would see these young men in, there'd be precious little dangerous about them, at least not in the way I was thinking. Even if there were, Daphne and the duchess together would frighten them silly if they tried anything. They won't allow such things. At least there's one thing they agree with the War Office on. 'She'd be all right with those two in charge, believe me, Mrs. Wilkins,' he said."

"Do you believe him?" I ask.

"I think I do. I know Mr. Randall and I trust him. He's like us, from a good working family."

"But you don't trust Daphne."

"If Mr. Randall does, then I will. He's known her a long time."

I'm thinking she's changed her mind, until she says, "But none of that matters. You haven't told me why you want to go. It can't be because someone says you'd be good at it. That's no reason."

So I tell her that it's because that night at the colonel's I vowed I'd stand up for myself. It's because at Hartcross Park we went on strike and got our own way, and when they fired all of us, it was the best thing that could have happened. It's because I saw what Jack was like when he came home, how I helped him and made him talk to me so that he got the horrors off his chest. It's because of Archie and how I was so powerless when I saw him go and so wretched when he was killed. It's because Jack told me about how Miss Bakewell did so much for him without even realizing it. It's because Enid didn't flop down defeated when her brother was killed; she stood up and took charge of her own life. That's why I went to London Fields, because I didn't see how I could go to France and this was the next best thing. So meeting Daphne was the answer to my prayers.

Ma listens to me and then she says, "If you go, Ellen, I'll never sleep."

"I know, Ma," I reply, thinking my reasons have all gone for nothing.

"But I didn't sleep when Jack volunteered. I didn't sleep when you went to Hartcross, nor when you came here. I'm used to not sleeping, Ellen. All mothers are. One day when you've children of your own, you won't sleep either."

I sit there imagining what it must be like to be my

mother, what it will be like one day when I'm a mother, whether I'll watch my children go away from me into dangerous places from which they might never return. And I cannot quite imagine any of these things, though the thought of them makes me cry, both for Ma and for myself.

She stands up and kisses me on the forehead. "Ellen," she says, "go to France, and go with my blessing."

Then she walks quickly away, and I watch her figure dwindling through the hospital gates on her way home.

PART 6

·1918·

ABBEVILLE

Chapter Thirty-seven

April's here. After Ma and I talked, it took a few days to sink in that I was really going. Daphne sent instructions on getting my uniform (a long gray dress with a red cross on the chest, white apron, white cap, and blue cape), a travel warrant for Boulogne, and money, made available by Lavinia.

I had big doubts in my last days at London Fields. "You're bound to now that the time's near," said Enid. The children and old men and women I'd nursed seemed silently to say, "Stay here. We need you more." Perhaps they were right. They would always be here, not just in London Fields, but in hospitals everywhere. One day there would be no more dying soldiers, though the news said that day might be a long time off. The Germans were breaking through, the first time the war had stirred out of the trenches for three years. Sister Agnew and Sister O'Leary came to see me, and Sister Jamieson arranged a little leaving ceremony on the ward, in which Dr. Pewsey made a lovely speech. On my last day, Matron presented me with my certificate, and suddenly London Fields was in the past.

Home was more difficult. Ma might have changed her mind, but she wasn't happy about it. I thought about her not sleeping, and it meant I couldn't sleep. Now it had come to the point that Pa wasn't happy either. Jack was as encouraging as ever, but the last night at home was a sad one.

Now I'm on the troopship. I'm traveling with another of Daphne's recruits. Her name is Lily Hobson, and she's from Birkenhead. Lily has reddish hair, pale, freckly skin, and looks five years older than me. She worked in a military hospital near Liverpool and wrote to Daphne asking if she could join. "How did you know about Daphne?" I asked. "We've all heard of the Flying Circus," she said. She wasn't the only nurse to apply, but she was the only one Daphne took. "She makes her mind up very quickly," she said. "I hope she sticks to it."

We met at Victoria Station, traveled to Dover, walked from the Marine station to the harbor, and there stood our somber gray troopship. We walked up the gangplank, and a ship's officer escorted us to a roped-off area on the top deck. "So the soldiers can't get at you," he said. The ship was crammed with soldiers, mostly British, but also some American doughboys, with broad-brimmed hats like Boy Scouts. No crowds cheered and waved flags to see us off. Good-byes were said long ago, and troopships were as regular as omnibuses. A hospital ship lay at the dockside with men on stretchers being carried off. "That's our life from now on," said Lily.

Though the sea was only a few miles from Lambsfield, just over the Downs, I'd never sailed before, not even on a Thames pleasure boat on days out in London. It was a bright April day with a brisk wind, and as we left Dover

Harbor and came out into the open, choppy sea, I felt queasy. But hearing the soldiers singing as though on a day trip, feeling the salty wind in my face, and thinking of the great adventure ahead, I soon forgot my sickness in favor of a daydream about being met by the duchess to drive us to Abbeville.

We docked in Boulogne, the singing stopped, and the soldiers poured down the gangplanks. Sergeants major roared and shouted at them. The harbor at Boulogne was a mass of men in khaki, army trucks, horses—I wondered how order could ever come out of such chaos. I saw a line of ambulances with big red crosses painted on their sides and beyond them the railway. The soldiers were now lined up in ranks, packs on their backs, rifles at the slope, ready for the march to the huge base camp at Etaples. I knew from Jack and from Archie's letters that they were in for a grim time there before going up to the front line.

Lily and I weren't allowed off the ship until the last soldier was gone. Two women in sisters' uniforms were waiting for us at the foot of the gangplank. They looked tired out, their faces pale, with shadows under their eyes. I supposed they couldn't be much more than thirty, but they looked sixty. "Are you Hobson and Wilkins?" said one.

We said we were. "I'm not going to say we're pleased to see you because we hoped you wouldn't be here," she continued. "I suppose you didn't get the matron's telegrams."

Lily and I looked at each other. "What telegrams?" Lily asked.

"Telling you to stay put. The Hun's not three miles from Amiens. That's too close for comfort. Matron said it was too dangerous for new nurses to come into this mess."

The other woman said, "You'd have been near as a toucher to ending up German prisoners. We thought the end had come."

"I heard the Germans were advancing," I said. "Lots of people were talking about it. But they said we were beating them back easily."

"Lots of people don't know the half of it," said the first. "If they break right through, there's nothing in their way before Paris. We're not a base hospital anymore, we're a casualty clearing station. The men come straight to us from the front in a terrible state. The war nearly ended last week, and we'd have lost it."

"No time for talk; now that you're here, you're on duty," said the other.

"It's straight to Abbeville on the train," said the first. "We have to swab it out and clean it up before the next batch comes on board. I'll detail a couple of orderlies to pick your luggage up."

The hospital train may have been empty, but everything in it spoke of suffering and death. For a split second, I saw a stretcher with a soldier in it, and I thought he was Archie. "We're in for a slow journey," said the first nurse. "We'll be stopped at every signal for ammunition trains to get through. I doubt if we'll see the hospital before tomorrow morning."

"We don't know who you are yet," said Lily.

"No more you do," said the first nurse. "I'm Sister Grogan and this is Sister Ellis. So much for introductions; we've got to start the swabbing down and disinfecting."

"You've had your anti-typhoid injections, I hope," said Sister Ellis.

We assured her we had. "Good," she said. "Matron wouldn't allow you in if you hadn't." Matron. I won't be calling her Daphne out here.

Abbeville was hardly thirty miles from Boulogne, but the journey took six hours. We either crawled or stopped in sidings while long trains rumbled past us loaded with big guns. It took all that time to clean the train, swab it down, and mop up blood and the other things best not thought of from the floor. Soon the smell of disinfectant covered the human smells still in the air. It was dawn before we finished.

When we stumbled out on the platform, I was so nearly unconscious after twenty hectic hours without sleep that I didn't realize I'd gotten my wish, and we were being driven to our destination by a duchess in an ambulance.

It wasn't until we were bumping along in the dark that I realized that if Ma and Pa had received that telegram, then Ma certainly wouldn't sleep. Sister Ellis must have known what I was thinking. "Don't worry, Wilkins," she said. "Matron will sort it all out."

CHAPTER THIRTY-EIGHT

Perhaps the people who used to live in the château before the war had fled the country, and to have a duchess buy their estate just in time had been an amazing stroke of luck. I never found out. But I saw what a lovely place it must have been: gray stone, wooden shutters on the windows, high-pitched slate roofs, and round it an overgrown garden where soldiers could lie outside on warm days and take their first few steps before they went home—or back to the fighting if they were deemed sufficiently patched up. I couldn't imagine them lying outside now. Once, Sister Ellis told me, the war was thirty miles away, seemingly locked forever in the trenches, and the guns were no more than a quiet thunder. Now they were close, and a pall of smoke hung over the horizon to the east, toward Amiens. By night, lurid flashes lit the air, and sleeping men groaned and cried out as if the noise and light outside were part of their dreams as well.

I woke that first morning into bright sunlight. It was past midday. I was on the top of a hard, narrow bunk bed and looked down to see Lily asleep directly below me. The room was very small, with a sloping ceiling. I jumped out of bed and looked out. We were high up in a little attic. Below were gnarled apple trees and unkempt bushes, weedy paths and unmowed lawns. To the left were the old stables. An ambulance stood in the yard, caked with mud and with bullet holes in its roof. The hood was open, and two people were bent over the engine. One was a thin, dark man and the other a large woman. They were speaking earnestly and urgently to each other. Monsieur Sagnol and Lavinia, I presumed. The woman's loud voice said, "All right, Alphonse, you crank her up and I'll start her." The man turned the starting handle, the woman clambered into the driver's seat, and a moment later the engine burst into noisy life. As it chattered and clattered, the woman jumped out with a whoop of triumph and shook hands with the man, who took over in the driver's seat and drove the ambulance away.

So they'd let us sleep, then, which was nice of them. There was a washstand, a bowl, and a big can of water in the room. I washed, put my uniform on, and nudged Lily. "Wake up," I whispered. "It's late."

Soon we were ready to go downstairs. We walked through corridors from which doors opened to wards with lines of beds in rooms that were once drawing rooms, sitting rooms, a library, even a ballroom. They had high windows, ornate plaster ceilings, and oil paintings on the walls. We walked down staircases wider on each succeeding floor. It was almost like being back at Hartcross Park. Sister Grogan saw us as we passed her ward. "You must report to Matron," she said. "I'll show you the way."

Matron's office was not very large, and sheaves of paper

clipped together and hanging on nails in the walls made it look even smaller. Daphne sat at a little desk, two piles of neatly stacked paper in front of her, together with a single framed photograph. She was writing with a black fountain pen in a big ledger and wrinkling her forehead as if working out difficult sums. Then she looked up with a smile. "There may be a war on, but accounts must be kept," she said, and waved her hand airily at the papers on the wall. "That's my filing system." She stood up. "Hobson and Wilkins, welcome." No "Ellen" here, I noticed.

"Good morning, Matron," we both said.

"You slept well? You deserved it. You had a jolly hard night's work the moment you landed. And don't worry. I telegraphed to your homes again last night: DANGER OVER. GIRLS ARRIVED SAFE AND WELL." I felt thankful. "Of course, the danger's not over at all," she went on. "Today is your baptism by fire."

She wore a uniform like ours—apron, cap, the lot— with nothing to show she was in charge. "Don't think I sit in here all day wielding a pen," she said. "I'm out on the wards. I don't get the leisure dear Cora has." She smiled again. She was the same as when I saw her at Colonel Cripps's, except that she wasn't Daphne anymore—at least, not within our hearing.

"There are so many coming in that we've opened up a new ward," she said. "Getting it equipped and staffed was why I gave myself leave over Christmas. Sister Ellis, who you met last night, is in charge of it, and the other nurses, Ferguson and Smollett, are old hands." Then she looked stern and serious. "Before I take you there, I have something important to say. This hospital may be Lavinia's show, but we aren't the Flying Circus anymore. The price of our independence is to fall in with War Office orders, and this, as far as you're concerned, is one of the most important: You know what people say. Male patients fall in love with their nurses, and nurses fall in love with the doctors. That may be true at home, but it mustn't happen here, because the War Office doesn't like it. There are to be no liaisons, no confidences shared with orderlies, patients, or doctors. Ordinary conversation is permitted off duty, but while you are working, nothing will be said that is not necessary for the job at hand. There will be no fraternization with soldiers either. That is the first rule of the hospital, and I rely on you to keep it. I do not look kindly on any nurse who breaks it. Is that quite clear?"

"Yes, Matron," we both said.

"Good. That's got that out of the way. Now I'll take you to the ward and introduce you to my other great catch at Christmas. Follow me."

As we left the office, I snatched a quick look at the photograph on her desk. It was of a man. His face seemed familiar, but I couldn't place it.

Daphne led us through the kitchens, full of women stirring pots, tending the huge ranges, and jabbering away in French. "The kitchen staff are all local," said Daphne. "They're marvelous. You won't go hungry here." We passed through the kitchen into the yard where Lavinia and Monseiur Sagnol had started the ambulance. The open square was churned up with mud and tire tracks.

The stable block reminded me of the night we tried to get Beatie out of Arthur Dunhill's bedroom. Most stalls for horses had been stripped out, except for a few with curtains over them at the far end. The walls were newly white-washed and the stone-flagged floor scrubbed. Unshaded electric lightbulbs, all lit, hung from the roof beams. Close by a big motor throbbed monotonously.

"That's the electricity generator," Daphne said. "A diesel engine. I suppose our German friends did one useful thing by inventing it. If it breaks down or we run out of fuel, this place is finished."

There were no windows, and the only natural light came from three skylights in the roof, which explained the lights being on. No high windows and oil paintings here. But the main feature was thirty beds, fifteen on each side, and every one occupied. Some men slept, others cried out, one moaned incessantly from pain or his memories. "Most have had surgery," said Daphne. "Arms, legs off, shrapnel out, stomach wounds patched up as best we can. Now we must keep them alive."

We stopped by a young man with a stethoscope round his neck bending over a man whose face was twisted with pain.

"Here he is," said Daphne. "My great Christmas prize, as valuable to us as you two." The young man looked up. "Captain Stevenson, here are two new nurses, Hobson and Wilkins."

Captain Stevenson's face was round and rosy, almost like a small boy's, with fair hair cut very short. He wore a white coat, but there was a light khaki uniform underneath. "Sure pleased to make your acquaintance, ladies," he said. The first American I'd ever met.

"Dr. Stevenson is a gift from Uncle Sam," said Daphne.

"He takes a great load off the shoulders of Major Withers, Captain Davies, and the others. The trouble is, what Uncle Sam gives he can take away. Captain Stevenson might be ordered away at any time."

The soldier in the bed whispered, "It hurts, sir." A notice at the end of his bed showed his name as Private Lodge, P. (British).

"The bullet will soon be out," said Dr. Stevenson.

He walked a few paces away and beckoned us over. "He's just come in. The bullet's in his neck. They couldn't do more at the advanced dressing station than make him comfortable enough to be brought here. We're the nearest place with an operating theater." He fiddled with his stethoscope. "It's a miracle they got him here alive. A jolt could have killed him. Where are the orderlies?"

"Sergeant Oldroyd," Daphne called.

Sergeant Oldroyd was in charge of the medical orderlies. He looked far too old to be in the army, though they took men of fifty now. The other orderlies were younger. Most were very small, none looked strong, and one had a clubfoot. Not fit to be at the front. But they worked very hard.

"Get this man into the theater, Sergeant. Tell them to get him anesthetized. I'll be there as soon as I've checked these poor fellows," said Captain Stevenson. "Hedges, leg amputation. Spencer, stomach wound. Won't last out the day, I fear." And so it went on, broken body after broken body, and by the time we'd been to the top of the ward and come back down again, I knew exactly what I had taken on. Seeing soldiers on the military wards at London Fields was nothing compared to this: they'd been through the worst already in places like ours. Daphne said, "That's an introduction. When the ambulances come, you'll know what work really is."

There are tents outside, and the orderlies are putting up more. A rumor has gone round that there'll be a big rush tonight. The Germans are still trying to take Amiens, and casualties will come here straight from the front.

Dusk came, then darkness. Candle lanterns and paraffin lamps were lit in the tents. "They're coming," said someone. The first ambulance turned into the yard. Soon the orderlies were bringing stretcher after stretcher and laying them down on the groundsheets. Sister Ellis stood by me. Now that the time had come, there was a knot of fear in my stomach. I'd been told what to do, and some things I'd done already at London Fields. But this was like nothing else in the world. I should have stayed at home.

In the weak yellow light, I saw distorted bodies, remnants of blood-soaked uniforms still clinging to them. I heard a cacophony of groans, screams of agony beyond bearing, and yet some little pockets of silence that seemed louder than any cry. Ivy Turner had sometimes tried to make me see things her way by telling me the punishments that awaited me in Hell. If she'd described this, I might have believed her.

Two orderlies put a stretcher down in front of me. A body, strangely small, covered by a rough gray blanket. I tried to draw the blanket back but couldn't bring myself to touch it. "You have to, Wilkins," said Sister Ellis.

I took a deep breath. His legs ended above the knee. Jagged bones stuck out of both ends, and torn flesh like scraps of paper hung from them. They had done a rough cauterization at the advanced dressing station to stop the bleeding, but the stretcher was red with fresh blood. He shouldn't still be alive, but he was.

I wanted to vomit. The tent seemed to go round and round, I was muzzy, and suddenly I blacked out, thinking, *Please God, don't let me fall on top of the poor man.*

When I came to, an orderly was saying, "Hold up, miss." Sister Ellis did not look sympathetic. "You'll have to do better than that, nurse."

I was too ashamed to answer. That must never happen again if I want to stay here.

CHAPTER THIRTY-NINE

I've been here a week now. The press of ambulances bringing men has become worse. There are British, Irish, Americans, Australians, Canadians, South Africans, Indians, New Zealanders, West Indians. As a German attack was beaten back, long lines of ambulances waited to get in.

I learned quickly and never fainted again. We worked all day, all night, with hardly any time to eat and sleep, making men as comfortable as we could, knowing who had no hope of staying alive, who needed old dressings taken off, wounds cleaned, washed, powdered with Iodol powder, and given clean new dressings, and who must have surgery. Those for surgery were put in a line because the doctors worked nonstop in the theater amputating limbs, removing shrapnel and bullets. This was work such as I never thought possible, even in nightmares. Yet after this first week, I've become so used to three hours' sleep at any time of day or night that it's as if I've been here all my life.

Lily and I have become quite close. There's no room for squabbling here. The hospital works like a machine, and over it all is Daphne. She works like any nurse much of the time, but she knows the progress of every patient and they soon know her. She's wonderful at putting them at ease, and I watch her carefully because I want to be the same. Yet she's in her office as well, keeping the place going. Nobody slacks, with her example.

What of the doctors? The two older ones are both British. Major Withers is probably about fifty. Captain Davies is in his thirties. Captain Stevenson looks younger than I thought possible for a doctor.

One day when there was a few hours' lull, Sister Ellis took me to the operating theater, a room off the ballroom. The walls were hung with white sterile cloths, and an unlit chandelier hung from the ceiling. Three unshaded bulbs were always on, despite the large window.

A soldier lay on one of the four operating tables. He had been anesthetized, and swabs were placed round an open wound in the side of his chest. With infinite care and slowness that I could hardly bear to watch, Captain Stevenson brought out a bullet with a pair of forceps, looked at it with disgust, dropped it into a bowl, and said, "I don't think he'll want it as a souvenir, but if he does it's here."

The wound was dressed, and I felt quite proud to be cutting lengths of bandage. Then the orderlies took the soldier gently back to the ward and a proper bed. Sister Ellis told me to go with them to make the soldier comfortable. He was still unconscious, and blood had already seeped through his new dressings. I changed the bandages again and touched his cold forehead, thinking of Jack and Miss Bakewell.

All night we worked. I heard Sergeant Oldroyd say that if the Germans didn't break through now, they'd lose the war and that he reckoned there were nearly as many casualties as there were at the Somme.

Next night I was back in the tents. I was beginning to get into a routine. It was the orderlies' job to get the men's filthy, blood-soaked uniforms off, wash them, and get rid of the dressings put on at the front, but there were too many coming in for that, so the nurses had to do it as well. Most men not unconscious were shy about this and said they'd do it themselves, but we wouldn't let them even if they were fit to, which most weren't. Then we cleaned out the wounds and put new dressings on them over and over again, time after time, until I was working in a daze.

At two o'clock in the morning, a man was brought in sorely wounded. His right arm was gone, but he was still conscious. I'd thought about how young Captain Stevenson seemed, but this one looked hardly older than Bully Straker. His uniform wasn't khaki; it was gray. He looked up at me and tried to say something, but I couldn't tell what it was. Sergeant Oldroyd stood next to me. "Bleedin' Jerry," he said. "I'll have to get him up to the German ward when the doctors have wasted good time sorting him out."

"You mean there's a special ward for German soldiers?" I asked.

"We get too many of the bastards in here," he replied disgustedly. "We put them in their own ward, where they can't do any harm. We have to look after them, so they tell us. Me, I'd let 'em die where they drop."

I looked at the German's weary, blood-drained face. He was no more than a boy, and he'd lost his right arm. I couldn't picture him as one of the hard men with spikes on their helmets who'd killed babies in Belgium, or so they told us. I remembered Jack telling me about Loos, how when the British came out to collect their dead, the Germans stopped firing and stood with bowed heads out of respect. I told Sergeant Oldroyd that, and he replied, "Who killed the poor sods in the first place?"

When I finally fell into my bed at five in the morning, I dreamed of Archie being brought in on a stretcher and me bringing him back to life.

I only got two hours' sleep. At seven o'clock I heard a shout of "Fall in" and had to be up again. Another convoy was here, and there was just me and the little orderly with the clubfoot, Private Jenkins, in the tent to receive six wounded men. We stripped their uniforms off and washed them. Then Private Jenkins picked up what was left of the uniforms and took them outside, some to be washed and repaired, others burned. I cleaned out wounds and put dressings on. Three men would need amputations, one had a terrible shrapnel wound in his stomach, another died before we could undress him, while the last had only a flesh wound. He was quite talkative. "Don't worry, miss. It looks worse than it is." He sounded Australian.

"I don't know about that," I replied. I looked at his identification. Private Walker, J., New South Wales Rifles.

"I didn't mean my little graze," he said. "I mean all of us coming in at once. You must think we're getting a right shellacking out there. Well, we're not. We're beating the buggers back, miss. We're being blown to chops, but the Jerries won't get any nearer. They've got kids in their army now. Shows they're nearly finished."

"I know they have," I said. "We've got one here."

"See my mate Fred there?" he said, pointing to the man with the shrapnel wound. "He doesn't think he's been wounded at all."

"He has," I answered. "It's terrible. I just hope he'll be all right."

"They kept trying to put him on a stretcher, but he wouldn't have it. 'What d'you think you're doing?' he said. 'There's men needing them more than me. I can walk.' They had to pretty well tie him down, miss."

Fred's eyes were closed. For a terrible moment I thought he'd died, but then I heard shallow, hoarse breathing. "There'll be a doctor here soon," I said. "I hope Fred's going to be all right. He deserves it."

Major Withers came round soon after. He took one look at Fred and said, "He goes to the front of the line. Jenkins, get someone in and take this man to the theater as quick as you can, and for God's sake don't jolt him."

"See what I mean, miss?" said Private Walker.

The three for amputation soon followed. Then Major Withers examined Private Walker. "You're a lucky man, soldier," he said. "Regular dressings back at base, a week's leave, and you'll be in the firing line again by next month."

"Suits me, sir," said Private Walker. "I don't mind going back now that we've got them on the run."

That was the strange thing. Though so many wounded men were being brought in, there was a sort of jauntiness about them. Perhaps the tide really was turning. It was evening before I was relieved, and then only for an hour. But before I went to get a bite to eat, I went round to the German ward. The boy had died.

Chapter Forty

For four days the convoys came. I was moved from the tents back to the ward, into the operating theater, and back again. I cleaned so many wounds and applied so many dressings that my hands automatically made the movements even in snatched sleep. We ate when we could. Just as suddenly as the rush started, it slowed. Some tents were taken down, and the rest of May was almost peaceful. The hospital was full but never overflowing. Then, as June approached, it all started again.

It wasn't until the first rush was over that Lily and I were introduced to Lavinia. "What do you call a duchess?" I asked Lily. "Search me," she replied. "Would 'my old Dutch' do?"

Anway, it didn't matter. When we were called to Daphne's office, there stood a large lady in a Women's Auxiliary Army uniform with a red cross armband. "Call me Lavinia," she boomed. "Remember, I'm only the chauffeur round here." Then she shook us both by the hand, so hard that I heard the bones crack. "It's a bit late to say it, but welcome, welcome, my dears. I'm so grateful to you for coming to help us."

So no "Your Grace" or "Your Highness" and no curtsying either, which I'd been practicing when nobody was looking. You'd never believe that back at home Lady Launton herself would look up to her, nor that she paid for the hospital and all of us. I hoped people in Britain understood, and the War Office as well, though I often heard Major Withers say that lot never understand anything. She asked us how we found things here and what we'd done, and when we'd told her, Daphne said, "They're good nurses. They've been wonderful since the day they came."

"Like everybody else here, I'm glad to say," said Lavinia. "Even dear Monsieur Sagnol. He and I fight like cats and dogs over those ambulances, you know." She put her hat on. "Ah, well, no peace for the wicked. The good monsieur and I must drive up to the front and see if we can pick up a few that the others have missed."

I haven't seen her since. She's been too busy with the ambulance.

Private Walker was wrong. The Germans weren't being beaten back—they attacked again and seemed to be stronger than ever. I hoped Private Walker was still on leave. Once again the wounded flooded in; once again we had no sleep and hardly time to eat. The main battle was farther south now, round Rheims and Soissons, they told us, and this time the French were taking the worst of it, but it didn't seem to stop the flow of casualties.

It's June, and we've got a new problem. Some soldiers are coming in with flu, and it's not like any old flu that can go of its own accord like a bad cold. This is bad, and we can't

seem to do anything about it. Three soldiers last week were
getting better from their wounds, but then they went down
with it, developed pneumonia within two days, and were
dead the day after. "It's a bad business. After all that time
at the front, they've got no resistance," Captain Stevenson
said as I covered the face of yet another victim. "The poor
fellows go through so much that to be taken by this is more
than human beings can bear."

The worst thing is to hear the men trying to breathe
with their lungs full of phlegm and rubbish. I've been
taught how to relieve the congestion. I take a heavy glass
cup and a stick tipped with cotton wool. I soak the cotton
wool in pure alcohol, set fire to it, and dip it into the cup.
Then I put the cup on the man's chest so it stays there by
suction, and it draws the muck out. If it won't, I call a doctor, and he makes a little cut in the skin. This brings the
stuff out, but it brings blood as well. The man can breathe
easily for a while, but he's soon gasping, so I do it all over
again. I'm glad when I'm back in the tents. I'd rather clean
out wounds.

Last night was awful. We worked without pause for eight
hours, then Sister Grogan said to me, "You're wanted in
the operating theater, nurse."

"What for, Sister?"

"Silly question. Get on your way."

Six of us were sent up there. All the operating tables
were full. I was put to helping Major Withers, handing him
instruments, cutting bandages, swabbing blood. There
weren't enough doctors to do the anesthetizing, so a sister
had to do it instead. I was used to seeing that, but the sister,

whom I didn't know, was urgently called out, and Major Withers said, "You do it, nurse." I was horrified.

"I can't, sir," I cried.

"Yes, you can. You've watched it done, haven't you? I've had the hospital chaplain anesthetizing patients before now, and he knows less than you do. I'll guide you through as I'm taking this fellow's shrapnel out."

He didn't stop working as he told me what to do. But I'd seen it done before, so I knew the different stages. I took a sort of wire cup lined with gauze and put it over the next patient's face. His left arm was shattered: it would have to come off. His eyes were wide with panic. Trying to look as if I did this every day, I took a bottle of chloroform and dripped the liquid on the gauze—drip, drip, drip— like a leaky tap.

"Nurse, pour it quicker if you please," said Major Withers, hardly looking up from his work.

"I can't, I'll kill him."

"No, you won't. I want him well under. And don't stare at him like a frightened rabbit. That's far more likely to do him in."

I forced myself to hold the bottle more steeply so the drops came faster, and soon the man was asleep. Next time I'd feel better about it.

"If ever the chloroform makes them fighting mad instead of putting them under, call an orderly," said Major Withers as he started the amputation, which didn't make me feel any happier.

We're two weeks into June. Another busy night. From inside the tent, we hear the ambulances come in, the confused shouting and near panic outside, the sounds I once dreaded. The first stretchers are brought in and laid on the groundsheet. The smell of blood and filth drowns out the paraffin stink, and groans and shrieks of pain fill our ears, but we just get on with the routine. Cut away uniforms, pull off the casualty centers' rough dressings, clean and drain wounds—thank God there isn't much pus now that the armies are on the move and not locked in trenches. Then take a clean swab soaked in disinfectant, place it in the wound, bandage it securely. Dressing finished, doctors take over. The next soldier is waiting. Hour after hour it goes on, head wounds, chest wounds, stomach wounds, leg wounds. Every soldier looks the same, and all of them like Archie. One man dies as I put his new dressing on. Another comes in. At first I think he has a black mask on his face, then I see the entire lower part of his face is shot away. A sudden dreadful vision: could Archie have been like that? I can do nothing for this man. The stretcher bearers pick him up and take him to the theater, though he'll have no hope there. I am past all feeling by now: these poor creatures are just jobs to do.

Another stretcher is brought in and placed in front of me. I look down and have a presentiment that this one will be different. A voice inside says, "It's not Archie, none of them are, and they never will be."

The boy has fair hair, and I guess he is about my age. I take away the blanket that covers him. There is a rough dressing on his shoulder: there must be a bullet there. But there is a much bigger, blood-soaked dressing on his thigh. I cut away the rest of his tunic to make sure there are no other wounds. Even in the light of the lamps, I can see that what isn't dark with blood is gray. He's German. He's conscious and his face twists with pain. But he manages to smile and for a moment seems to relax.

I take off the dressing on his thigh. The wound is deep, ragged, and oozing blood. I prepare swabs and bandages and set to work cleaning and draining it.

Suddenly a fountain of blood jets up, splashes in my face, and runs warm down my cheeks. "Oh, God," I cry. "His femoral artery's ruptured." I know what to do, though I never thought I'd have to. I feel around for the rupture and, when I think I've found it, press down with my thumbs to pinch the artery closed. If I haven't got the right place, he'll die in front of me from loss of blood. It jets again, not so much, then stops. I stay with my thumbs pressed down, shrieking, "Someone help me. Raise his leg." I have to do this so his leg is higher than his heart. "I'm here, miss." Private Jenkins. He takes the man's heel and lifts it. Sergeant Oldroyd watches. "He's only a Jerry," he says. "Leave him be. Let him bleed to death."

I yell at him. "Get a doctor, Sergeant. Tell him, *tourniquet*." Sergeant Oldroyd doesn't move. "*Now!*" I scream. He's gone at once. He must be quick, or I'll be standing here, thumbs pressing down, until I can do it no longer and the soldier will die. I despair. It will be my fault.

It seems an age, though it cannot be more than a few seconds. Questions pour into my mind. Why is the wound in his thigh? Bayonet wounds are usually stomach or chest: even if the soldiers get here alive after one, they don't last long. I remember Jack saying how he stuck bayonets into sacks of straw during training and his fear when ordered to fix them before going into battle. Bayonets are horrible. I have a sudden clear, terrible vision of this German soldier facing a bayonet charge. Did he have a bayonet too? Did he plunge it into an Englishman's stomach? Might that man also be here in the tent? Or did he, with no bayonet, frightened out of his wits, shoot his enemy, who then ripped his thigh open with a last despairing lunge as he died? The thought makes me shiver. But the wound is jagged, not the clean cut I'd become used to with bayonets. Whatever it was, this hospital is full of ordinary nice men, both allies and enemies, forced to do such things to each other, and as I stand here, I cry with the pointlessness of it all.

Then a soft American voice says, "All right, nurse, hold on." Captain Stevenson. "Sergeant Oldroyd," he shouts.

"Sir," Sergeant Oldroyd answers.

"I want you to lift the end of the bed so the blood can flow to his head. 'When the head is pale, lift the tail,' as they say. Private Jenkins, find a box, block of wood, anything to rest the end of the bed on so we can keep him stable." Private Jenkins runs off, returns in a moment with what look suspiciously like two beer crates, and Sergeant Oldroyd rests the foot of the bed on them.

Captain Stevenson looks at the soldier. "Yes, he needs a tourniquet," he says. "A stick and bandage must do for now. It should stop the blood well enough. Primitive, but it will keep him alive. We'll do better later. I'll take over now."

Thankfully I take my hands out of that terrible gash. My thumbs and both hands up into my forearms are numb. My wrists ache, my hands and forearms are covered in blood—my sleeves and apron are drenched in it, and the red cross on the front of my dress has disappeared. I step back and see the man's frightened eyes watching me.

"Keep his leg still, Private Jenkins," says Captain Stevenson. "Bandages, please, nurse." By the time I've cut them and handed them over, they're red too, but Captain Stevenson says, "At least it's all his blood, and he's strong and healthy so he'll soon make up the difference." I watch him working so calmly and neatly, until he says, "He'll do for now. I'll give him morphine. Get him up to the theater, and I'll take that bullet out." He steps back and says, "Good work, nurse. With any luck he should be OK. I hope he thanks you."

I'm trembling. That's the worst thing yet to happen to me, but it's over and I've come through. I take a last look at the German. His eyes are still open, and I wonder if it's gratitude that I see in them. *Will you last the night? I wonder if, when this rush is over, I'll find you again in the German ward.* All these thoughts pass through my mind as I turn to the next wounded soldier.

Chapter Forty-one

Two days have passed since the young German's tourniquet. This morning I was in the flu ward with Captain Stevenson. He was going round the beds, and I followed him, doing the cupping. Suddenly he started talking. This surprised me, because he was an officer and a doctor. But he was so nice and easygoing. He told me all about himself—how he came from Massachusetts, how his father had put him through medical school, and how he'd started as an intern in a hospital in Boston.

"Do you know," he said, "I thought we should have joined this war two years ago, after the *Lusitania* was torpedoed and all those Americans died. I even thought of leaving the hospital and enlisting in the British Army, or the French. But then Mr. Zimmermann, the German foreign secretary, decided on a piece of mischief and sent a secret telegram to the Mexican president suggesting they invade Texas and get the good old U.S. of A.'s dander up. Revenge at last for the Alamo. But you British decoded it, so President Wilson had to join in the war whether he wanted to or not. So I came over here with Uncle Sam.

But when Lavinia and Daphne got ahold of me, I couldn't avoid coming here."

Greatly daring, I asked him how old he really was. "Twenty-five," he answered. "That's not too young, is it?" Then he looked at me. "How old are you, nurse? To me you look like a little girl."

"Nineteen," I answered.

"I thought you nurses were supposed to be twenty-three. Just a minute, don't tell me. Lavinia fixed it. Am I right?"

"Yes," I said.

He whistled and said, "Wow! What Lavinia wants, Lavinia gets."

"You don't think I'm too young, do you, sir?"

"You, Nurse Wilkins? Never. I judge people by what they do, not how old they are." He looked at me hard. "What you did that night for the German was amazing."

"Do you know what caused his wound, sir?" I asked.

"We dug a huge piece of shrapnel out of it. It's a wonder he didn't lose his leg." He took a flu victim's temperature, looked at the thermometer, sighed, and said, "Less of the 'sir,' please. I'm no stiff-upper-lip Englishman. By the way, what's your first name? Mine's Chauncey."

"Ellen," I replied. "But—"

"Right, Chauncey and Ellen it is, though not when those starch-front English doctor colleagues of mine can hear or any other nurses. But when we're working together, then OK. Anything else makes me uncomfortable."

"All right, sir," I said.

"*Chauncey,*" he insisted. He passed to the next bed. "By the way, our tourniquet case not only survived—he's doing really well."

I went off duty that night with my head reeling. I was so pleased for the German soldier. But if Daphne heard about Captain Stevenson talking to me, would she say I'd broken her rule about nurses and doctors? I was happy and elated, but a bit guilty and worried as well. It would be a long time before I'd call Captain Stevenson "Chauncey."

A fortnight has passed. This morning I'm on the German ward. We take turns coming here. Daphne doesn't want the same nurses in every day lest they get too friendly. I'm always uncomfortable here. It's hard when we can't talk properly to the soldiers. Some of the older ones are grim-faced, saying little, grudging about the care we give them. We try to treat them fairly, but it can be very hard. They know that when we discharge them, they'll go to England as prisoners, and that must hurt their pride. Sergeant Oldroyd is no help. My heart sinks when he comes into the ward.

The young ones are usually nice. Some manage a few words of English. They're thankful to be out of the war. Knowing that they'll go to England makes some of them happy because at least they'll be safe. Because of them, I almost started to like working on the German ward.

My tourniquet man was in the bed by the door. I looked at his wound. It was healing well and, though pale, he seemed in very good spirits. I was so pleased to see him. Yes, he was no older than me, with fair hair and an open, honest face. *"Guten Morgen, Schwester,"* he said.

I knew *schwester.* It's German for "sister." The Germans call us Schwester just as all the others call us Sister whether we are or not. "I'm not a sister, I'm only a nurse," I said, though I didn't think he'd understand. But he answered, "I do not care about that. To me you are Schwester. I watched you as you stopped my blood. You saved me, Schwester. I can never thank you enough."

"You can speak English," I cried in surprise.

"Of course," he said. "I have an uncle who lives near Northampton, in a village called Peterspury. I have often visited him there."

"Is he still there?" I asked.

"I think so. We have not heard. I hope he keeps well. I think he may be in some sort of prison."

"They'll have sent him to a place for enemy aliens because he's German."

"Now that the war is near its end, I may hear from Uncle Friedrich soon."

"Why do you say that?"

"Because my uncle will write as soon as he is able."

"No, I mean the other thing, about the war being near its end. How do you know?"

He sighed and looked sad. "Believe me, Schwester, I know."

One of the grim-faced men heard him and said "traitor" in English, I expect because he wanted me to understand.

"I am no traitor," the young soldier answered hotly. "You are the traitor, wanting to keep the war going when it will ruin our fatherland."

At that moment, Lily came into the ward and said, "Ellen, you're needed in the theater."

"Good-bye, Schwester," said the young soldier. "Good-bye," I answered, and Lily looked at me strangely. I followed her out of the ward wondering what sort of argument I had stirred up between the German soldiers and whether the young man whose uncle was in an internment camp would give as good as he got. I believed that he would.

Ten days later I was in the German ward again and felt even more uncomfortable. The young soldier was sitting up looking very cheerful. He was still in the bed nearest the door, so I saw him last. Some men were not doing well, and I took a note of their names for Sister Grogan. When I came to the young soldier, I looked at the notice at the end of his bed: Vögler, Matthias.

"How are you this morning, Private Vögler?" I asked.

"Private?" he replied. "What is this 'private'?"

"It's what they call ordinary soldiers." I shouldn't have answered, but my good resolution was slipping away, and I couldn't seem to help it.

"*Soldat?* I am not *Soldat.* I am *Gefreiter.*" I must have looked puzzled, because he continued, "Next up from *Soldat.*"

"Lance corporal," I said, thinking of Jack. "So how are you this morning, Gefreiter Vögler?"

He smiled. "Very well, Schwester Ellen."

"I told you, I'm not a sister, and you certainly mustn't call me by my first name. Besides, how do you know my first name?"

"I heard the other Schwester say it last time I saw you."

First an officer, then an enemy calling me Ellen. If Daphne found out, I'd be out of here before my feet could touch the floor.

"I must look at your wound," I said. It had almost

healed. He must be very strong. "The doctors will be discharging you soon."

"Then they will send me to England until the war ends," he said.

"I don't know. I think some prisoners go to camps in France."

"I am lucky. I was not killed. It was only a bullet in my shoulder."

"But you had that terrible wound in your thigh. It nearly killed you," I said.

"But you saved me, Schwester," he said. "My hurt is now cured, and I will go to England and see Uncle Friedrich again. When at last I go home to Germany, I can still play football." *More than poor Jack can,* I thought, but I didn't tell that to Gefreiter Vögler. "I can be a goalkeeper again. It's thanks to you, Schwester Ellen."

A soldier in the next bed muttered something in German, and it didn't sound very friendly. Gefreiter Vögler looked him straight in the eyes and answered with one short, angry-sounding word. There was a tense silence, so I got out quickly. Once the door was closed, another argument would break out. Gefreiter Vögler certainly knew how to annoy his fellow soldiers. Perhaps I should ask Sister Grogan not to send me to the German ward in the future. But when I asked, she said, "Certainly not, Wilkins. We can't chop and change duties to suit you."

I had a letter from Ma this morning. Jack's business is doing well. He's taken on two more men because there's nearly as much car work as bike work now. Colonel Cripps says he will pay for a proper motor pit, and Jack can repay

him out of his profits. Dr. Pettigrew has sent Madge to
learn how to type so that she can be a real secretary. Betty
still works for Mr. Brayfield. Pa is well, though worried
about how the war is going, and Ma herself is feeling fine,
though she's tired with all the extra work now that Madge
and Betty aren't there. If she was trying to prick my con-
science by hinting that I ought to be home helping her, it
didn't work.

Lily had a letter from a friend in London. She showed it
to me. Ever since the Germans seem to be winning, there's
a lot of what the girl who wrote it calls "Hun-baiting" going on. There are angry rallies and meetings calling for revenge, and I find I'm worrying about Gefreiter Vögler's
uncle Friedrich. I look through Ma's letter again to see if
she says anything about it happening in Lambsfield, but
she doesn't, so at least the Strakers aren't up to their old
tricks. I must stop worrying about Gefreiter Vögler and his
uncle.

The flu epidemic gets worse. The ward in the stables is
now an isolation ward, and only a few nurses are allowed
in. Thank goodness, I'm not one of them. Dr. Stevenson
works there all the time. I've hardly seen him, let alone
worked with him, since the time he called me Ellen. It's just
as well. Gefreiter Vögler is quite enough to be dealing with.

I try to ignore Gefreiter Vögler, but he won't let me. He
talks to me even when I'm seeing to another soldier. "I'm
nineteen, Schwester Ellen. I've been in the army for two
years. They pulled me in the moment they could. I didn't
want to go, but it's for the good of the fatherland, so I
must. They take boys of fifteen now."

The soldier whose stomach wound I was cleaning up gave a sort of growl that did not sound friendly, though I knew it wasn't aimed at me.

"I come from a place called Regelstein. It is a lovely town in the Taunus, a place of great beauty with wooded hills and castles. One day soon I shall be back there. Where do you live, Schwester Ellen?"

I didn't answer as I saw to the next man's shoulder. Gefreiter Vögler said nothing more. *He's taken the hint*, I thought. Three more to go and then it's his turn, the last to do. All three were making good progress, so I turned to Gefreiter Vögler. The gash was still healing nicely. "You've done really well," I said. That was all right to say because he ought to know how he's getting on. But he took it to mean I'd talk to him properly. "Where do you live in England, Schwester?" he asked again.

I had to answer. "A place called Sussex, in the south, by the sea."

"Ah, the sea. You are never far from the sea, you English. Is Sussex a lovely place, like the Taunus?"

"I don't know about the Taunus, but I love Sussex. Woods and fields and the South Downs, round hills with short grass, dew ponds and not a single tree on them, and the sea is on the other side."

"I should love to see Sussex, as you would the Taunus," said Gefreiter Vögler. I thought that was a rather forward thing to say, but perhaps that's how they speak in Germany. "My father works on the railway. He is, what do you say in English, the locomotive engineer."

"An engine driver," I said. "My father works on the railway too. He's a signalman."

"So we have something in common, Schwester Ellen. For myself, though, I do not want to work on the railway. Cars are the thing for me. One day I would like my own garage, where I could repair them."

"Just like my brother!" I exclaimed. It was uncanny how similar our lives seemed to be. But I couldn't keep talking to him like this. "You're fine now, Gefreiter Vögler. They'll soon be sending you away."

"Schwester Ellen, please do not call me Vögler. I am Matthias."

"We mustn't call patients by their first names," I said.

"That is a pity," he replied. "It is not right."

"I must go," I said. "I have work to do."

I paused outside for a moment to hear an argument break out. But there was silence, so I walked away feeling quite relieved for Gefreiter Vögler.

Captain Stevenson passed me as I was going to the ward in the stables this morning. "Hello there, Ellen," he said and seemed to veer toward me so that our shoulders touched. I felt uncomfortable and was glad when he was well out of the way.

When I walked into the German ward a week later, four beds were empty and Gefreiter Vögler's was one of them. I was greeted with a stony silence until a soldier older than the rest said, "They have been taken away to a prison camp. I have been told that you English shoot prisoners."

"Of course we don't," I said indignantly. "If we did, we wouldn't spend time trying to save your lives first."

That shut him up. But then he said, slightly more kindly,

"We do not know where they are gone. I am sorry. He wanted to tell you, but it was done very quickly. He did not know until the last minute."

When I left the ward, I felt strangely empty. I'm going to miss Matthias Vögler.

CHAPTER FORTY-TWO

July is here, and the flood of casualties is dying down. The main fighting is still farther south, where the French and Americans are trying to stop the Germans from doing what they aimed to do in 1914: get through to Paris. But there's a feeling that at last they may be crumbling. A few weeks ago, Gefreiter Vögler said the war would soon end. The German ward has gradually emptied. There are six prisoners left, all too ill to move. For the first time, more soldiers leave than arrive. Tents have been taken down, leaving yellow patches on the grass. Last week we began to work in proper shifts. "Make the most of it—it won't last," said Sister Ellis.

Yesterday Daphne saw each shift separately. "Now that it's a little less hectic, you'll be allowed time off outside the hospital," she said. "I've brought you all together to give you a reminder." I knew what was coming. "You remember what I said when you came here. There is to be no social contact between you and the males in this hospital, whether doctors, orderlies, soldiers, or Frenchmen outside. Absolutely forbidden." She looked at us sternly, then softened. "We're still on active service. There must be no"—

she stopped as if searching for the right word—"no distractions. If I hear of a liaison developing, I shall send the offending person home at once."

I saw one or two disappointed faces. I didn't mind because I didn't want a liaison—not here, anyway. Daphne continued. "Don't think I'm a killjoy. I don't see myself as some old schoolmarm. But we must keep our discipline. This is a War Office order, not Lavinia's or mine."

One of the younger sisters put up her hand. I knew her: Lorna Bilson. She worked in the flu ward. "Yes, Sister Bilson?" said Daphne.

"Matron," she said. "Captain Stevenson told me that there aren't such rules in American hospitals."

"The Americans can do what they like," Daphne replied. "We know all about the Americans. All ragtime and skyscrapers. They've only been here five minutes." We laughed, and Lorna Bilson muttered, "I wish I was a Yank." I wondered why Captain Stevenson told her that. He must have asked her to go out with him sometime and she said no. *Good,* I thought. *Safety in numbers.*

Lily and I are on night duty, so after a few hours of sleep this morning, we thought we'd go to Abbeville for the afternoon. We asked Sister Ellis, and she said she'd tell Daphne. We wore our best uniforms—the ones that weren't washed nearly white to get the blood out—and capes. Monsieur Sagnol was driving an ambulance to town to pick up provisions, and we asked him for a lift. He looked doubtful, and Lily said, "Don't worry, Monsieur Sagnol, it was worth a try."

Then a big voice boomed out, "It's all right, Alphonse.

You take 'em, they deserve it." I couldn't tell where the voice came from until a head emerged from under the other ambulance, and Lavinia appeared in oily, grease-stained coveralls, looking less like a duchess than ever.

"But I must return as soon as I have collected the provisions, madame," said Monsieur Sagnol. "I cannot wait for them."

"Oh, they'll find some way to get back. It's only four miles, and the roads should be safe now. Perhaps there's an omnibus. Anyway, they can walk. Nothing's beyond the ingenuity of our nurses."

It felt good to have a duchess so confident in us, though I wasn't so sure about getting back on our own. But we couldn't miss this chance, so we got into the ambulance and sat uncomfortably on a bunk while Monsieur Sagnol cranked the starting handle. The engine started with a bang and a hiccup, he climbed in, and we slowly drew out of the yard onto the potholed road to Abbeville.

He dropped us at the marketplace. The stalls were loaded with beautiful fruit and vegetables, better than anything in England, even out of our own back garden. Joints of meat hanging on hooks, chickens in coops clucking away, sausages, pâtés—you'd never think there was a war on. "This market has nothing in it compared to peacetime," said Monseiur Sagnol disgustedly. "Ah, the terrible penalties the *Boche* have brought." We left him haggling with a stall keeper over a pile of huge red tomatoes.

Abbeville was noisy with cars and horses and full of soldiers—British, French, American—some sitting outside in pavement cafés, others with ladies on their arms. All round was a babble of French and occasional raucous English laughter. A few eyes turned toward us, and Lily said, "We could have trouble shaking this lot off." But nobody came near us. "Are we that ugly?" I said.

"It's the uniforms," Lily replied. "They don't set the pulses racing."

"I think they're afraid of us," I said. "I never thought I'd frighten anyone." But it didn't matter. Just to be out of the hospital and walking freely was quite enough, until Lily said, "Do you know the way back?"

I looked round. Houses, squares, streets, shops, cafés all round us, and we had no idea where we were. "Do you speak any French?" she said, and I replied, "Where would I learn French?"

"France might be the best place," said Lily, and I answered, "I've been here nearly four months, and so far Monseiur Sagnol is the only Frenchman I've seen."

"Oh, dear," said Lily. "I think we're lost."

"Let's retrace our steps," I said. But we couldn't agree which streets we'd come through, and soon we were more lost than ever. "We could ask one of the Tommies," I said.

"No, we couldn't," said Lily. "You know what soldiers would think."

We were beginning to argue when a Klaxon horn sounded *parp* behind us, and a small car drew up. "Good afternoon, ladies," said the driver. "May I be of help?" He took his goggles off. It was Captain Stevenson. "To me, you two look lost."

"Yes, sir," we said together.

"None of the 'sir,'" he said. "I told you, Ellen, I'm not a stuffed-shirt Englishman." Lily looked at me sharply, and I felt really annoyed with him.

"I guess you don't know Abbeville," he said. "Let me show you the old place." He looked round. "We're in the place Sainte-Catherine. I'll lock the car. I rely on you not to forget where it's parked."

So we started on our tour of Abbeville, and nobody could say that Captain Stevenson wasn't the soul of politeness. He knew a lot about the town. We saw St. Wulfram's cathedral, St. Gilles with its lovely church, and the new bridge over the river Somme. Then he took us to the port, where the Somme opens out into the sea. Sailing ships, fishing boats, and a small steamer were tied up by the dock. Gulls flew screaming overhead in the sea breeze. No troopships, no hospital ships—it was hard to believe we were at war, or that this lovely, slow river had had the fiercest battle ever known fought over it a few miles away and that one of its victims was my dear Archie.

As the afternoon wore on, I noticed that Captain Stevenson kept close and addressed everything he said to me. I wished he wouldn't, especially now that Lily was trailing behind us. A little farther on from the harbor, there was a small beach. "We could go for a paddle," said Lily.

"I'll sit on the pebbles and watch you," he said.

"We can't," I said. "We'll get our uniforms wet."

"Fancy worrying about a little seawater when most of the time they're covered in blood," Lily replied.

"I don't want to paddle," I said. But it wasn't wetting my skirts that worried me—I didn't want Captain Stevenson watching us.

"Let me buy you some refreshment," he said. We sat at a table outside a café on the dock. He bought ice cream for us and a glass of red wine for himself, stretched back in his chair, and said, "This sure is nice. Would you like a crêpe, Ellen? And you, of course, Nurse Hobson."

Lily and I looked at each other. We had no idea what he meant. When they came, though, the little pancakes were lovely.

He looked at his watch. "Four thirty," he said. "Time to get you back. Don't want to annoy Daphne, do we?"

His car had a seat beside the driver and a little dickey seat high up on the back and I wondered who'd sit where. We had no choice. He handed Lily up to the dickey seat and ushered me into the seat beside him. "You sit here, Ellen," he said, and I felt a slight squeeze to my hand.

The air blew quite cold through the open car as he drove. My hair was all over the place. It would have been lovely to have a proper hat with a scarf tied under my chin to keep it on, like the ones you see rich women wearing in the illustrated magazines. The car was too noisy for much talking, but Captain Stevenson did ask if we had enjoyed the afternoon, and I said we had and thanked him. Well, we had—though I still wished he hadn't met us. "What would you have done if I hadn't chanced on you like that?" he asked.

"I suppose we'd have wandered up and down until we got tired," I said. "Then we'd have walked back because we couldn't afford a taxi."

"What a waste that would have been for two such lovely ladies as yourselves, Ellen," he replied.

He had been very gallant and had perfect manners, but I thought that sounded a little forward. I tried to get out of the car before he came round to help me, but I was too late. Once again I felt that slight pressure on my hand.

When he handed Lily down from the dickey seat, her face was like thunder, and I wasn't surprised.

"I'm sorry," I said when he'd gone. "That wasn't my doing. I was embarrassed."

"How do you think I felt?" Lily said indignantly. "I don't like being a gooseberry. Did you two arrange that?"

"No!" I cried, upset. "I didn't like the way he behaved."

"How long has this been going on behind my back?"

"It hasn't. I've only really talked to him once, and he only noticed me because of Gefreiter Vögler's tourniquet."

"Enough to call you Ellen. What's his first name, then?"

"Chauncey," I said without thinking.

"There you are; that proves it."

Lily didn't speak to me after that. The night shift seemed to last a very long time, and I almost wished a line of ambulances would draw up outside and I'd have some really bad wounds to see to.

When I came off the ward in the morning, Sister Bilson was waiting in the passage. "Matron wants to see you in her office," she said. "Now."

When I went in, Daphne sat behind her desk looking stern. "I've been told something very disturbing about you, Nurse Wilkins," she said. "You were seen in Abbeville yesterday with Captain Stevenson, on very good, even personal, terms with him. Do you deny it?"

"I can't deny I met him, Matron," I replied.

"What have I impressed on all you nurses? The first, most basic rule, the one thing the War Office and the army together insist on. No liaisons."

"It's not a liaison. I've hardly spoken to him. We weren't

alone. Nurse Hobson was with me. He met us and offered us a lift home."

"Yes, after escorting you all round Abbeville. My informant, whom I trust, said nothing about Nurse Hobson."

I was angry. Lily herself must have told Daphne. Nobody else knew, and she obviously wouldn't say she was there as well.

"You put me in a difficult position. I said that a nurse flouting this rule would be sent home. Can you give a reason why you should stay here?"

"I hardly know Captain Stevenson."

Her manner changed. "Ellen," she said. "I can't tell you how disappointed I am. You're a good nurse, you've done well here, but now you've let me down. How can I trust you if you disobey my specific order? I should ask you to leave now. I'll see you have a travel warrant."

I couldn't help it. I burst into tears right in front of her. "It's not fair. I've done nothing wrong. Someone's trying to get me into trouble."

"This won't do you any good, Ellen."

"Coming here was the one thing I wanted above all, and now someone's ruined it for me and I don't know why."

"You should have thought of that before."

"Please, Daphne, won't you reconsider? You think I've let you down, and the colonel as well, but I haven't—I haven't, honestly. I didn't want Captain Stevenson anywhere near me. He embarrassed me in front of Lily—Nurse Hobson—by paying me so much attention."

She looked hard at me. "I'd so much like to believe you," she said. "But my information comes from a good source." A moment's silence—then, "Look here, old thing, I don't like this any more than you do. See me tomorrow at the same time for my final decision. And just hope and pray that something turns up to help me change my mind."

Blinded by tears, I stumbled out the door, up the stairs, into our room. I climbed up to the top bunk and sobbed my heart out. I couldn't believe it. Just like London Fields. History repeating itself.

"I'm trying to sleep." Lily's voice from the bottom bunk. I hadn't even noticed her.

"What did you do that for?" I stormed. "Thanks to you, I'm being sent home. There was no need for it."

"What are you talking about?"

"Telling Daphne I was alone with Captain Stevenson yesterday."

"I did no such thing," said Lily indignantly. "Why would I?"

"Because your nose was pushed out of joint."

"No, it wasn't. Well, I was a bit annoyed at first, and it spoiled the afternoon, but since then I thought, who cares? It's no business of mine."

"I don't believe you. You told her out of spite."

Lily got out of bed and looked over the top of the bunk straight at me. "Look, Ellen, I didn't do it, and I'm sorry you could even think it of me. I'll go to Matron right now. I'll tell her that I was with you all the time, that it was pure accident Captain Stevenson saw us, and that he behaved like a complete gentleman all afternoon."

"She'll ask you why you've changed your mind."

"I haven't changed my mind. I didn't tell Matron in the first place, and if I tell her what really happened, how can you still believe it was me?"

"Well, if it wasn't you, who was it?"

"I don't know," said Lily. "But I'm going to see her now."

She left. I curled up and went to sleep and didn't hear her come in again. I didn't wake up till three o'clock, and when I went down to the canteen, all the food was gone.

Well, it's the next day, and I can't believe what's happened. I went to Daphne's office this morning. "Sit down, Nurse Wilkins," she said. "You have a good friend in Nurse Hobson. She confirmed your version. To put your mind at rest, she was not my informant. It was a person senior to you both. But this doesn't mean I've changed my mind. Of course Nurse Hobson will defend her friend. I need less biased evidence."

"Captain Stevenson will tell you."

"Anything Captain Stevenson says would be subject to the same criticism. Besides, I can't ask him. Yesterday he was ordered to report back to the American Army as we feared, and he left at once. So your case is not proved, I'm afraid, Ellen. What will it do for discipline if I give you the benefit of the doubt? I gave you your chance, I brought you here, I made an allowance for your age, but I dare not be suspected of favoritism."

"I don't know, Matron," I said miserably. Oh, what possessed us to go to Abbeville?

Suddenly there was a terrific hammering on the door and a large figure wearing dirty coveralls burst in. "Sorry I didn't knock, old girl," said Lavinia. "This is too important to stand on ceremony."

"What is it, Lavinia?" said Daphne, almost wearily.

"What do you think you're doing to this young lady?"

"She's committed a breach of discipline and has to go home, I'm afraid. I don't like it, but you know our agreement with the War Office."

"Bosh," said Lavinia. "They can't do without us. Besides, what is this famous breach of discipline?" Daphne started to tell her, but Lavinia said, "Don't bother explaining; I know what it's all about."

"How do you know?" said Daphne.

"Because this young lady's friend and roommate came to see me this morning, quite distraught. She said she tried to tell you, but you wouldn't listen and now she's desperate. That's not good enough, old girl."

"But, Lavinia—"

"'But, Lavinia' nothing. Whatever rule she's supposed to have broken, who cares? What right has the War Office to treat these wonderful people like machines? That's half the trouble in this war. And why we, of all people, should knuckle under to them beats me."

"It's the agreement, Lavinia."

"I know it's the blasted agreement. And now we're breaking the agreement, and I daresay the bigwigs with pips on their shoulders will be outraged, and I dare them to do anything about it. I want my wonderful nurses to be happy. I don't expect this place to be a brothel, but I do want a place where people can behave to each other like human beings."

"So do I, Lavinia, but you know our position."

"Come on, Daphne, this isn't like you. We've been good girls for four years, and in all that time we've been too busy for that sort of thing. Now we've got a lull, though God knows it will soon change. What is this but a storm in a teacup? Completely unreasonable."

"I know the War Office is stupid and thinks it's still dealing with Florence Nightingale, but we have to keep its goodwill."

"Daphne, I gave you full power to run this place and said I would take a backseat. Now I shall do something I never thought to. I'm giving you an order. You are not to send this girl away."

I couldn't believe this argument was going on in front of me. They seemed to have forgotten I was there, until Daphne said, "Nurse Wilkins, please step outside for a few minutes."

What they would say next was important. Nobody saw me standing by the door to listen. The voices were muffled, but I heard enough. Daphne said, "Lavinia, how dare you undermine my authority in front of a nurse?"

"I believe you did wrong, Daphne. These girls aren't inhuman. They've put up with worse things than any young women in history before them, and we mustn't put them to an impossible discipline."

"You've got a short memory, Lavinia. If we hadn't agreed to go by the War Office's rules about women on active service, we wouldn't be here now. We picked those we would follow and ignored those we didn't like, but we can't start adding to the list now. They nearly threw the Flying Circus out of Belgium because they said we got in the way. It was a small price to pay to keep our independence, and I don't want to risk it."

That was the gist of it. They said a lot more that I

couldn't make out, though most of it sounded angry. I'd
hoped they'd have a short discussion and then come out to
tell me I could stay after all. Instead, Daphne opened the
door and said, "Wilkins, go to your room and stay there."

Wilkins. More than anything that showed what a mess I
was in.

I'd never been so miserable in my whole life. Three jobs
I'd had, and I'd left each one under a cloud, none of them
my doing. The world seemed stacked against me. When
Lily found me in the room, I was in such despair that I
couldn't speak. She soon gave up on me and didn't stay
long. She didn't come back until deep into the afternoon.

"Do you want to know what's happened?" she said. I
didn't answer. "Daphne's leaving and Sister Ellis is taking
over as matron. They say Lavinia's sacked her, and
everyone knows why. Now that she's going, they might let
you stay."

"I couldn't. Not now."

"No," said Lily. "I didn't think you could." I buried my
face in the pillow and cried until I was empty. Dusk began
to fall, and I thought I'd better get my things together. Just
as I started packing the suitcase, there was a knock on the
door and Sister Grogan entered. "Here's your travel warrant," she said. "It's all been signed. If you hurry, Monsieur
Sagnol will drive you to the station at Abbeville. You might
get a train to Calais tonight if you're lucky."

She left. A few minutes later Lily returned. "It's all over
the hospital," she said. "Your name is mud."

"You don't need to tell me," I replied.

"There's someone outside who wants to see you. I'll
leave you to it."

"I don't want to see anyone," I said, but Lily had gone. I turned my face to the wall so I wouldn't have to see who it was.

"Ellen?" said a voice.

"Go away," I answered.

"Ellen, this is important. We've got to do something, you and I."

"It's too late. There's nothing anyone can do."

"Ellen, there's something you ought to know. Look at me, please."

I turned my head. There stood Sister Bilson. "You don't know the half of it," she said.

"What do you mean?" I asked.

"It was me who told Daphne."

I sat up. "Why?"

"I thought Captain Stevenson liked me. He kept on saying he did, calling me Lorna when nobody could hear, telling me all about himself, touching my hand. It made me uncomfortable. I know the rules. But I really, really thought he liked me, and that one day it would be all right."

"He was like that to me too, Sister Bilson."

"Please call me Lorna. We're both in the same boat."

"No, we're not. I'm sacked; you aren't. Please go now."

"Hear me out," said Sister Bilson. "He asked me to go with him in his car to Abbeville. We were together there all morning, and he was lovely, so attentive and polite. But we were sitting outside a café in the afternoon when he suddenly got up and said, 'Excuse me, I have to do something,' and walked away. I waited and waited, and then thought something bad might have happened, so I went to look for him. Then I saw you both. You two looked really close, and Nurse Hobson was trailing behind looking like she'd lost a sovereign and found sixpence. I was livid. I nearly made a scene in the street, but I was afraid to because he's a doctor and an officer. I could do something about you, though, so I picked up my skirts and walked all the way back to the hospital and straight to Daphne."

"Did you see Captain Stevenson before he was ordered away?"

"Ordered away? You surely don't believe that. Big coincidence, isn't it? I bet you he never showed Daphne the order. He's just driven off back to the Yanks, and they'll welcome him and ask no questions. Well, I've told you everything, so we have to do something about it."

"It's too late."

"Not if we hurry. I don't expect Daphne's left yet."

"There's nothing we can do," I said.

"Yes, there is. We can try talking to Lavinia."

"What good will that do?"

"Then she'll know how it happened and ask Daphne to stay."

"But Lavinia didn't sack Daphne because of what Captain Stevenson did. She did it because Daphne wouldn't do what she told her," I said. "If we tell anyone, it should be Daphne."

"Daphne's the one who's going. She can't ask Lavinia for her job back now."

"Then it's no use doing anything."

"Yes, it is. You've missed the point, Ellen. The point is that this man's making fools of us, and it's not right. I don't see why we should suffer because he's a rotter."

I remembered Beatie and Arthur Dunhill. She called him a lot worse than a rotter. That's Beatie's problem, I'd thought then—it'll never happen to me. Now it had, even though I hadn't wanted Captain Stevenson's attentions in the first place. "It still won't be any use," I said.

"Come on, Ellen; try it. Perhaps you're right; we will see Daphne first. I'm truly sorry for what I did. I don't know what got into me." I could see she meant it; she wasn't Sister Bilson anymore; she was Lorna. I was ashamed, for me, for us, for the whole hospital, that this silly business mattered so much compared to the suffering we'd seen here. I told Lorna so.

"I know," she said. "But that doesn't mean it's not important. Our hospital is special. Why should we let that man ruin it? For a start, we'll look for Matron."

Daphne wasn't in her room. We knocked on the door until our knuckles were sore and then, because it wasn't locked, daringly looked inside in case she was asleep ("Or worse," Lorna said), but she wasn't. An open suitcase stood on the bed, so she was still here. We ran to her office.

The noise of furious activity sounded from inside. When we knocked, Daphne's irritated voice called, "Who is it?"

I opened the door, and we stood together in the doorway. She looked at us coldly. "What do you two want?" I could hear anger in her voice, yet somehow she sounded more like an elder sister than our matron.

"There's something you ought to know," said Lorna.

"I am aware of all the facts," she replied. She was clearing the drawers in her desk and dropping everything into a wooden tea chest.

"I lied to you," said Lorna.

"What did you say?" Daphne's tone was dangerously angry.

"I said Ellen and Captain Stevenson were alone. That's not true. Nurse Hobson was with them."

"She's right," I said. "Lily told you the truth."

"That makes a difference, doesn't it?" said Lorna.

"Yes, it does. It means I cannot trust my staff. I really have overstayed my time here."

She swept more objects into the tea chest and took a last look through the drawers. Then she picked up the photograph on her desk, the one I'd noticed on my first day, of the man whose face was familiar. Now I recognized him, and for a moment I forgot my worries. Edmund, Major Cripps. It was the same photograph as the one I saw in the colonel's sitting room way back in 1914. Why should Daphne's cousin's photograph be the only one on her desk, where she saw it every day?

Cousins often married. There were several in Lambsfield. I'd never thought of Daphne with a man friend, let alone being in love. But why should I be surprised? One thing I knew: Major Cripps would never behave like Captain Stevenson, not if he took after his father, the soul of honor. Lorna was right. Perhaps this was the way to change Daphne's mind.

"It's Captain Stevenson who's caused all this," I said. "He's a rotter." Daphne looked at me uncomprehendingly. "Rotter" was Lorna's word. Perhaps it should be stronger, though perhaps not as strong as Beatie's. "A rat," I said. "Not all men are like that. I know."

She was just about to drop the photograph in the tea chest. But then she stopped, looked at it, said, "So do I," and put it back where it was. Her voice softened. "Ellen, my uncle told me about your young soldier who was killed. Were you thinking of him just then?"

Lorna said, "It's all Captain Stevenson's fault. He made us look like fools, and now he's run away because he's afraid to face us."

"Captain Stevenson was ordered away by his superiors. We always knew that might happen."

"Matron, did he show you the order?" Lorna asked. Daphne didn't answer. "Matron, this must make a difference."

"The Duchess of Faringdon has dismissed me. I shall not grovel to get my job back. That is the end of the matter," said Daphne. She put the photograph gently in the tea chest and said, "I appreciate what you've tried to do. But I have been given a direct order, and I cannot see it being rescinded. I must ask you to leave now."

"I knew it was a waste of time," I said when we were outside.

"If Daphne won't grovel, then Lavinia will have to do the rescinding," Lorna replied. "This is my fault too, and I'm going to sort it out. Come on." She ran down the passage and outside toward the stables, and I followed. "She'll be with her beloved ambulances," she said.

But she wasn't. "She can't be far away if both ambulances are here," said Lorna. There was nobody in the stables either, not even Monsieur Sagnol. "Where does Lavinia live?" I said.

"She has a sort of flat on the floor above," said Lorna. "We'll knock."

"We don't know where the door is," I replied.

"Can't you see her curtains?" said Lorna. I looked where she was pointing. Three windows had curtains, and even from here I could see they were heavy and expensive.

We found the staircase and the door. Lavinia opened it the moment we knocked. If she was surprised, she didn't show it. "Come in," she said. "Welcome. I do believe that in all the time this hospital has been running, no sister or nurse has ever been inside here. Isn't that shameful?"

The room made me gasp. It was furnished like the drawing room at Hartcross Park: lovely chairs and tables with curved, spindly legs, the sort that I'd spent so many hours polishing. She saw us staring. "A few little things I had brought over from home when the duke wasn't looking," she said. "I didn't want to rough it completely out here. Sit down."

I'd rubbed away at chairs like these until I knew every little bend and cranny in them, but I'd never sat in one before. They weren't all that comfortable. "Now, what can I do for you?" said Lavinia.

We blurted out the whole story. She listened without saying a word. "So, please, can you tell Matron to stay?" Lorna finished.

"Even if I did, I don't think Daphne would budge. We stay independent by accepting certain conditions, and I understand how Daphne thinks that sticking to them is a point of principle."

"But it's not," I said. "Nobody's gone against the conditions. It's what Captain Stevenson did that's caused all this. None of it would have happened without him. He's a rotter and a rat."

Unexpectedly, Lavinia started laughing, and once she'd

started, she couldn't stop. "I believe you," she said at last, wiping her eyes. "Thousands wouldn't. Besides, how do I know what the duke's up to behind my back? He could be having the time of his life with all those little fillies running around London. That would put our Captain Stevenson in the shade, would it not? Though, looking at my dear old hubby, probably not. All right, I'll do it. Let's find Daphne."

So back we marched, the three of us.

CHAPTER FORTY-THREE

I'm still here, Daphne's still here, and the lull is over. It's the end of August, the western front has swung north again, the British Army is advancing, and the ambulance convoys are coming back. I don't think that Daphne's really forgiven me. She's cold and looks right through me when I pass her.

I've dreamed a lot about Archie lately. Night after night I meet him in a dream Barnsley, and then I see him in a stretcher and I'm cleaning deep wounds and, one dreadful night, pressing down on his severed artery. I scream for help, just as on that real night, but it isn't Captain Stevenson who comes, it is Gefreiter Vögler. "What good are you?" I say, and he answers, "I am all the help you need. Nobody knows better than me what to do. Schwester Ellen, why will you not call me Matthias?"

Summer dies; autumn comes. The soldiers tell us of hard fighting, great victories. Places round the Somme with names we'll never forget from 1916 are captured—Thiepval Ridge, Mametz Wood, Delville Wood. They are pushing the

Germans back, they have breached the Hindenburg Line, and the way is nearly open to Germany. They come to us in better shape now, their wounds not so raw. But there are so many of them: this war is bitter, as if everyone knows it's coming to an end and wants to finish it off as soon as possible. More Germans are brought in than ever, and they seem to get younger—seventeen, sixteen, fifteen, a few look no more than twelve. They are sad, frightened little creatures, and if they die, we feel deep sadness at how futile all this is. I remember what Gefreiter Vögler said when I asked him why he thought the war was nearly over. "Believe me, Schwester, I know."

One day, one night, merge into the next. We are back to how we lived before the August lull. I've stopped seeing Archie in every new stretcher; in fact, I hardly see the soldiers' faces anymore, hardly register them as separate human beings, and this makes me feel guilty. At the end of September, there is a great British victory when they cross the St. Quentin Canal. The soldiers are excited and triumphant, despite their wounds, with tales of how they swam over the canal at night on life preservers taken from cross-Channel steamers and caught the defending enemy by surprise.

"Poor loves, it must be so wonderful to be out of those everlasting trenches, able to think for themselves again and know they're winning, even if just as many still die," said Sister Ellis to me one night. But Sergeant Oldroyd, curmudgeonly as ever, said, "Don't speak too soon. Fritz won't give up that easily. He'll fight like a tiger till there's none of him left."

*   *   *

It's October. Incredible stories are flying round the hospital. "Haven't you heard?" Lily said to me. "There's a Bolshevik revolution in Germany. All the German soldiers are talking about it. They want the war to stop now."

"It's too much to hope for," I said.

But new stories circulate. The Germans are ready to give up; they want an armistice; this time it really will be all over at Christmas. And still the broken soldiers flood in.

It's the last week in October. The night is busy. Stretcher after stretcher is brought in. One is placed in front of me. Even before I twitch the blanket off, I know what I will see. Both this man's legs are shattered. It is amazing that he is alive. His face does not yet have the unmistakable death pallor, and he is breathing, just about, and I realize I know him. He spoke to me in a tent at Hartcross Park. He was sent home to a hospital in Edinburgh and had no need to go back to the fighting. A few weeks ago I saw his photograph.

"Quickly," I say. "Someone fetch Daphne."

Daphne is there in two minutes. She takes one look and says, "Give him to me."

"You take one end of the stretcher," Sergeant Oldroyd says to little clubfooted Private Jenkins. "I'll take the other. Where to, ma'am?"

"Theater," says Daphne, leading the way.

It was four in the morning before I could sleep. I woke at eight, jumped out of the bunk, and looked out of the window. The day was dark and overcast: there was rain in the wind. Dead leaves had piled up over the grass because there was no time to rake them up. All summer the garden had grown steadily more unkempt. Had Edmund survived the night?

Only a few people were in the canteen, and they were all talking about him. "He's her brother," said Nurse James. "Never," said Elsie Barton. "He's her husband, and they married in secret on their last leave."

"Well, Daphne's a dark horse and no mistake," said Lily. "I never put her down for the marrying kind."

"I know him," I told them. "You're all wrong. He's her cousin. His father lives in our village." They looked disappointed until Sister Ellis cheered them up. "Ellen's right," she said. "But he's her fiancé as well."

"How long has that been going on?" asked Lorna Bilson.

"He asked her before they put him under to take his legs off. He said he wanted something good to wake up to, and she said yes. I was there. He was still alive an hour ago. They've moved him to the officers' ward."

"One of the soldiers told me how he was injured," said Lily. "They'd come to this canal, and the Germans were on the other side going hammer and tongs with machine guns and bombs. He was organizing the crossing when a mortar shell exploded right by him. He's a good man, the soldier said. He looked after them, and they trusted him. They got across the canal without him, though they lost a lot of men."

As soon as I finished eating, I went to the officers' ward, once a sitting room with huge windows looking out over the lawns. A bed at one end had screens round it. I tiptoed up and peeped round them. There he was, still unconscious, with Daphne stroking his forehead. "How is he?" I whispered.

I half expected her to say, "It's not your business, nurse. Get back to your duties." Instead, she looked up and said, "We must wait. He's strong, but we won't know for some time if we'll ever give him back to his father." Suddenly she smiled. "Ellen, has it occurred to you that if this had happened in August, I would have had to dismiss myself as well as you?"

I didn't answer, but a great happiness welled up inside me. Captain Stevenson was forgotten. I wasn't here on sufferance anymore, and Daphne was once again the wonderful person who had brought me to Abbeville.

Edmund will be well. Soon he will be strong enough to be taken back to England and several months' convalescence. At least he is not dead, though it seems a terrible thing that he got through the whole war uninjured until its last few weeks, because those weeks are here now. The enemy still fights, but its leaders know it is hopeless. For so long we have yearned for an armistice. Suddenly, nobody talks about anything else.

There really does seem to be a revolution in Germany. People say that the Bolshevik red hammer and sickle flag flies from town halls, that the German navy has mutinied, that soldiers jeer at reinforcements as they come to take their place. It gives us no pleasure. If providence had not been on our side, that might have been happening to us.

November 11. It's really here. The war stopped at eleven this morning. Nobody cheered, hoisted flags, or danced on the wards. There was just a quiet relief that after today there would be no lines of ambulances at the gates except those taking men on the first stage of their journeys home.

Just after the clocks struck eleven, I overheard two soldiers talking. "Anyway, what is an armistice?" said one. "Time off to bury the dead, mate," said the other.

CHAPTER FORTY-FOUR

I never dared think that I'd be home for Christmas 1918. Even after all the horrors, it was a real wrench to say good-bye to Lavinia's hospital at Abbeville. But by December the last patient had gone, the beds were empty, and the operating theater deserted. Only ghosts remained: a hunched figure on a bed was no more than a trick of the light, the wind became groans and screams of agony and despair, and occasional little pockets of silence were invisible coffins. I'd only been here eight months, yet it seemed like a whole lifetime, and when the people I had shared so much with were gone, then nothing worthwhile could ever follow.

Two weeks before Christmas, there was a farewell party: sisters, nurses, doctors, orderlies—all ranks and duties forgotten. Monsieur Sagnol came with a huge four-generation family we'd never known existed. Lavinia brought in lovely fresh food from markets and farms that had escaped damage. There was dancing to cracked records played on a gramophone left behind in the officers' ward. Sergeant Oldroyd and Private Jenkins were attentive partners, if not exactly graceful. Even the doctors joined in. Lavinia gave a long and eloquent speech, broken by occasional "harrumphs" and gusts of breathy laughter. Daphne spoke movingly and gave us news of Edmund, who had survived the crossing to England and was now in a hospital near Aldershot.

It was hard to say good-bye to Lily, Lorna, Sister Ellis, Sister Grogan, and the others. But the time came, and three days afterward we stepped off the ship at Dover and went our separate ways, vowing to keep in touch. Next day I was home.

Getting off the train and seeing Pa run down the signal-box steps to greet me and Ma, Jack, and the girls waiting on the platform was almost too much for me. It was a joyful reunion, yet as we walked together along the familiar streets, which in the last months had seemed parts of an old dream I once had, I couldn't stop my tears.

"Your father said we should get a real big feast in to celebrate," Ma said. "I told him we'll have it later because it's the last thing you'd want after your journey. Did I do right?"

"Of course you did, Ma," I answered. "I'm so tired."

I slept for twelve full hours that night, and when I woke, it was Abbeville that seemed like the dream.

I shan't talk about Christmas, because it was almost too happy to bear. On Boxing Day we went to the Hartcross Hunt, all except Pa, who expressed his usual disgust for it, and I remembered how last year I'd seen Colonel Cripps with Daphne and my life had changed. He was there today, with Bonny but not Daphne.

"She's staying in Aldershot to be near Edmund," he

said. "I'm going there myself tomorrow. Shall I send them your regards?"

"Please," I replied.

"Daphne thinks highly of you," he said. "As do we all."

I didn't tell him how near I was to coming home in disgrace.

"I know Edmund and Daphne aren't in the first flush of youth anymore and Edmund is crippled for life, but it's my dearest wish that they should marry," he said. "It always has been."

So many others I saw that morning: Billy Fawkes the porter, Willy Doughty, who Jack took on to work for him, Dr. Pettigrew, Mr. Brayfield, Fred Straker, Bully Straker, Percy Pinkney, Oswald Langley, the Randalls, even Dottie, who gave me a strange look that seemed to say, "I don't care where you've been, you don't impress me, Ellen Wilkins." Seeing them made me think of others who weren't there—that roll call of people who'd walked through my life for four years: dear Archie, Cissie, Meg, Enid, and poor Beatie, everyone at London Fields, even Ivy Turner, and so many more. As I watched the hunt move off—hounds, horses, the Launtons at the head of it—I had a great feeling of peace. The war was over, and I was really home.

It's the first Saturday after Christmas. "Football on the Green this afternoon," says Jack. "Go on, Ellie, come down with me to watch it. It'll do you good. Lambsfield versus Ilfriston. Only a friendly game, but it gets the team going again now that the best players are coming back from the war."

"Why would I want to watch men kicking a scrap of leather around a field?" I answer.

"If your Archie were still here and you'd married him, he'd drag you there whether you liked it or not," says Jack.

That isn't the first time he's mentioned Archie. I don't mind now; in fact I'm glad he does. "Why do you say that?" I ask.

"Didn't you say once that when he was on his last leave he went to the Oakwell football field to watch Barnsley play Sheffield Wednesday? Barnsley won, I remember."

"I never said that."

"Yes, you did, when you told me about your day in London."

Then the penny drops. Of course. Walloping the Wednesday. At last I know what Archie meant. I wish I hadn't found out too late.

Jack sees. "Sorry, Ellie, that went a bit too far. Still, come anyway."

"All right, Jack," I say, and get my coat while he puts his false leg on, which he uses instead of crutches now when he goes out.

Outside, it's a cold, gray day, feeling like snow. As we walk, Jack goes on talking. "Of course, the team's not what it was. A lot of the players have gone, me included. It's all young ones and a couple of old-timers. We didn't even have a goalkeeper last week. But we've got one now. Guess where he came from."

"I've no idea."

"There's a few German prisoners working up at Gill's farm while they wait to go home. Farmer Gill took them on because he was short-handed, with all the land girls go-

ing home. He says they're terrific workers. He thinks the
sun shines out of them even if they are Jerries. Anyway,
one came to a practice match the other day and asked if he
could join in, so we said he could go in goal. He was pretty
good, so he's playing today."

"Didn't anyone complain?"

"Why should they? We've nothing against him. We were
most of us in the war, but the ones we didn't like were the
higher-ups who started it. The poor sods we were shooting
at were in the same boat as us. He's a nice chap and he
speaks good English. Mr. Gill says he works like three men."

A strange thought comes into my mind, but I damp it
down because it's impossible. Jack is still talking. "He
hadn't any gear, so we found him a goalkeeper's jersey and
some shorts and socks, and I gave him my old football
boots. They fit him all right, and I won't be needing them
again."

The strange thought returns once more.

We come to the Green. The trees are leafless skeletons.
The cricket square in the middle is roped off so nobody
can spoil it before summer comes. The football field is
marked out to one side of it, and about forty men wearing
coats, scarves, and caps stand round the touchline. The
match has been going a few minutes when we arrive.
Lambsfield wear blue-and-white stripes, Ilfriston red-and-
black quarters. A figure in a green jersey stands in the goal
at the far end. Now the strange thought won't go away,
and my heart is beating quite fast. *No; stop it; don't be silly.*
It's like looking for Archie among the wounded men coming
into the hospital.

Lambsfield is attacking, and one of the forwards kicks the

ball high toward the goal. The goalkeeper in the green jersey jumps to catch it. "Well done, Matt," shouts a Lambsfield player, and the knot of men watching from the touchline clap their hands. Jack joins them. I stand a little way off. Willy Doughty is there. "About time too," he says to Jack. "What kept you? Oh, hello, Ellie." Jack's talking already; he's forgotten I'm here.

I hesitate a moment, then walk toward the far goal, slowly at first, then quicker, as if a magnet is pulling me, down the touchline to the little flag that marks the corner of the field. Bully Straker, Percy Pinkney, and Oswald Langley, boys no longer but grown men who would have been in the army now if the war hadn't ended, are standing there, and I'm reminded of that far-off recruiting day. They ignore me, and I ignore them. I come nearer the goal. The play is at the other end of the field. I summon all my will to make the goalkeeper turn round and see me.

Twenty yards away. *Look round, look round.* But he won't. Now I'm right up close. I take a breath and say, "Matthias?"

Now he does turn round. A huge smile splits his face. "Schwester Ellen!" he exclaims. He runs out of the goal toward me, his hands outstretched.

Bully Straker, Percy Pinkney, and Oswald Langley have followed. They walk round the back of the goal pretending not to look. But as they pass, Bully Straker hisses, so only I can hear, "Hun-lover."

And with a cold, dull feeling about my heart, I know that one day everything we have just been through will start all over again.

But I'll be ready for it.